Ghost Walk

Ghost Walk

A Rose McQuinn Mystery

ALANNA KNIGHT

First published in Great Britain in 2004 by
Allison & Busby Limited
Bon Marche Centre
241-251 Ferndale Road
Brixton, London SW9 8BJ
http://www.allisonandbusby.com

A catalogue record for this book is available from the British Library

ISBN 0 7490 8301 8

Printed and bound by
Creative Print + Design, Ebbw Vale

ALANNA KNIGHT has written more than forty novels (including eleven in the successful Inspector Faro series), four works of non-fiction, numerous short stories and two plays since the publication of her first book in 1969. Born and educated in Tyneside, she now lives in Edinburgh. She is a founding member of the Scottish Association of Writers and Convener of the Scottish Chapter of the Crime Writers' Association.

For Camilla and Lorn, with love

'No living man I'll love again
Syne that my bonnie man is slain;
Wi' ane lock o' his black hair
I'll chain my heart for evermair.'
                    ('The Widow's Lament' – Old Border Ballad)

1

June 21, 1897:

The Queen's Diamond Jubilee should have been my wedding day, a momentous event, but with little impact on my future as a Lady Investigator, Discretion Guaranteed.

Jubilee fever was sweeping over the country. A rare opportunity for celebration and inebriation. That was in my future husband Jack Macmerry's words how the citizens of Edinburgh viewed it.

And who was to blame them, he added frowning over the extra work for the police in keeping order, dealing with drunkenness, loose morals and more sinister issues.

Jack's parents, however, were very patriotic and determined that this remarkable coincidence was to herald a day to go down in the annals of the Macmerry family. I could imagine his mother was already picturing the smiling faces of her unborn grandchildren on the mantelpiece. I shuddered...

His parents' delighted reactions that this would be a memorable occasion were reported to me by Jack who looked suddenly anxious.

And with good reason.

Ten years ago, the 1887 Golden Jubilee had been accompanied by Fenian assassination attempts discreetly kept from public knowledge.

When I said: 'Now that the Queen is so old, perhaps they won't consider it worthwhile and will let nature take its course.'

But Jack wasn't so sure about that. It seemed that not only the Fenians wanted rid of her.

There were those much nearer home, if I got his meaning.

My eyes widened at that. But truth to tell the old queen

wasn't all that popular with her English Parliament, keener on ruling from her Scottish retreat at Balmoral Castle. According to her son, the Prince of Wales, she was heavily under the influence of some questionable servants with peculiar interests, such as spiritualism. Bertie didn't care for them at all and was most eager to rule the country and Empire while he still had some life left in him.

Which was questionable considering his present life-style.

The excuse was that as youth veered into middle age and an increasing corpulence, so did his despair at ever becoming king. Most days he felt sure that his tiresome indomitable old mother was going to live for ever – and possibly outlive him. Faced with this gloomy prospect he had nothing more worthwhile to pass away the time of his unkingly days, months and years than to relax in the arms of a succession of mistresses, his long suffering Princess of Wales having learned to close her mind to such humiliation and even to manage a bleak smile when encountering these royal playthings at social events.

'Bertie would never... his own mother!' I exclaimed.

Jack shook his head and smiled. Whatever happened, Edinburgh City Police would have to do without him.

He didn't need to spell that out either. He'd be on honeymoon. Even a detective inspector, newly appointed, had his weak moments. And Jack had had plenty of them since we met two years ago, any excuse to lead me up the aisle and slip a wedding ring on my finger.

He little knew how near he was to that now. I had not yet shared with him my suspicion that I may be carrying his child. After all, we would be wed within weeks, and there would be time enough to tell him then. And I did not want to suffer the extra pressure that he would certainly impose on me to move the wedding date forward.

Let me make it clear. It wasn't that I didn't love Jack.

Friends nudged me and whispered that any girl would jump at the chance, sighing over his good looks, the fair hair and high cheekbones of the Lowland Scot, very different indeed to the black-haired, blue eyed Celtic warrior, my first husband – Danny McQuinn.

I was afraid. Afraid still of that dream in which a door opened and Danny, whose death I firmly refused to acknowledge, walked in with a perfectly simple and completely logical explanation of where he had been for the past three years since the day he walked out of our home in Tucson, Arizona, never to return.

I told myself that I could never ever love any man as much as I had loved Danny. The dream persisted and became an obsession, as well as providing an excellent excuse for not getting married a second time.

A more truthful reason was that I enjoyed my new life following in the footsteps of my illustrious father, Chief Inspector Jeremy Faro, and ignoring the occasional grim look in Jack's eye which clearly indicated that once we were married he would soon put an end to that nonsense.

Not because he feared rivalry of a wife in the same profession – unofficially – but because he loved me and feared for my life.

On two memorable occasions he had saved me from death at the hands of a killer who I had unmasked. Perhaps he felt that twice was more than enough and wasn't prepared to let my lucky escapes go to my head, feeling with good reason that he could not always guarantee to be around at the crucial moment.

And so, the wedding plans began with a long promised visit to Jack's parents who farmed just over the Border, a visit I had evaded for two reasons.

The village had remote associations with Danny. He used to

visit one of his relatives, a priest, who had brought him over from Ireland as a child in the late '40s. Good sense told me that was a mere excuse and that there was little chance of Father McQuinn still being alive.

The real reason was that any visit to Jack's parents meant that they would hear wedding bells for their one and only bairn. Two years without a formal engagement, neither fiancée nor wife and the revelation that we were lovers would be extremely embarrassing for devoted parents.

The Macmerry farm was in Eildon and constructed, like most of the village, from stones from the ruined Abbey, a beauty spot popular with lovers and families on summer picnics.

Eildon's days of glory had ended some 600 years ago when King Henry the Eighth, who was as enthusiastic about matrimony as I was to avoid it, decided how he would deal with the Pope's refusal to permit him the luxury of bigamy. He had responded to excommunication by chopping off a few heads and rewriting the rules. These included destroying the abbeys and transferring their wealth, which was considerable, into the Royal purse.

May blossom had become the buds of June and I sat in the garden with Thane, my deerhound, who had temporarily abandoned the yellow gorse to pretend to be a domestic pet.

He spent a lot more time with Jack and me of late and, stroking his head, I wondered if it was only trust or because he was getting old.

Where did he live on Arthur's Seat? I had long since given up trying to solve the mystery of his origins, how he existed and looked so well cared-for. And why there was a deep bond, a strange telepathy between us where he often seemed to read my mind or understand when I was in danger.

I was happy that morning, weddings were still far off and

the sun was warm on my arms. To a blackbird's serenade above our heads, I opened the newspaper Jack had left with me that morning.

It promised to be dull reading. The main item as usual was Jubilee fever, its spread infecting Edinburgh and its environs with a daily outcrop of summer fetes and fairs.

There was one just a short distance away, within walking distance or a bicycle ride from where I lived in Solomon's Tower, at the base of Arthur's Seat.

The Sisters at St Anthony's Convent were today having a 'Modest Charity Fair in aid of their Orphans.'

My interest was immediate. The Sisters were a teaching order of nuns. And Danny McQuinn had been one of their orphans.

When his parents died in Ireland during the Famine, the priestly relative heading for Eildon and, at his wits end about what to do with a little lad, had deposited him en route at the Catholic orphanage in St Leonard's.

Danny was clever and had grown up a credit to the Sisters who educated him. At 17 he joined the ranks of the Edinburgh City Police as constable and worked his way up to become the trusted sergeant of my father, Chief Inspector Faro.

When I was twelve years old, Danny had rescued me and my younger sister Emily from kidnappers during one of Pappa's most sinister cases. Suffering thereafter from a case of terminal hero-worship, I was determined to marry Danny when I grew up. And that is exactly what I did, completely oblivious of the existence of any eligible young men of my own age. It was always Danny – although I have to confess that marriage was never really his idea.

Not his strong point, he said as he tried to talk me out of it, bringing sadly to mind the old adage: 'There are those who kiss and those who are kissed and there are those who love and those who are loved.'

I had long realised sadly that where Danny was concerned I was in the latter category, but I was nothing if not tenacious, my mind firmly resolved to follow him out to America and share his life in the still untamed state of Arizona.

Danny wasn't strong enough to send me back home again. And so we were married. We had ten years together until the day in August 1894 when he walked out of the house never to return.

I was not unaware of the daily hazards of his life with Pinkerton's Detective Agency and the Bureau of Indian Affairs. He had enemies on both sides, he said, a timely warning to prepare me for the possibility of his disappearance. I had been left with careful instructions.

Wait six months only and then, acknowledging that he was missing presumed dead in some unmarked grave in Arizona, I was to return to Edinburgh where I would be safe.

What he did not know was that I was carrying his child.

I had not known for certain either, somewhat cautious after several miscarriages in our ten years of marriage. But the baby son Danny had longed for was born strong and healthy, only to die of a fever on a Navajo reservation where we had taken refuge from an attack on settlers by renegade Apaches.

Thoughts of Danny and that baby in its unmarked grave were still a bitter agony. I had a sudden wild idea that a visit to the orphanage and acquaintance with any of the now elderly nuns who might have known him might also offer healing or even exorcism, especially when I was on the threshold of a second marriage.

Not quite a new idea. In the two years of my life just half a mile away I sometimes felt guilty at not visiting the convent and asking the nuns to say a Requiem Mass for Danny McQuinn. A devout Catholic he would have wanted that, but I also knew that it would be like drawing a line across twelve years of my life. And so, always ready with excuses, telling myself next week, next month, I had pushed it aside, perhaps with the feeling that a Mass for Danny's soul would pull down the curtain of finality.

None of this, of course, did I confide in Jack. I doubted whether his strict Presbyterian upbringing could cope with such superstitious Popery. As it was his lips would tighten perceptibly and his eyes turn cold, his manner suddenly remote, at the least hint or mention of Danny.

With good cause, I recognised the signs and had learned to avoid any mention of my late husband whom Jack understandably regarded as a rival he could do nothing about, untouchable and deified by death.

Telling Thane where I was going and pretending that he could read my mind and the newspaper, he watched me take out my bicycle and saying no, he could not come with me, I left him looking quite dejected as I set off alone for the convent at St Leonards.

2

The Little Sisters of the Poor's Summer Fair had brought out the best in Edinburgh weather, warm and sunny with the merest hint of a breeze. I free-wheeled gracefully downhill towards the tall grey house which had once been Danny's boyhood home.

What had he been like then? I wondered, hoping that a class group photograph might at least provide clues to those early years lost long before we had met. The enigma of a lad who had hated England so passionately and chanted 'God save Ireland' but had yet joined the Edinburgh City Police. Although his nationalism did not waver, I knew that at Pappa's side he had helped to foil at least one assassination attempt on the Queen of England.

Such were my thoughts as I rode along the drive where figures, black-robed, white-coiffed, fluttered busily from stall to stall across the lawns.

I soon discovered plenty of pretty things to buy, witness to the nuns as excellent seamstresses and housekeepers. Not only homely pots of jam and vegetables from the gardens but delicate nightgowns and robes very suitable for a bride's trousseau. And, nestling coyly alongside, the inevitable baby layettes regarded as a discreet but necessary follow up to the honeymoon.

I moved away rather quickly. On to crocheted shawls, tablecloths and antimacassars which seemed appropriate gifts for my future in-laws next week.

As I made my selection, the best of Edinburgh's weather having overreached itself, the day went into sudden decline. A deluge had all the visitors racing for shelter.

The nuns had foreseen such an eventuality and were well

prepared as we were speedily ushered into the assembly hall of the convent where tea was being served.

Looking around, I saw fewer ladies than I had expected taking seats at the flower bedecked tables with their white lace cloths and I noted that the nuns were counting heads.

Doubtless, the well-trained Edinburgh Presbyterian matrons, casting nervous glances over their shoulders at sanctuary lamps and statues of the Virgin and Child had quickly decided that patronising stalls under anonymous non-denominational skies outside was one thing. But stepping under the sheltering roof of a Popish establishment with the sniff of incense was quite another.

I had no such qualms. I drank the tea and ate the sandwiches and cake. My life at Solomon's Tower tended towards the spartan and despite my lack of inches and small frame, I was always hungry these days.

Thoroughly enjoying this unexpected treat for a sixpence I looked around at the impromptu waitresses. The older girls from the orphanage wore neat grey uniforms while those attending the stalls were doubtless young novices who had not yet taken their vows. Here and there I identified accents other than local. French, Irish – But all had gentle serene expressions, faces empty of the marks that living in the world outside the convent leaves on women stressed by childbirth, the rearing of a family and its attendant responsibilities.

About to leave and inspect the weather, I was asked to sign the visitors book at the door. I could hear Jack's cynical interpretation of this invitation as a useful trap for the unwary.

'Very useful indeed having the names of sympathetic ladies when they do door to door with their collecting tins for the orphanage.'

As I lingered inside waiting for the rain to abate, I was approached by one of the older nuns. Making an opening remark about the weather, she smiled:

'I noticed you signing our little book – Mrs McQuinn.' Her pause was a question. 'An Irish name?' she smiled. 'Are you from Ireland, my dear?'

I said I was from Edinburgh. 'McQuinn is my married name.'

I looked at her. Perhaps she had known Danny, but it was difficult to attach ages to those smooth faces unlined by the passions and torments of domestic life.

'My husband was at the orphanage here. Thirty years ago. But that would be before your time,' I added gallantly.

She laughed. 'Not at all. I had just taken my vows. I am Sister Angela by the way,' she added. We shook hands. Less smooth and unlined than her face they told a tale of frequent encounters with hard rough work.

'Danny McQuinn.' She smiled. 'I remember how proud Sister Mary Michael was of him. I'm sure she would be delighted to meet you.'

This was an unexpected stroke of luck. 'She is still with you?' I had almost said alive, but remembering that Danny referred to her as an old lady over 20 years ago, that seemed highly unlikely.

'Yes, she is still with us.' Sister Angela nodded gently and sighed. 'But only just! She is past ninety and infirm in body but her spirit is quite indomitable as she waits patiently for the call to meet her Maker.'

As she spoke she considered me thoughtfully. 'She lives a life of meditation and sees few people. But I am sure she would make an exception in your case, someone with a connection to one of her past pupils,' she added enthusiastically.

'I would like that very much.' With a feeling that she was perhaps over-optimistic about the old nun's memory, I could not pass up even this remote possibility of a glimpse into the missing years of Danny's early life. 'Perhaps we could arrange a time for me to call on her.'

'How about now?' chirped Sister Angela. 'If you are not too busy.'

I said I wasn't and she nodded eagerly. 'Her room is close by.'

It was quite an ordinary large rambling house, spartan as became a convent, the sole decoration of stark walls and uncarpeted floors were a few holy pictures with here and there a sanctuary lamp glowing under a statue of Mary and Jesus.

She stopped before the open door of the chapel and alongside one with a notice 'Sister Mary Michael.'

'Wait here, Mrs McQuinn.' A moment later she emerged and I was ushered into a room as close as one could get to a monastic cell plus the homely addition of a fitted cupboard known to every householder as the Edinburgh press.

A quick glance took in a small bed, table, and sitting in an upright wooden chair by the window, her body bent almost double, an old nun.

As Sister Angela introduced us, my heart rebelled against such an appalling lack of comfort for a woman past ninety. A few cushions and and an extra blanket could hardly have offended against holy church.

'This is Mrs McQuinn, Danny's wife.' Sister Angela's voice was louder than when we had spoken together, tactfully indicating deafness.

Sister Mary Michael turned her head slowly towards me and smiled. I could not vouch for what she saw through eyes filmed and hooded with age.

Sister Angela had retreated to the door and I hovered wishing I had somewhere to sit down. That hard little bed would be better than nothing.

For a few moments I was aware of thoughtful scrutiny.

I guessed that the Little Sisters were probably well aware of all the Roman Catholics in Newington and she was exploring the sensitive ground of rarely speaking to someone whose religious inclinations were not her own.

I took a deep breath. 'Danny is dead, sister. I am a widow and have been for the past three years.'

This took her by surprise. Her hands fluttered. 'Surely not, surely not,' she murmured staring up at me.

'I'm afraid so.'

'Three years, you say.' Bewildere, she shook her head. 'But that cannot be.' And turning her head towards Sister Angela, she pointed.

'In the cupboard, please. Bring me the cardboard box.'

Sister Angela did as she was bid and I watched as she lifted the lid and a mass of folded yellow papers and notes overflowed.

'It is here somewhere.'

We watched patiently as she shuffled among the papers. 'I had it here,' she said helplessly.

Sister Angela's offer of help received an impatient gesture. With her hand restraining the unruly contents of the box, the old nun looked at me.

'I had a note from Danny,' she said firmly. And frowning, shaking her head at the effort of remembering. 'Now when was it? Yes, yes, just recently. I remember.'

That couldn't be. But my heart pounded just the same.

'How recently?' I asked.

She stared towards the window. 'Three weeks – yes, I am sure. It was three weeks ago. But I seem to have mislaid it.'

She had to be mistaken. I caught a sympathetic glance from Sister Angela and I interrupted those scrabbling movements among the papers.

'It isn't possible – the time, I mean. You see, Danny has been dead for three years,' I said patiently.

As if she didn't hear me, she continued pulling out papers

24

and thrusting them back again. Some fell on the floor and were retrieved by us.

'It is possible, Mrs McQuinn,' she said. 'His note is here somewhere.'

I told myself she was very old, obviously confused and upset as she kept protesting, mumbling:

'It was definitely here, just a short while ago.'

'Would you care to borrow my spectacles?' asked Sister Angela, producing them from her pocket.

'If you insist. If you think that will help,' was the icy response. 'But I remember perfectly what Danny's note looked like.'

We waited patiently for another search aided by the spectacles but with no better result. Finally thrusting the box aside with a despairing and angry glance, she took out a large brown envelope.

We watched hopefully. A triumphant sigh. 'These are class photographs. I am sure there is one with Danny.' Adjusting the spectacles, she took out the cardboard mounts.

'Ah yes. Here is the year Danny came to us. I remember it well, the very day it was taken.'

A group of small boys sitting cross-legged in the front row. One unmistakably a very young and beautiful child. Danny. Even before her finger directed me to him, my heart leapt in recognition and tears welled in my eyes.

Here was Danny as I had never known him. An image I had hoped would one day be that of our baby son, had he lived.

'An older relative, a priest brought him to us from Ireland. He used to look in and see the boy and he has kept in touch with us –'

Her voice was fading. Her breathing growing heavy, eyes closing. All this undue excitement was too much for her, falling asleep as she spoke to us and Sister Angela was just in time to seize the cardboard box and its contents before they slid to the floor.

The action alerted the old nun, who jerked awake.

'We are just leaving,' Sister Angela whispered.

Sister Mary Michael gazed up at me. 'I am sorry I couldn't find Danny's note to show you, Mrs McQuinn. But I do remember the exact words. It said: "Forgive me. I have sinned. Pray for me."'

Once more, as if the final effort had been too much, her chin sunk to her chest.

I stared at her. It couldn't be. Wanting to stay, to argue, as Sister Angela put a gentle hand on my arm and with an apologetic glance led me towards the door.

Outside she said, 'That often happens these days. She tries very hard, you know.'

I leaned against the wall. I wanted to know so much more.

'Don't upset yourself, Mrs McQuinn. Gracious, you have turned quite pale.'

My head was whirling as I tried to set my thoughts in order.

Danny – three weeks ago. And I, who had lived through years of horror and danger in Arizona and never turned a hair, fainted away for the first time in my life.

I was conscious of being supported to a bench, a glass of water. Sister Angela's face looming over me. 'Take a few sips. That's better.' She patted my hand gently.

'I'm sorry. Three weeks ago – it just isn't possible.'

'Now don't you be worrying yourself, my dear. You must remember that Sister Mary Michael is different to the rest of us. Time gets like that for old people. Three weeks, two or three months.' She shrugged. 'They are much the same to her.'

'But not three years, Sister. She was very definite about

that. And three years ago was the last time I saw Danny. I have every reason to believe that he is dead.'

Sister Angela shook her head. This experience was beyond her. She didn't know what to say, who to believe.

'And that note,' I insisted. 'If that was true, what she remembered. Why should he ask forgiveness, that he had sinned? I don't understand. It doesn't even sound like Danny –'

Sister Angela seized on that gratefully. 'There you are then. You are probably right. The note was from someone else. After all, Danny isn't such a rare name, is it. She saves all her prayer notes. Yes, that could be it. From some other Danny,' she added consolingly.

But I wasn't convinced. 'She recognised him in the photograph, pointed him out. She didn't seem mistaken about that.'

There was a note of hysteria in my voice and Sister Angela looked anxious.

'If it was Danny then why hasn't he got in touch with me?'

She looked away, embarrassed. The ways of married people were an unknown territory, far beyond her.

I stood up swaying. I felt deadly sick.

She took my arm. 'Now, Mrs McQuinn, I know it's all very upsetting, but remember what I've told you.' And suddenly confidential: 'It's getting worse. Just last week even, she was absolutely certain that she had never met our parish priest before – and he comes every week to say Mass –'

But I was no longer listening, deaf to these examples being trotted out for my benefit. I was aware of the overpowering smell of incense. I almost ran outside to breathe in the fresh air.

'At least the rain has stopped,' said Sister Angela, eagerly grasping normality again. 'Have you far to go? You're still looking very pale,' she added regarding me anxiously.

I straightened my shoulders with effort. 'I'm fine. I have

my bicycle. Over there by the wall. I live just half a mile away.'

Regarding the machine with considerable trepidation she said, 'Perhaps you should contact Father McQuinn. I'm sure we have his address somewhere. I can go and look for it,' she added helpfully, 'if you wait a moment."

Thanking her, but saying that wasn't necessary, I was aware of her anxious expression as she watched me ride away, down past the stalls deserted after the rain.

3

The fresh air didn't do much good. I still felt dreadful by the time I reached Solomon's Tower. Dreadful – and angry too.

If Danny McQuinn was alive, for heaven's sake, why hadn't he got in touch with me, his wife, first of all. Did I no longer matter? Was I less important than the orphanage who had brought him up?

I told myself it couldn't be true. There had to be a mistake otherwise the implications of the prayer note Sister Mary Michael had received were the stuff that nightmares are made of. And I was back in that constant dream made manifest by that renewed longing to see him again, the frail hope of the joy of opening the door and seeing his smiling face. He was taking me into his arms...

And then I woke up.

Now that fleeting moment of madness, of dream fulfilment, had been replaced by a sense of impending doom and I remembered the solemn pagan warning: Take care what you ask the Gods for. Their answer may not be quite what you expected or even find acceptable.

Despite the now bright day, the Tower seemed suddenly brooding and desolate, and I realised why local people thought of it as a sinister haunted place. In no mood for empty echoing rooms I sat on the wooden bench outside making the most of the soothing comfort, the solace of warm sunshine.

It was all I had. In a sudden orgy of self-pity I decided that when I needed tenderness and reassurance, a banishment of my fear, Jack Macmerry wasn't there. No doubt he was busy tracking down criminals on Leith Walk. Even Thane had disappeared too when I yearned for a friendly welcome.

Should I tell Jack about my strange experience? I quickly

decided against that recalling tight lips and cold eyes at the mention of Danny McQuinn.

I closed my eyes and rested my head against the wall, letting the gentle scent of summer flowers and fresh cut grass drift over me.

Oh Danny – it can't possibly be true. You would have come to me first. Sent me a message before anyone.

And that was the unkindest cut of all. I thought again of his life with Pinkerton's Detective Agency and the Bureau of Indian Affairs, remembering his warning that there were plenty of hazards, for he had enemies, as he described it, in both camps. They were the unquestionable reason for his precise instructions about that six months waiting time before I returned to Edinburgh.

Or how he never knew that day he walked out of my life for ever that I was carrying his child after a long history of miscarriages and false alarms. Then when pregnancy had seemed beyond belief I bore the baby son we had both longed for, only to lose him with fever.

As I prepared to quit Arizona my frequent and frantic enquiries to Pinkerton's branch in Tucson met with little response even, I thought, with cruel indifference. Either they knew something they were not at liberty to tell me, or they were speaking the truth, equally baffled by Danny's disappearance.

If only I could have talked to someone, a friend who knew him, but there was little hope of that for, always on the move, staying in Arizona's infamous shack towns, we had little chance to form lasting friendships.

There were none of his colleagues I could turn to. He had always been seriously noncommittal about his activities. An occasional visitor with an Irish accent about whom no information was volunteered made me aware that Danny's sympathies lay with the Caen na Gael, a group of Irish Americans who funded a movement to free Ireland from British rule. There were other secret visitors and when my offered hospitality was unceremoniously declined, I suspected that Danny was also a secret Government agent.

On one occasion I made the accusation. How he had roared with laughter at such an idea.

Jabbing a finger at me he said: 'Ask me anything about Pinkerton's and I'll tell you what you want to know. Go on, ask me.'

And that invitation was irresistible. There was one matter concerning my own future I was most eager to discuss.

'I know for one thing that they employ female detectives.'

Getting it wrong, he raised a mocking eyebrow. 'So you think I have a fancy woman.'

I gasped for I had to confess that the thought had never occurred to me.

Taking my astonishment for anxiety, he kissed me gently. 'No one but you, my Rose.'

'I'm just interested, that's all.'

Eyeing me doubtfully, he sighed. 'Sure, Allan Pinkerton employs a few brave women. He is keen to employ females as he believes them to be at least as clever and daring as men in detective work – and more imaginative.' His somewhat sceptical tone regarding Pinkerton's confidence in this novel and daring procedure had raised a hue and cry within his organisation. And none was more concerned than Danny McQuinn, alarmed that his own wife might have inherited her famous father's talents. He often said Pappa had wished for a son, interpreting this as a wish that I had been a boy rather than the wistful ache and guilt for the stillborn baby that had cost his dear Lizzie, my Mamma, her life.

'If Mr Pinkerton approves why can't I – I mean – you could recommend me, Danny. Please. I would love to try my hand at catching criminals. You know I was well trained in observation and deduction by Pappa at a very early age.'

'Observation and deduction!' He shook his head, then added seriously, 'And how far do you think that would get you in this lawless land where criminals shoot first and answer questions afterwards?'

'But –' I began indignantly.

Danny held up his hand. 'No, Rose. Definitely not – now or ever. You don't know what you are talking about. I wouldn't consider such a thing –'

'But Danny,' I pleaded, 'I wouldn't be alone. We could work together.'

He leaned back in his chair, regarding me narrowly, a searching gaze of critical assessment. As if seeing me for the first time, his look asked was I to be trusted, and made me feel not only uncomfortable but afraid.

The moment was gone in a flash. He laughed, took my hand. 'So you think you're a brave woman, Rose,' he said softly. 'You think you could deal with outlaws and murderers because your illustrious father taught you some clever method of observation and deduction.'

Shaking his head, he went on, 'Believe me, you'd need a lot more than that in some of the situations you'd find yourself in, or the sort of criminals I encounter on a daily basis, little more than animals, the very dregs of humanity. Situations where I might not be around, or even in a position to protect you from rape – from torture and slow death.'

Ignoring that I said defiantly, 'Whatever you say, I'd still like to meet Mr Pinkerton.'

Leaning forward, he laughed again, tenderly cupping his hand under my chin. 'Is that so now? And don't think I haven't any idea what this famous meeting would be all about. I can read your mind.'

'I would like to talk to Mr Pinkerton,' I insisted. 'He is from Scotland, after all. We would have that in common.'

'Yes, he's from Glasgow. Know why he came to America?'

'I expect he thought like many emigrants that it was a land of opportunity.'

Danny shook his head. 'Of necessity, in his case. His militant activities in the '40s on behalf of the rights of the working man brought him to the close attention of the law and he was forced to flee the country.'

I knew some of the story from his autobiography, *Thirty Years a Detective*, published in '94 (the year he died), which I had read avidly.

In Chicago, he found like-minded thinkers, sympathetic folk and a job in what was a very rudimentary police force. A brave dogged hardworking lawman, he was soon rounding up small time criminals, powerful gangs and counterfeiters. Such was his success that after having been in America only eight years, he was able to set up his own agency.

From '60 to '62, Pinkerton was responsible for the personal safety of President Abraham Lincoln and for a time spymaster as Head of Intelligence to General McLennan, operating behind the enemy lines during the Civil War.

When the war ended the General was removed from office, his activities no longer needed and Pinkerton also returned to his detective agency.

Danny however, in common with many other Americans, had his own theory about Lincoln's assassination. Had General McLennan stayed in the secret service, they felt certain that the quick-witted Pinkerton might have got wind of the plan and averted what was, for America, a national disaster.

'Pinkerton was ruthless too,' said Danny. 'The end justifies the means if the end is justice, was his slogan. He behaved outrageously outside the law and was well known to have authorised illegal burglaries on behalf of clients. And the killing of bank robbers on the grounds that had they ever come to court, juries might not have convicted them.'

Pinkerton wrote several other books and, after his death, the agency he had founded went on, grew in splendour and fame. Known to the world by its slogan "We Never Sleep" with its logo of a wide-open eye, they were always on the lookout for experienced lawmen like Danny McQuinn whose last word on the subject was a firm:

'Detective work is no job for a married woman.'

His words had come home to roost with a vengeance. History was repeating itself with Detective Inspector Jack Macmerry who, whatever his emotions regarding his inaccessible and dead rival, would have shared his sentiments on that particular issue.

I had no idea what were the views of Edinburgh City Police on the subject of female detectives or the milder term 'lady investigators', but I could guess that they regarded criminal investigation as a 'men only' province.

I felt so impatient with authority. Would a day ever dawn when women ceased to be treated as playthings or breeding machines, when they would be given equal rights with men. My hackles rose in anger at the suffragettes' gallant struggles as portrayed in a recent pamphlet which I had been at pains to keep concealed from Jack.

Watching him eat his supper that evening, I observed that this had not been one of his good days. He was in a bad mood, his perplexed frown told me all I needed to know. His current investigation was not going well and it would not be a clever move on my part to bring up the subject of Sister Mary Michael's mysterious note from Danny.

So in my mind I went over and over the details of that brief and frustrating interview and realised that she had told me something of importance. That his relative Father Sean McQuinn, whom I had presumed would be dead by now, was not only alive but occasionally came into Edinburgh and visited the convent.

And suddenly I was quite eager to visit Jack's parents on the off chance that the priest might have news for me.

Jack was surprised by this burst of enthusiasm but my preparations in the days that followed were accompanied by ghosts of the past, the agonies of the last three years with their false hopes and dreams.

Reason and pride – of the wounded variety – insisted that if Danny were alive, he would never have allowed me to suffer so. We were a devoted couple. He was my only love and my despair, for I thought that love awakened when I was twelve years old would last forever.

I had never imagined the remotest possibility that I could love again, desire and marry another man – and yet, Jack Macmerry was on the threshold of disproving that theory.

I believed that Danny had loved me too, although doubts crept in sometimes that he was not quite as passionate or single-minded in his devotion as I had been. After all, I had pursued him to America and rather forced his hand if truth were told. That did arouse feelings of guilt, but I told myself firmly that such overwhelming emotions were more natural to womankind who stayed at home, raised families and waited on their men. Feelings which I had to admit sat uneasily alongside the women's rights I so fervently supported.

In the end, it all came back to that inescapable wounded pride and the reassurance I needed that if Danny were still alive and well and in Scotland, I was the first he would have got in touch with, the most important person in his life.

And on days when logic needed extra sustenance I told myself that the old nun had been mistaken and for her, confused by the passage of time, three weeks could have been three years. So taking comfort and refuge in Sister Angela's consoling explanation regarding common Irish names I looked forward to Eildon and meeting Father McQuinn.

He would confirm that Danny was indeed dead and that there no longer existed any impediment to my marriage to Jack Macmerry.

4

As it turned out, I was to travel alone by train to meet my future in-laws for the first time.

Jack was summoned to appear as a police witness in a Glasgow court. This last minute change of plans put me in an ill-humour, recalling as it did childhood occasions in the household of a Chief Inspector where my sister Emily and I soon realised that Pappa was never there when we needed him.

In despair and anger, I thought, was this to be the set pattern of my life as a policeman's wife – for the second time. Was I being foolish, indeed insane, to expect anything better?

I should have realised when I followed Danny to America that life was to be no romantic bed of roses. Hazardous and uncertain, it had eventually made me a widow. I had now learned to live with that bitterness and grief but was I in my right mind even to consider a second marriage to a policeman, especially since I was independent, with a successful career?

Although Jack certainly did not approve of my choice, he knew when to keep his mouth shut and to accept that I could deal with 'discretion guaranteed' cases that were outwith the scope of the Edinburgh City Police.

Domestic incidents involving the thrawn behaviour of relatives, cheating husbands and wives, betrayed mistresses. My logbook was full of them. Where the arrival of a uniformed policeman would have caused alarm and despondency, a respectable young woman could, without suspicion, gain access to houses to track down thieving servants, or fraud by close relatives. Such a convenient arrangement thus avoided scandals well-to-do Edinburgh families were eager to avoid at all cost, which also meant paying handsomely for my services.

Such were my thoughts as I sat in the train awaiting its imminent departure from Waverley Station.

However, even here it seemed that there was no escape from the Little Sisters of the Poor. At the last moment, a young nun ran down the platform and entered my compartment. As she sank breathless into the seat opposite, I greeted her sympathetically about being just in time.

She merely nodded and fixed her gaze beyond the window.

Not wishing to be unfriendly I tried another tack and said: 'Your summer fair was extremely successful I gather, apart from the change in the weather.'

She stared at me and nodded vaguely as if she had no idea what I was talking about. She looked embarrassed and I realised I was presuming she was from the convent. Such institutions were hardly thick on the ground in Edinburgh and I was certain that St Anthony's was the only one of its kind.

She turned towards the window again and did not sink back into her seat until the train began at last to move.

Feeling rather uncomfortable I realised that my presumption was a natural mistake since all nuns at first glance look alike in their dress and hoods.

This one looked young enough to be a novice and as her attention was clearly elsewhere I made some mental notes. She had not uttered a word but surely a novice would not yet have taken a vow of silence.

There was something in her expression, not nun-like serenity but an expression furtive and anxious. I thought about her urgent attention to the windows not as trying to avoid conversation with me but perhaps expecting someone to join the train. She had now relaxed. Was she pleased – relieved even, that we were now under way?

Her nun's garb too was incomplete. No cross or rosary and as she leaned back more comfortably and closed her eyes I caught a whiff of perfume. A quite exotic perfume. I could have accepted incense or lavender water but this was much too worldly for convent life. It aroused thoughts of seduction, of amorous evenings with a suitor.

My eyes travelled downwards to an elegant silk clad ankle in a fine leather shoe, far from the hard wearing practical footwear of the sisters.

I didn't look away hastily enough. Opening her eyes with a start as we came to the signals, she saw the direction of my glance and hastily thrust her feet out of sight under her robe.

But I kept thinking about those shoes and stockings. Perhaps they were a present, and as a novice, this might indicate her last worldly fling before entering the cloisters. Her slim ungloved hands as she had rearranged her robe also gave cause for comment. Such nails neatly manicured, pink and shining, slightly longer than was usual, and I was observing the hands of a middle or upper class Edinburgh young lady who had never done a day's manual work in her whole life.

I was intrigued for I would never know the answer to this piece of observation, having fallen into the pastime I had learned from Pappa long ago. To while away the time on train journeys he had encouraged me to scrutinise fellow passengers secretly and make up character studies. After they left the train, we would discuss the results and decide who they were and what were their professions.

For me there was only one conclusion. The young woman sitting opposite, despite her garb, was no nun, novice or otherwise.

When the train reached our destination, to my surprise it was hers also. Which suggested the faint hope that she might have some business with the local church.

Seeing her hurrying out of the station while I waited on the platform for the Macmerrys how I regretted that wasted train journey. It was unlikely that a Border stronghold of the Scots kirk would have more than one Roman Catholic church and had I been tenacious enough to discover where she was heading, I might have learned something to my advantage about Father McQuinn.

An elderly man hurried breathlessly through the barrier, red-faced with the bewildered and anxious look of one who is meeting a passenger for the first time.

His complexion suggested the farmer despite the smart bowler hat, apparently seldom worn, since his hand went to it constantly as if its rare presence nagged him. Then walking along the platform he tugged at the jacket of that handsome tweed suit, suggesting Sunday best made long ago for a fitting now considerably more ample than the tailor's original measurements.

Although shorter and more thickset, Andrew Macmerry's resemblance to Jack was unmistakable. I smiled in his direction and he hurried towards me.

'Rose, is it?' His hand sought the familiar farmer's bonnet and instead encountered the bowler hat. Raising it politely, face sweating with anxiety, he clasped my hand in a powerful grip.

Introductions over, he laughed and picked up my luggage. 'What a relief, I would have kenned you anywhere, lass. You're exactly like Jack told us.' A sideways approving glance. 'Except that he didn't do you justice.' Added shyly, with a slightly embarrassed cough, 'You're far bonnier, lass, far bonnier that we thought you'd be.'

'We' indicated the missing Mrs Macmerry. As I paused and looked around, interpreting my glance, he said hastily:

'The farm's a wee step from the station so Jack's ma has taken the chance of a bit of shopping. Ah, here she is now.'

40

The picture in townsfolk's mind is of farmer's wives rosy and rotund. Jess Macmerry however was as far from that description as could be imagined. Taller than her husband and considerably thinner, her grey hair in a tight no-nonsense bun above a deep frown and a long rather sharp red nose, the kind that suggested a perpetual drip in winter weather.

As we shook hands there was a smile that might have come through a tea-strainer and walking towards the station exit, the shrewd all-enveloping glance told me much about her character, as I read her summing up her son's intended.

She was a disappointed woman. She had firmly decided long ago that had this Rose McQuinn even sprouted angel's wings and borne a message from heaven itself she would still have been no fit mate for Jack Macmerry. A widow woman, I was soiled goods, second-hand, while she had set her heart on a fresh young virgin as daughter-in-law, the only decent and suitable choice for her one and only beloved bairn.

Seated together with Mr Macmerry in the driving seat of the dog-cart, she resumed her relentless scrutiny.

'You're much smaller than we thought you'd be,' she said candidly and, with the expert eye of the farming community, that quick glance over my figure was assessing whether it was strong enough to produce – among an assorted bevy of lively and healthy grandchildren – a lad to some day inherit the farm.

'There's grand stuff in small bundles, Jess.' I detected mild reproach as Mr Macmerry came to my rescue. 'And that's a right bonny head o' hair ye have on ye, lass,' he added gallantly.

It was my turn to be embarrassed by my wild mop of yellow hair inexpertly tamed under a small and now, alas, unfashionable bonnet bought in a moment of optimism in an Edinburgh millinery sale.

'I've always been told that a lot of hair drains your strength away.' Mrs Macmerry's sniff was a stern reminder that a man's admiring eye could be deceived and turning to me: 'Jack tells us you're living alone in Edinburgh. In some old tower on Arthur's Seat.'

Her tone conveyed that living alone was not quite the done thing, and the tower unseen was exceptionally squalid and extremely ruined.

'I would be terrified sleeping in a place like that all on my own. Doesn't it scare you?'

'It doesn't bother me in the least. I feel quite safe.'

She seemed surprised by this and I could hardly confess that most nights Jack slept by my side.

'Rose is a right bonny name,' said Mr Macmerry desperately.

His wife regarded me solemnly. 'Rose? Not very Scotch though, is it,' she reminded him.

He shook his head, his gentle laugh indicated that I was not to be offended. 'I don't suppose you know, Rose, but your father was once on a case in this area. I canna mind exactly, it was a fair time ago.'

Pausing, he smiled. 'But we never imagined then that our wee lad would one day be marrying the daughter of the famous Inspector Faro –'

'Oh, did you meet him?' I interrupted eagerly, ignoring Mrs Macmerry's stony glance and grasping this new talking point for what it might open up.

'Nay, lass, it was market day in Peebles that Friday.' He sounded disappointed and as I was left wondering what the case had been, Mrs Macmerry put in sharply, 'Of course, it was nothing involving any of our friends or the farming folk, thank goodness.'

Mr Macmerry frowned. 'Something to do with Fenians. I think that's what it was.' His vague tone suggested that national politics were beyond the range or interest of local farmers.

42

As a silence ensued above the horse's clip-clopping along the leafy road I suppressed a sigh. What I would have given for Jack's presence at that moment.

Surprisingly, his father must have sensed my anxiety. 'The lad shouldna be long now,' he said heartily, as if Jack had just gone down the road for a message from the shops.

I smiled weakly, hoping that he was right. How little he knew the machinations of the criminal courts, where days were known to stretch into weeks and even months during trials. Again I suppressed that burst of resentment against the absent Jack for I didn't relish the immediate future of unspecified days at Eildon Farm under his mother's relentless gaze.

'Jack said you were a teacher,' said his father.

'Yes, that was before I went to Arizona.'

'Arizona?' queried his mother.

'That's America, Jess, over in the west,' she was told.

'Ariz – ona,' she repeated making it sound what it was to folk who had never travelled further than the nearest town: the very ends of the earth, beyond imagination. 'How long were you there?"

'Ten years.'

'You must have been just a bairn at the time,' said Mr Macmerry kindly.

'Not quite, I had been teaching for a few years.'

And I was conscious of Mrs Macmerry at my side. She was moving her lips in some sharp mental arithmetic, shocked to realise what Jack maybe had not told them; that I must be at least thirty, perhaps even older than himself. Another altogether appalling revelation.

A rather more uncomfortable silence followed, in which I received some searching glances. I was no doubt expected to carry on the conversation with accounts of my life in Arizona, what had taken me to this remote wilderness.

I was saved. Crossroads and a signpost loomed into view. A

sharp turn to the right and the leafy lane revealed distant houses, a village nestling in the folds of the Eildon Hills.

Soon be home now, I was told.

I felt a warming of the heart, my natural affinity to living in the shadow of ancient hills. There had been hills too, gigantic ranges of prehistoric red rocks, in Arizona, fringed by red desert. Perhaps that was what had endeared it to me, a place of destiny that I would never again see in this world.

A life and a child lost forever.

A husband too. For at that moment I did not doubt that the old nun had been mistaken and I would never see Danny again.

5

A skeletal ruined abbey drifted into view, carefully railed off, its remains much abused by time and the removal of its stones from which most of Eildon had arisen.

Mrs Macmerry drew my attention to a rather ugly modern church which had not been so fortunate in its architects.

'That's where we were married. Our Jack was baptised there. As you're not attached to any particular church in Edinburgh,' a sigh bravely lamented such a shortcoming, 'we were sure Jack would like you to be married here among the people who have known him all his life.'

A pause for a polite smile to indicate my approval as she went on: 'The minister and his wife are close friends. They are very understanding.'

'He won't worry that you aren't a regular churchgoer,' Mr Macmerry put in hastily.

While his wife took up the theme of similar weddings with bride and groom of different persuasions, I listened politely thinking, Well, well, Jack, I have been much discussed over your kitchen table. Our marriage has been a *fait accomplait* in this particular family long before I said yes to your proposal. A brand new version of the tough strong man who was my lover arose before me and I even wondered if Detective Inspector Jack Macmerry, in the role of obedient son, had asked his parents' permission first.

'Is there a Catholic church?' I asked.

Looks of horror were exchanged.

'Oh, you aren't an RC, are you?' cried Mrs Macmerry in a voice of doom.

'No. But my late husband was Irish and very devout.'

'You didn't turn, did you?' she whispered asked in sepulchral tones.

'Of course not. That was never expected of me.' And taking the plunge headlong, 'I'm only interested because one of Danny's relatives was a priest down here.'

Further mention of my late husband by name raised a sudden acute and embarrassed silence, broken at last by Jack's father.

'Would that be Father Sean McQuinn?'

'Yes,' I replied, expecting the worst.

Mr Macmerry smiled. 'Was and still is, lass. Been here for years. Ever met him?'

'No, but I'd like to look in on him. Say hello.'

Mrs Macmerry had recovered from the shock that I was remotely connected with RCs. She shook her head, regarding me tight-lipped to make it quite clear that visiting a priest indicated feet trembling on the very threshold of Popery.

'I'm sure he'll make you welcome,' said Jack's father, his magnanimity earning a scorching look of disapproval from his wife.

'We don't need a Catholic church. There's just a handful of them in the village. Nothing like our own congregation,' she added proudly.

'Nothing like. He has to go out to the remoter places and take services in the house for Catholics who don't have a church,' said Mr Macmerry, a piece of information which caused Mrs Macmerry to open her mouth in protest and then close it sharply again as we entered the road to the farmhouse.

'There are still some old families like our laird Lord Verney who never turned at the Reformation and stayed loyal to the Stuarts. His carriage was at the railway station meeting that young nun who was on your train,' said Mr Macmerry, handing me down from the dogcart.

So that was the explanation, I thought, of why she looked so well-groomed. My mind raced ahead, picturing her visiting her family for the last time before taking her final vows.

Setting foot for the first time in the house where Jack had been born and bred, square-faced and unimposing on the outside, I was pleasantly surprised by the interior. Dating from the beginning of the century, the kitchen was large and comfortable, originally intended to seat a large family and servants round an immense table, the size of a room in itself.

When I remarked upon this I learned that the Macmerrys lived very economically in a positively feudal system. Nothing was wasted. The wives of their farm labourers dealt with Mrs Macmerry's domestic requirements. Without wages. This service was expected of them as part of the rent-free accommodation they enjoyed in the tiny row of dwelling houses along the roadside and the model cottages on the Verney estate.

Mrs Macmerry added to this account by telling me proudly that the younger members of the workers' families were also recruited and expected to follow in their parents' footsteps, if they were willing and had no other ambitions.

If, however, they yearned for pastures new beyond the confines of the Eildon Hills, her disapproving expression told me that this was regarded as a sense of betrayal. She might have deplored the laird's religion but she approved of his politics. The slave owners of America's deep south could have learned nothing new from Jack's mother.

'We've put you in the best room, next to the bathroom and WC,' she told me proudly as I followed her up a wide uncarpeted stair. 'Come down when you're ready. We have our supper at seven.'

Left alone, the room met with my immediate approval; whitewashed walls and low ceiling beams, an oak floor well-polished, spread with a few bright rugs. Made by Mrs Macmerry with help from the farm labourers' wives, I fancied that the church's annual sale of work would be an event not to be missed.

Untouched walls were a pleasant change from the present fashion prevalent in most Edinburgh houses for heavily embossed wallpapers where every inch of floor was adorned by some small table or potted plant.

Very agreeably, Jack's home had changed little in the passing years and still clung to the uncluttered style that had existed before Queen Victoria ascended the throne, apart from the laird's modern installations of running water and gas. Looking around approvingly at mahogany furniture, a large bed with snowy white covers and an armchair, chest of drawers and a vast wardrobe, I had been honoured indeed. This best bedroom was the one Jack and I would have after our wedding.

The bow window with its upholstered seat looked towards the Eildon Hills. In the foreground and reaching as far as the eye could see before lines of trees intercepted, were fields of sheep. I had never seen so many, certainly their presence would be a singular advantage should I ever find myself sleepless and need to count them in the recommended manner.

Unpacking my valise I withdrew my most recent purchase: 'The Leavenworth Case' by Anna Katherine Green, and the latest exploits of Amelia Butterworth assisting a middle-aged police constable whose 'sense of probability' and specialised knowledge in cigar ash and different grades of writing paper I found immensely satisfying. Despite his contempt for what he dismissed as 'women's fiction' I felt that Pappa would have thoroughly approved of PC Ebenezer Gryne.

Like a guilty secret, I tucked the book away at the back of the drawer, alongside 'Thou Art the Man' featuring female detective Carolis Urquhart, a one-time lady's companion. The life of the author, Mrs Braddon, was almost as sensational as her books and certainly more scandalous. Rumour had it that she lived with her London publisher John Maxwell, a married man with two children, whose wife was confined in a lunatic asylum (shades of *Jane Eyre* and Mrs Rochester, indeed!) Mrs Braddon bore him two children, showing an independence of convention to be met with the approval of the women's rights movement.

This was the country of the 'shilling shocker' scorned and shunned publicly and vociferously by upright intellectuals but, according to gossip when we were in America, authors like Robert Louis Stevenson found them vastly entertaining leisure reading.

Danny went so far as to wonder if in his days of hardship in California, Stevenson added to his meagre income by writing 'such tongue-in-the-cheek nonsense', under a pseudonym, all traces of which would have been destroyed by high-minded Fanny Osbourne, who spent sleepless nights guarding her husband's literary reputation.

Danny had encouraged my leisure reading. I could never find enough books to read and he certainly wasn't afraid that they were secretly encouraging my 'morbid' ambitions, as Jack called them.

We had both encountered enough violence and bloody deaths first-hand to realise that no fictional representation could ever equal the horrors of real life, but I recognised the resolve, the ambition that burned within me, in the heroines of these books.

The seeds were there in my blood waiting to be cultivated and long before I read '*Lady Audley's Secret*', smuggled into Gran's house in Orkney, those seeds had been helped to grow and thrive with Pappa's help. Our games of 'observation and deduction' on railway journeys had certainly helped me solve my first case.

And had I been a boy, my constant moan, I would most

certainly have been encouraged to follow my illustrious father into Edinburgh City Police. No one would have had anything but praise and commendation for my decision. It would have been expected of me.

But a female. Shocking, outrageous! Life was so unfair.

And thinking of Pappa I knew that I could no longer delay writing to Vince and Emily to inform them of my impending marriage. They would be delighted, both were very fond of Jack, but I doubted whether my sister, with a young baby, would even contemplate the journey from Orkney. True my stepbrother might have news of Pappa's present travels with his companion Imogen, but as junior physician to Her Majesty's household, it seemed unlikely that Vince would be free to make the journey from London.

With letters, short and little more than invitations, hastily written, I went downstairs and was rewarded by an open door and a glimpse of the farmhouse parlour where doubt-less important and influential visitors were entertained.

Here, alas, Mrs Macmerry had bowed to the conventions of the day and provided a well-off hostess's background of hos-pitality: Wax fruit and tropical birds under glass, some rather sombre thundery landscapes encased in heavy gold frames seeing their reflections in a gleaming highly polished table and a set of rigid chairs daring visitors to lean back and relax.

I headed towards the kitchen, identified by the pleasant aroma of roasting meat. As a future member of the family, indications were that meals would be served here, for which I was truly thankful.

Mrs Macmerry's brief nod acknowledged my presence while two old labradors lying by the fire idly glanced in my direction. Even before her sharp warning to: 'Bide now!', deciding I wasn't worth the effort of an exploratory sniff, they feebly wagged tails and resumed their slumbers.

Informed that it was early yet for supper but would I like a cup of tea, I accepted gladly.

After I had consumed two cups and my second scone with jam and cream plus a large slice of fruit loaf, a performance Jack's mother watched with some astonishment – having politely declined a third cup – she asked weakly:

'What would you like to do now?

I asked for directions to the post-box.

'There's no collection until morning.'

This was a mere excuse as I had already decided I was going in search of Father McQuinn who would soon settle that most urgent question and prove that Sister Mary Michael could not have heard from Danny three weeks ago.

'I think I'll take a walk,' indicating the letters and my sketchbook.

'Jack didn't tell us you were an artist,' she said accusingly.

Was this hint of bohemian loose living to be held against me, I thought, as modestly declining such aspirations I wondered whether Jack had revealed my true vocation and I hoped earnestly not to be present when he launched that thunderbolt on his family.

I met his father at the gate with two collies, his working sheepdogs trailing obediently at his heels. I hadn't enough wool to make me interesting to them either.

'Where are ye off to now, lass?'

I told him and was given even more precise instructions about the post-box.

'There's a grand view of the Abbey just down the road there.'

Off I went. As soon as he was out of sight, I turned the opposite way clear of the house and made my way into the village we had passed through in the dogcart.

At once I saw my destination. Father McQuinn's church, its

exterior somewhat shabbier than the prosperous Presbyterian kirk.

The door was open. Empty pews, a few candles bravely burning and the lingering smell of incense.

I called: 'Hello?' No answer. Back across the path to the modest and minute cottage adjoining the church, raising my hand to ring the bell, the door was opened by the priest himself.

At first glance I was disappointed. I had hoped he might look like Danny but there was not the least family resemblance.

He was on his way out, in a tearing hurry, formally clad in biretta, stole, clutching a rosary and leading a scared looking lad of about twelve years old.

'Father Sean McQuinn?' I said smiling and introducing myself. 'I am Danny's wife.'

'Danny? Danny who?' He stared at me for a moment before realisation dawned. 'Oh – Danny. You must be Rose, of course.'

Shaking my hand briefly, he indicated the small tearful boy at his side. 'Sorry I can't stop now. The lad's father,' he whispered. 'He's dying. Can we talk later.'

'Of course. I'm here for a few days.'

And rushing down the path, he shouted over his shoulder. 'I'll be in church later this evening. After Mass. We can talk then.'

That would be fine I thought. Just an hour or two.

But it was not to be. As I walked back towards the farm, the rain began and so it remained, unyielding in its ceaseless downpour and holding me trapped for the rest of the evening.

The Macmerry's main meal was at midday. Supper was a lighter version, meat and potatoes again but without the soup and with cake or scones substituting for a dinnertime rich plum duff or bread pudding served with cream.

Afterwards I looked out of the rain-streaked window.

'Oh dear, I could do with a walk.'

Jack's father came to my side. 'Ye canna go out in that, lass. Ye'll catch yer death.' And shaking his head. 'Set in till the morn, I'm afraid, lass.'

And so it was. With neither excuse nor opportunity to leave the house I discovered that Jack's parents obeyed the ancient country laws, bed at sundown to rise with the dawn.

I wasn't sorry to retire early either, rather than remain sitting idly at the kitchen table watching as Mrs Macmerry attended to the final chores of the day.

My offer of assistance was declined with considerable embarrassment by his father, his 'Bide where ye are, lass,' managing to indicate that they might both be answerable to Jack for allowing me to get my hands dirty.

I went upstairs gratefully deciding that I was more tired in Eildon than I ever was in Edinburgh. Something to do with the air, I thought.

I would see Father McQuinn in the morning, get it over with, my mind at rest before Jack arrived. Snuggling down into white linen sheets and snowy pillows smelling of lavender, I realised that Jack knew no such luxury under my spartan roof at Solomon's Tower.

My last thoughts before I slept were of him. Curiously I dreamed of Jack too which I did very rarely. Opening a door, he was waiting and, smiling, he took me into his arms.

For the very first time, my familiar dream had forgotten Danny.

I awoke haunted by a feeling of guilt that Jack had now replaced him.

6

Next morning I came downstairs to the sound of female voices in the kitchen.

Mrs Macmerry had a visitor, a neighbour, Mrs Ward.

'Pleased to meet you, Miss Faro,' she said with a polite smile that made no bones about looking me over very candidly, so that I had the curious feeling of being well-discussed before I made my entrance. Her subsequent manner indicating that she had heard a lot about me, and none of it very good.

It happened that Mrs Ward was also a long-time friend of the Macmerrys, as she revealed with a somewhat triumphant smile that her daughter and Jack had been friends since they were in the cradle together.

I needed to know no more after that. The drift of the talk I had missed was instantly revealed that Mrs Ward, her daughter and Jack's mother had entertained hopes that the cradle would be exchanged in due course for the wedding bed. Hopes that this wretched intruder across the table had blighted.

Mrs Ward had taken all there was to see of me in a glance – wild cloud of hair, a sleepy and dishevelled look – and I knew that once she took her departure, that first meeting would be the talking point of the village for a long while to come. It would make no matter how I shaped out in the end, first impressions were what counted and I would never redeem myself in their eyes.

Leaving, Mrs Ward again shook my hand, formally polite. 'It has been a pleasure, Miss Faro.'

I looked sharply at Jack's mother whose expression was impenetrable. She made no attempt to correct the mistake.

Watching her take Mrs Ward to the door, where they stayed longer than was necessary, I wondered if she had not mentioned that her future daughter-in-law was a widow.

Surely Jack must have told her, I thought desperately, as she returned and asked with careful politeness how I had slept.

'You'll no doubt be wanting just a slice of toast and a wee cup of tea, a mite of porridge, rather than a farmer's breakfast.'

She couldn't have been more mistaken. From under covers on the kitchen range delicious smells of fried bacon drifted towards me and, always hungry, I sat down to a hearty farm style breakfast, the kind I did not doubt that labourers frequently consumed at a much earlier hour.

Jack's mother watched, clearly astonished. Having expected a lady-like refusal she was utterly taken aback at my ready acceptance of second helpings.

'For such a wee lass, you certainly have a big appetite,' she said as I demolished the second slice of thickly buttered toast.

I treated myself to a little mind reading and decided her alarm was justified. She was picturing all Jack's hard-earned pay going on food. I could hear her telling his father: 'She'll be eating him out of house and home.'

I didn't bother to apologise or to explain the reason why I ate so heartily when food was set before me. So often in Arizona I had gone without eating for days on end. Square meals were not at the forefront of my mind as I trudged across the red desert with a baby, bent on survival and trying to keep ahead of the renegade Apaches. With only a fast-emptying water skin to keep us alive, I knew all about starvation.

'What would you like to do today?' she asked briskly clearing the table and making room for a flour bowl and an assortment of baking dishes.

'I realise you will be very busy and I don't want to disturb your routine. I think I shall explore. Or,' indicating the appearance of a bag of flour, 'perhaps I could make myself useful,' I added with a brave attempt at a smile at Jack's father who had just come into the kitchen.

'Nay, lass, there's no need for that,' he said. 'You're here to enjoy yourself, have a nice wee holiday and get acquainted with Jack's homeland. You could start by having a look at the Abbey.'

The offer to make myself useful had not gone past the canny Mrs Macmerry. 'She could always gather a few eggs later, Andrew. That would be a help.' Clearly she wasn't rapturous either about the prospect of having to entertain me until Jack arrived.

I said yes to eggs and, their usual hiding-places indicated from the kitchen door, regretting the absence of my bicycle, I set off down the farm road.

Not for the Abbey but in the direction of Father McQuinn's church.

The door was open. This was a Friday and I had a fleeting notion that today all good Catholics went to confession.

Greeted by incense, sanctuary lights gleaming on statues of saints, but no Father McQuinn, I decided I would try the house next door. Presumably he had a housekeeper or someone I could make an appointment with.

A rotund, rosy-cheeked middle-aged woman came to the door. Flourishing a duster and scrubbing brush she presented a picture of bustling health and energy.

'The Father's out on his morning calls at the moment, dear. He shouldn't be long. Call back later, a couple of hours, say. He'll be delighted to see you then.'

She made that sound like an agreeable prospect and I was almost tempted to ask her if she knew Danny. However, at that moment, a young girl with the appearance of a serving maid poked her head out and enquired anxiously about the state of the oven.

56

I left them to their domestic crisis. The sunny landscape beckoned and I decided to wander off and make the further acquaintance of these Eildon Hills. Another piece of legend, their mysterious depths and caverns were attributed as a peaceful sleeping place for King Arthur and his knights.

I had to admit that the king and his noble lords had a very busy time back yonder in the Dark Ages, they certainly covered a lot of ground across Britain from Cornwall to Scotland. In a time when travel was no easy matter apparently he and his knights had had as many resting-places as beds royal queens were alleged to have slept in.

Eventually I climbed a path overlooking the village, little more than a sheep track which led up the hill. With the warm sunshine across my shoulders and an abundance of birdsong and shady trees, after wandering another mile, I came to a fence and, across a field, looked down on a large squat mansion nestling in a picturesque glen sheltered by the hills.

It was not an imposing building for a noble residence, lacking the fashionable Balmorality that would have immediately rated it as a castle.

Gates and a long drive between trees hinted at local aristocracy. A busy scene with a great deal of activity in the grounds, servants scurrying back and forth in front of the house. On sweeping lawns, awnings hinted at an important event about to take place. A family wedding or yet another manifestation of the Queen's Jubilee celebration, perhaps.

I was enjoying the scene. It would make a great drawing from this angle. I took out my sketchbook, balanced it against a post. Then I almost jumped out of my skin.

A growl at my side and a sheepdog bounded towards me. This was no Thane. There was nothing of my mysterious gentle deerhound in the bared yellow teeth and the snarl that menaced me.

Where was his owner? Even as I tried placating words like

'good dog' and wondered how I was going to convince this brute and get out of his way in one piece, a man materialised from over the ridge.

He had the look of a gamekeeper and demanded: 'What do you think you're doing here, miss? This is private property.'

Relieved at the presence of a human being, I apologised and pointed to my sketch book. 'I didn't realise. I came over the stile –'

His angry glare was quite unbending for a moment, then he began looking me up and down with a rather unpleasant leer that registered a change in his approach. As I turned away, pretending to ignore that hot look, he repeated: 'This is private property.'

I was truly scared now, aware of my danger in this isolated spot. Quite defenceless, miles from any help, faced with a fierce dog who continued to growl at me and a fierce man licking his lips in a very unpleasant manner.

He came towards me, held out his hand. I backed away.

'Come on,' he said impatiently, 'What's that you've been drawing? I want to see it.'

'I haven't started yet,' I stammered pointing to the house. 'It's – it's a rather lovely view.'

The man stared over my shoulder and said: 'His lordship doesna like strangers on his property and he doesna care for artists either, unless he has given them permission.'

'Indeed.' I was feeling braver now, eyeing the dog who continued to regard me fiercely but had settled down at the man's side, obediently awaiting his next command. 'And how does one get permission?'

His glance suggested a dog considering a very tempting bone. 'Not from me, if that's what you're thinking. You take that up with the estate office in the village. See them about it.'

I felt that my immediate danger had now evaporated and

as I prepared to leave the scene with as much speed as dignity would allow, curiosity overcame me.

'Everyone seems very busy at the moment. Are they preparing for the Jubilee celebrations?'

An angry look. A growl his dog might have envied. 'None of your business, miss. Just you keep away – keep out of trouble, if you know what's good for you,' he snarled and the dog leapt to its feet at this change of mood to add a warning bark of its own.

I needed no more persuasion. I left without another word, my thoughts regarding his lordship of a very uncharitable nature. What supreme arrogance not to allow anyone to draw a distant view of his home.

But curiosity remained undefeated, one of my particular failings, and I resolved to find out all about that pompous gentleman and his grim gamekeeper from Jack's father.

Making my way back down the hill, with every hedgerow full of the anxious twittering of nestlings, I opened the sketchbook in a determined effort to capture an ancient tree by a picturesque gate.

Above my head a chorus of corbies lent raucous accompaniment to the occasional bellowing of a cow or the baa-ing of a distant sheep in distress, while below in the world of humans, a horse rider clattered along the road. A distant rumble of wheels and a hay cart moved lazily aside to allow access to a rather grand carriage, which I suspected came from the direction of the stately home.

Perhaps this was the carriage I had glimpsed at the railway station, returning the young nun to her life in the cloisters. But as always while drawing, I was completely absorbed, the rest of the world abandoned as I lost myself in the task before me.

At last a church clock's chime echoed up from the village.

I had been absent two hours. Father McQuinn should be

back by now. Gathering my pencils and book, ten minutes later I was outside his house. There was no response, no one in the church either.

I would try again later but I was frustrated as my sense of urgency suggested that I should get this matter settled before Jack arrived. I did not imagine him taking kindly just before our wedding to anything that remotely involved my former life, my long and happy marriage to Danny McQuinn.

The farmhouse too was empty. Everyone was busy out of doors at this time of day and a note on the table told me to make myself at home. Bread, cheese and milk in the larder.

I wasn't hungry and in my bedroom I moved a comfortable chair to the window with its splendid view of the undulating Borders landscape and took out the book I had been reading on the train.

I was quite addicted to the new fashion of daring mystery stories by lady authors. Especially as none of them had the remotest idea of what murder was like, of what was involved. Such a messy untidy business in real life, these literary ladies with their genteel female detectives would have wilted away in horror at meeting bloody death head-on at first hand.

I think I dozed for a while and hearing footsteps on the path below the window, I hurried downstairs to see Jack's father carrying an injured sheep across his shoulders.

At my commiseration he said: 'Found her way up the hill there, far from the rest of the herd. Fallen on her back, poor beast, and couldn't get up. Poor craiter's lain there for days.'

'Will she recover?' I asked although she looked near death to me.

'Nay, lass. Bad lambing, too old ye ken, and then a broken leg.' He sighed. 'Just brought her back to get my gun,' he said, walking over to a rack above the fireplace.

'Your gun?' I echoed, realising what he had in mind.

'Aye, lass. We've known this craiter a long time. Jess fed her as an orphan lamb. I couldna leave her out there, a mile away, in pain –'

A clatter of churns approaching announced Jack's mother who had been milking the cow.

'What's this, Andrew? Another for your hospital.'

'Too far gone,' was the sad reply as he went out with the gun and his sickly burden.

I was intrigued by the conversation. 'You have an animal hospital?' I asked.

Mrs Macmerry laughed scornfully. 'We havena, but it's no, from lack of trying. The man's daft about animals and folk come from miles around to have him cure their sick beasts. He certainly has a way with them, healing hands they'd call it if they were treating folk but his gift doesna extend to God's created human beings.'

This was a new dimension to Jack's father and having already decided that I liked him very much, one that raised him further in my estimation.

'He would have liked Jack to go to the university to be a doctor but no, the lad had a mind of his own, he didna care for the sight of blood.'

I found this somewhat ironic. The father who saved animal lives and the son who set about pursuing those who destroyed human lives.

That I wasn't hungry was hardly surprising and declining the offer of soup on the pretext of further acquaintance with the village, I set off once again for the Catholic church.

Nearby a group of women were gathered, one of them Mrs Ward whom I had met earlier. She recognised me. With my hand on the church door, I lost my nerve.

It would be all around the village like wildfire. 'Did ye see that? Ken where she was going? Dinna tell me that the lass who is to marry Jack Macmerry is an RC!'

61

I couldn't quite face that imagined Greek chorus and fled in the opposite direction. There, by a stroke of luck, the priest's housekeeper was emerging from the post office with a basket over her arm.

When I greeted her, she stopped, looked a little puzzled and then smiled at me apologetically.

'You were wanting to see the Father? He's been delayed. It often happens.' And then with a curious expression, 'You're a visitor here?'

It was a great chance. Telling her that I was related to Father McQuinn by marriage, I had to repeat that several times as she listened with the intense watchfulness that indicated deafness. At last I was hearing what I most wanted to know. She had met Danny.

'Aye, long ago, when I was a lass. Only the once, he was on a case with an inspector –'

That would be Pappa, I thought.

'– and he looked in for a chat.' Pausing a moment, she added: 'I heard that he had gone to America.'

At this stage I had no desire to embark on the sad story of my widowhood and merely asked if Father McQuinn still heard from him.

'Letters, you mean.' She frowned. 'There might have been some – yes, I think there were –'

And there our conversation ended as a farm cart laden with produce rolled along the street. Presumably this was what all the women were waiting for and the housekeeper stared anxiously in its direction.

'Come and have a cup of tea with me. I'm usually at home in the afternoons, and if you want to be sure of seeing the Father, after mass at eight o'clock is the best time –'

Her eyes fixed on the group of women round the cart, I asked, 'If you could remember when Father McQuinn last heard from Danny –'

But she didn't hear me. She was turning away, I touched her arm and she stared at me blankly.

'It's very important,' I said, repeating it.

She nodded briefly, a puzzled look. 'You can ask him yourself, when you see him later on.'

And with that I had to be satisfied as I made my way in the direction of the Abbey, a magnificent scene worthy of my sketchbook.

As I walked among the ruins, I thought I was alone.

I was wrong. A shadowy figure lurked, then, as if anxious not to be seen, ducked out of sight.

A moment's unease. Was I being stalked? How absurd! I was certainly mistaken. With a shrug, I took out my sketchbook.

7

I had little idea of how long I had been drawing the Abbey ruins before I became aware that I was certainly being watched, my movements carefully followed.

Awareness might have come earlier except that, after firmly dismissing my overactive imagination, I had seemed to have the place to myself; alone with the lavishly decorated masonry far above my head, shreds of broken arches and empty windows imploring the heavens for those long lost days of grandeur.

A post near the entrance held a short history, that the original building had been founded during the reorganisation of the Scottish Church in 1126 by King David the First. Intended for the Cistercian church which, while dedicated to poverty, contrived as did the great abbeys of the period to create unprecedented wealth. The truth of this lay in the tiny hamlets and villages which had sprung up alongside.

The original abbey was a place of worship but after its destruction by the English army following the Scots raid over the Border in 1385, rebuilding was in stark contrast to its former simplicity and the new edifice's ornamentation marked it out as one of the most opulent Border monasteries.

Now only the village of Eildon remained, a cluster of houses arising from a systematic pillaging of the Abbey's scattered stones. There was something here for the philosopher in all this, I thought, choosing a broken cloister wall as the vantage point for a sketch of the ruined chancel.

Engrossed in my task, the silence was shattered by a bird rising screeching into the sky. I looked up and saw the faint outline of a watching figure high up, gazing down.

A tall man. The light behind him made identification uncertain.

But there was something in that stance – something familiar.

'Jack!'

Had he come back unexpectedly and guessing where I'd be, was trying to surprise me.

Jack? No, that wasn't Jack's style at all.

Shading my eyes, I looked upwards. He immediately stepped back.

Definitely not Jack.

I went on drawing, curious but not in the least alarmed – not yet.

A few moments later, conscious again of distant eyes intent upon me, I looked up knowing that he was back once more.

This time I waved, called a greeting. Immediately he ducked out of sight. And that furtive gesture was enough to scare me. I no longer felt safe sitting alone in this vast ruin.

There was worse to come. As I made my way towards the entrance, I passed the spiral stair which led to the ruined gallery and heard stealthy footsteps descending.

A braver woman would have stayed until the mysterious watcher appeared. But aware of the isolation and now certain that I was being stalked I hesitated no longer.

I took flight and did not stop until the gate clanged shut behind me. Only then did I pause to look back.

The abbey grounds were deserted and whoever was on that spiral staircase had not appeared across the lawns.

I am not nervous by nature, nerves of steel had been forged by the constant everyday dangers of a pioneering life, but there was something sneaky and furtive about this encounter that touched a raw edge of nightmare.

Conscious that my heart was beating fast, I was overjoyed to be hailed by Jack's father in the pony cart.

He was taking the younger of his two collies, Rex 'to a farmer up-by' he said, indicating the area I had explored earlier. There was a fine bitch to be served. Did I fancy coming with him?

Saying that I thought animals made their own arrangements about such matters, as I jumped aboard, he said,

'Valuable breeding bitch, great pedigree, had some wee trouble with her innards, while back. But I've managed to put it right, a few of the right herbs and a bit of nursing. Aye, she'll have plenty litters yet awhile. This'll be Rex's first siring – officially,' he added proudly.

Asked what I had been doing I told him I had explored the abbey and listening to a full account of its history far outpacing the small notice I had read, I decided against mentioning my sinister watcher.

In fact, the further we travelled from the ruined abbey, the sillier it sounded, the product of an overwrought imagination. And what was more important, we had now reached a part of the track where his lordship's mansion was faintly visible.

To my question he said: 'Verneys have lived there for 200 years. From Ireland originally, they stayed loyal to the Stuarts. Loads of money, staunch Catholics – bit of a thorn in the side in a Church of Scotland area but they keep themselves to themselves.'

I said I could imagine that it might cause problems, having a local laird who is of a different persuasion.

He nodded. 'Particularly when this laird also has connections with our Royalty by marriage. It doesn't make good news to local folk either that a goddaughter of the Queen is about to become a nun.'

That must be the nun I had travelled with from Edinburgh.

He went on: 'I have always tried to keep out of local politics, especially where religion is concerned. His lordship lets me run my sheep on his land and so I say live and let live.'

And with a 'whoa' to the pony-cart, 'Well, lass, what do you think of the view from here?'

It was magnificent. We were so high that it felt almost like being a bird staring over the undulating landscape of the Border counties, right down to Northumberland and north to Midlothian. Far below us, a great moving tide of sheep.

To my question he answered proudly, 'Aye, they are ours. I suppose all sheep look alike to you, but this herd are different from the general rule. Our border Cheviots with their white faces and Roman noses take their names from these hills. The early Celts who in settled this area got the sheep as well and the Roman noses are thought be a throwback to sheep from the East, first domesticated by folk from the Mediterranean and brought north west through Europe.'

I said I promised never again to dismiss every sheep I encountered as a rather dull dumb creature, interesting from my viewpoint only for its wool.

He laughed. 'Lass, no other creature has made anything like the same contribution to the prosperity of our land as sheep, although we know little for certain of the ancestry of the various breeds. Monastic establishments of the Cheviot area, like our abbey back there, had their own flocks in the 13th century with sheep runs over most of the area which evolved with traces of the Blackface from the Pennine hills.'

Pausing to urge on the ponycart down a twisting farm track, a mile further on and our destination loomed into view. Andrew said:

'I'll only be a wee minute, lass,' and I watched Rex trot smartly ahead towards the farmhouse, occasionally pausing to sniff the air, ready and eager for what was expected of him.

A door opened, voices, a bark of greeting and then silence. As I waited alone once more, I wondered if I should mention the stalker in the abbey. Again it seemed quite ridiculous.

The thing that troubled me most was that fleeting second, an illusion of familiarity, that the watcher knew who I was. If so, and if this was an innocent encounter, why was he so anxious not to be seen?

And then to return again, to watch once more. But worst of all was the fact that there was no encounter at the foot of the spiral staircase where our paths should have crossed.

Even if he did linger in his descent I should have seen whoever it was just behind me, as I turned at the exit gate. That vast empty stretch of green lawn, so innocent seeming had taken on a sinister image.

Jack's father returned faster than I had anticipated. We set off again and he said: 'Where was I? Oh aye, the sheep. It wasn't until the 18th century that scientific breeding began. When a Belford man, James Robson, bought three rams of the Lincolnshire breed – another ancient strain – and crossed them with native ewes according to the Cheviot Sheep Society, there was a vast improvement in the fore quarters, while the wool clip increased 20 per cent. The result was that Belford rams became very popular well beyond the Cheviot area.'

Glancing sideways to see that he still had my attention he added, 'Wherever you go among these hills and see sheep feeding, one of the most interesting characteristics is that they show less inclination to stampede than the majority of other breeds and flocks can usually be seen working up the fell sides as evening approaches. Know why?'

I hadn't the least idea.

Pleased he pointed with his whip. 'It's believed to be bred in them, from the old days of the Border raiders when the sheep were herded well away from the vicinity of reivers' tracks before nightfall.'

I was soon to learn that talking about animals was Andrew Macmerry's favourite subject. As a man who, with further education and his inborn gifts of healing, might have been a successful veterinary surgeon, it did seem a waste.

When I said so, he laughed. 'There's advantages to living in the country, a simple life, lass. I never had any notion for the big cities. I'm well content here, like my fathers before me, but since the farm's been in Jess's family for a hundred years, she reckons it's a pity there's none to inherit after we go.'

Back at the farm, having done justice to a very substantial supper of roast lamb – I did not enquire its origins – I told them I would take a walk before retiring. I was glad they did not ask any questions and at eight o'clock I set off to visit Father McQuinn.

The old door creaked as I opened it. The sun had sunk behind the hills and the interior was dim, the steady line of pews and overall the smell of incense and wax candles.

A sudden movement, a flutter of candles in the dark area near the altar with its crucifix.

'Father McQuinn?' I called.

The response was a faint swish of a curtain on one of the closed booths which I guessed were the confessionals.

Embarrassed, I decided I had come too early but I called his name again.

No answer, no movement anywhere. A heavy and profound silence.

My scalp began to tingle. There was something wrong. I knew these feelings of old.

I went forward down the aisle towards the altar, footsteps ringing on the stones, my progress illuminated by candles fluttering under holy statues which gave those serene saintly faces sudden life and cast great shadows against the walls. At the altar steps, a figure lay prostrate, arms outstretched.

Father McQuinn in prayer.

I edged towards a seat in a nearby pew to wait discreetly for him to rise but, deciding he must have heard my approach, I cleared my throat gently to indicate my presence.

Although the sound was magnified and seemed to echo around the church, he did not move.

I felt I could hardly turn retrace my steps. So again I whispered his name.

Again no movement.

I went closer, stood beside him. His face was turned towards me. One look and I knew that he was dead. I had seen too many dead people in my time to be mistaken about that.

As I knelt beside him, I saw blood on his temples. Had he had a heart attack, struck his head on the stone step? That was my first thought but then I saw the candlestick beside him. A thick trickle of blood led across to where the priest lay.

I stood up, shaken, horrified.

Father McQuinn had been murdered!

And recently, remembering the swish of a curtain, the fluttering candles. There was someone else in the church. I called out.

'Who's there? Will you help me, please.'

My answer was the faint sound of footsteps and the sound of the church door creaking as it closed.

I ran up the aisle threw open the door, rushed to the gate. But the street was empty. There was no one.

The local constable. I must find him. But where was the police station?

I must find someone to help. So I ran to the house across the path from the church, hammered on the door. There was no reply. The housekeeper was not at home.

I stood outside wringing my hands. What to do next?

My thoughts frantic as a rat trapped in a cage, I decided that I'd get Jack's father. Surely he would know what to do.

Of course, questions would be asked about what I had been doing in the Catholic church. But I no longer cared about that. The prospect of Mrs Macmerry's tight-lipped disapproval had ceased to matter.

A man, a relative of Danny's, had been murdered.

As I ran up the track to the farm, there were voices raised. Mrs Macmerry's shrill, protesting. Dogs barking.

Above them all, I recognised Jack's deep voice.

Jack!

Thank God. Jack would know what to do.

The door was flung open. A huge grey shadow hurtled towards me.

I screamed!

8

'Thane!'

Even on three of his four feet, he was much faster than Jack, desperately clinging on to the rope around his neck.

'Thane,' I yelled again as he reached me, threw out those three anchors and stopped just in time, at my feet. There he sat down. Even sitting he reached my shoulder as he gazed at me adoringly and blissfully attempted to lick my cheek.

'Thane – what on earth –?'

As Thane, however willing, was incapable by nature of human speech, it was Jack's turn. Regardless of his parents at the door, he pushed Thane aside and swung me off my feet in a lingering passionate embrace.

Thane regarded this with the human equivalent of a heavy sigh. He had seen all this before. He yawned.

'I've missed you,' said Jack tenderly. 'How have you been?' he added glancing nervously over his shoulder at his approaching parents while the two labradors, Whisky and Soda, who had been roused from their apathy by the arrival of Wonder Dog peered out of the kitchen door like disgruntled dowagers.

'Jack, for heaven's sake. Are you mad? What on earth is Thane doing here?'

Thane, who was following this comment closely, held up a heavily and somewhat inexpertly bandaged paw by way of explanation.

'What happened to you?'

'You might well ask,' said Jack. 'Just look at him. I couldn't leave him in Edinburgh. He has a badly cut paw, caught in a snare or something. You weren't at home, so who was to take care of him.'

As he spoke, a series of images floated rapidly through my mind. Thane, whose habitat was Arthur's Seat, brought into a strange environment miles from home. How he lived on Arthur's Seat, who fed him and groomed him was one mystery we had never solved. How would he react and live in Eildon was immediate and our responsibility, as imagination prompted a ghostly tribe of panic-stricken woolly sheep streaking across the fields –

'Jack, what have you done?' I wailed.

Jack stamped an impatient foot. 'You aren't listening to me, Rose. I'm telling you I couldn't leave him. He was at the back door when I called at the Tower, and I'm pretty certain he's been sitting there every day, waiting for you to come home.'

Pausing to stroke Thane's neck, he said, 'Looking so poorly, too. You wouldn't have wanted that, you'd have been worried sick.'

That at least was true.

I made no comment and Jack beamed. 'Then I had a brain wave. All I could think of was that Da is fantastic with animals, a real animal doctor, he missed his vocation. As anyone around here would tell you. So I knew exactly what I had to do,' he added firmly.

I looked at Thane who was studiously avoiding my eye. I patted his head. He turned and winked at me, and Jack said in wounded tones. 'I thought you'd be pleased'.

I was trying to think of a suitable reply when his parents decided to join us. His mother said quickly, a no-nonsense tone, firm and decisive. 'That Dog can't stay here.'

Thane and Jack both looked at her and Jack said patiently but rather proudly. 'He isn't a dog, Ma, he's a deerhound.'

Mrs Macmerry considered this correction, shrugged and said, 'Whatever he is, he can't stay in my house, that's for sure. He's far too big for one thing, for another, Whisky and Soda wouldn't tolerate it.'

And neither would Thane, I thought as Jack's father beamed on us, rubbing his hands in an excited way.

'What a fine chap he is. We haven't seen a deerhound in this neighbourhood for donkeys' years, have we, Jack?'

Thane gave him an approving look, that injured paw thrust forward once again.

'Aye, aye, a great animal. He can sleep in the stable with Charity.'

Thane and I exchanged nervous glances. Who was Charity? Then I remembered the old mare who pulled the pony cart.

I wasn't sure how Thane would react to this strange bedfellow as Jack, a latter day Pontius Pilate, washed his hands of the whole affair, the problem solved as far as he was concerned.

'That's settled, then. It's just for a day or two.' This for his mother's benefit, 'Then we can take him back with us.'

'Leave it to me, son. We'll have that paw sorted in no time at all, won't we, Thane,' said Mr Macmerry with comforting reassurance.

'There now, Rose,' Jack all smiles repeated. 'I knew you'd be pleased. After all I couldn't leave him back at the Tower – to die –'

'To die.' The terrible words echoed the shocking event that Thane's unexpected arrival had banished completely from my mind.

'– Sorry for not being here when you arrived, Rose but things have been tricky and Glasgow took longer –'

I was no longer listening. I clutched his arm.

'Jack, I'm so glad to see you. You must come with me, right now! Now. Father McQuinn – the Catholic priest down the road. He's dead –'

'Dead,' echoed Mr Macmerry. 'Sad, that.'

'Not just dead,' I shouted. 'Someone killed him!'

From Mrs Macmerry a shocked exclamation of disbelief.

Mr Macmerry recovered first and asked. 'What makes you think that, lass?'

'Because I've just been there. I found him in the church.' And aware of Jack's warning hand on my arm, I added lamely: 'I wanted – to talk to him.'

These words said, I could see questions like 'What on earth for' forming in balloons above their heads.

'Never mind about that.' I could hardly tell Jack that according to the Little Sisters of the Poor there was a strong chance that Danny might still be alive. And in danger of being branded a bigamist, I wanted to talk to his only relative, the priest who had brought him to Scotland on the off chance he might know the truth.

'Please, Jack – let's go. I'll explain later.'

Jack needed no second bidding. Thrusting Thane's rope into his father's hands he raced at my side across to the church.

The door was closed. I was sure I had left it open.

Inside the candles still fluttered. We ran down the aisle. But there was no man lying prostrate in prayer, alive or dead, by the altar steps.

'Well, Rose, where is he?' whispered Jack.

I took in the scene. The huge candlestick was still there, but where was the body? The bloodstain too had gone, washed away very energetically by the look of the still wet stone floor.

At my side, Jack sighed. It was a familiar sigh, long-suffering and patient but implying that he didn't believe a word of it. 'Rose, what's this about? Is this some kind of a joke?'

'A joke! Jack Macmerry, you know me better than that.'

He sighed again. Again I knew what he meant.

History was repeating itself. Once I had found a dead woman at the ruin of St Anthony's Chapel on Arthur's Seat. Summoning Jack, by the time we got back to the scene, the body had disappeared. Refusing to accept any logical explanation that might be forthcoming I went stubbornly headlong into an investigation that almost cost me my life.

Jack had gone strangely quiet. 'Well, what are we supposed to do now, Rose? Any ideas?'

He saw my frightened expression, took pity on it and put his arm around me. Leading me to the nearest pew, he said gently, 'Let's sit down for a moment, shall we?'

'No,' I protested. 'I'm all right. If you'll be patient and listen I'll tell you exactly what happened.'

'Go ahead. You have my undivided attention.'

I pretended not to notice the hint of mockery. 'I came in to see Father McQuinn to – to talk to him about Danny.'

I ignored that familiar wince, the sudden coolness as he said:

'An odd time of night for a social visit.'

'No, it was the right time. I'd been told he would be here after Mass. I came in, the church was empty but I heard movement and thought he was in the confessional. Over there, those boxes. A curtain moved. I called out but when he didn't answer I came down to the altar – the light was very dim –'

'Still is,' said Jack looking round, his tone denoting that anyone could make a mistake.

'So I came down to the altar and then I saw him. He was lying – just there.' I indicated the wet place on the floor with my foot. 'He was dead.'

'How could you know that?' Jack demanded.

'Because maybe it has slipped your mind, Jack Macmerry, but I have considerable knowledge and experience in that direction. In America, long before we met, remember, I saw plenty –'

I walked over to the altar candlestick. 'This was lying beside him. There was blood on it and a trickle of blood leading from his forehead, the blow that had killed him.'

As I spoke Jack inspected the candlestick 'Is this the same one, do you think?'

I said of course it was and Jack shook his head. 'No sign of any blood here, Rose. Or on the floor. But it's a mighty heavy object,' he added weighing it in his hand. 'It could do some damage if you got hit over the head with that –'

I was intrigued by that still damp area near where the priest's body had lain. Someone had cleaned up the blood not only efficiently but very recently.

Shivering at what that implied, I said, 'I think I missed his killer by seconds. When I opened the door I called 'Father McQuinn.' As I told you there was movement from the direction of the confessionals. At first I thought he was still hearing Mass and I didn't want to interrupt. So I thought I'd wait.'

Pausing I looked at Jack. 'You realise that it must have been his killer. As I knelt beside the body, I heard footsteps. Someone ran out of the church.'

Jack tried not to look sceptical and failed. 'All right, Rose, so where is the body then?'

'We'd better try to find out, hadn't we?'

Jack sighed. 'Maybe we should have brought Thane with us. Used to scenting blood and that sort of thing –'

I had personal doubts about Thane's expertise in that area and said, 'He can't be far away. I wonder where they took him –'

That mystery was soon solved. When we got outside there was considerable activity around the church house.

The door was open. Mrs Aiden came out wringing her hands.

'Oh, it's you, Miss Faro.' In her agitation she had forgotten that I was Mrs McQuinn. 'Something awful has just happened. The Father – the Father is dead.'

'I know, I know,' I said.

She gave me a surprised look, shook her head from side to

side. 'So sudden. So terribly sudden. He must have had a heart attack after the Mass. I went in to tell him his supper was ready and – and there he was – lying by the altar.'

In a state of shock, she obviously didn't want to add that he had been murdered.

Suddenly she broke down, gave way to heavy sobs. 'Oh the poor dear man, God rest his soul. He was kneeling at the altar steps, as he always did before he came home, a final prayer. He'd hit his head on the stone steps as he fell forward. I didn't know what to do. I couldn't carry him. I ran outside for help and a man who was passing by carried him here, into the house. He went for the doctor.'

'What was he like?' I asked.

She stared at me frowning, shaking her head. 'Who – the Father?'

I had to repeat it. 'No, this man who helped you.'

Leaning her head forward, listening intently, she seemed surprised by the question. 'I didn't take much notice of what he looked like. Just an ordinary-like man.'

'He must have been strong to carry Father McQuinn into the house.'

She shrugged. 'Yes, I think he was quite tall and strong looking.'

'You didn't know him, then? He wasn't from here.'

'No. I'd never seen him before.' She kept watching me as I spoke, dazed and distressed, and wondering what all these questions were about. 'I expect he had been visiting the Abbey.'

At eight o'clock, when it closed at four? I thought that very doubtful and my stalker leapt to mind. He was tall. But before I could ask any more, a door opened across the passage and a distinguished looking man emerged closing his bag, presumably the local doctor.

Trailing behind him was a uniformed constable. Adjusting his helmet with an air of importance he hurried out.

Calling after him, the doctor said: 'I don't think you need trouble, constable. The Fiscal wouldn't lose any sleep over this one.'

And apologetically to Mrs Aiden: 'My condolences, a sad business. A very nasty accident. But these things happen. The church can be a dangerous place.'

Noticing Jack and I standing by the door, he beamed on us both. 'Well, well, Jack, we don't see you often. Visiting your folks, is it? Preparing for the happy day, eh? I presume this is your fiancée, Miss Faro.'

Jack smiled proudly and didn't bother to correct him as, smiling, he introduced Dr Dalrymple, who shook my hand warmly.

'What happened to the Father?' I asked.

'Heart attack. Took us all by surprise, as he's a very fit man for his age. Walks miles and miles every week, seeing that his parishioners are fairly well spread about the countryside. Nasty accident though.' he repeated and shook his head. 'When he fell he split his head open on the stone steps,' he added, confirming Mrs Aiden's statement.

There were others arriving. Some of his congregation had heard the news and were there to support the distraught housekeeper.

We took our departure, I following Jack reluctantly and lingering beside the doctor, wanting to question him about the stranger who had carried the priest into the church house. Most importantly, had he ever seen this man before.

Jack however, as if he read my mind, kept the conversation on a light social level about the changes in Eildon since his last visit and walked me firmly towards his parents waiting at a discreet distance from the church.

They knew Dr Dalrymple well. I learned that he had brought Jack into the world and we left them chatting philosophically about mortality and how it strikes without a second's warning, the young and the not-so-young alike.

'Natural causes, was it?' Mr Macmerry sounded relieved.

'Of course, Andrew. What else? Happens every day,' was the doctor's cheerful reply but I was aware of curious glances following from Jack's parents as they remembered my hysterical outburst that someone had killed the priest.

It was all very depressing. And very unreal, I thought as Jack took my arm and we went into the kitchen.

Thane had been removed to the stables for his medical attention and to get acquainted with Charity. Mr Macmerry's faithful sheepdog Rex, newly returned from his brief honeymoon in the farm 'up-by' and having done his duty, was basking by the fireside alongside the two ancient celibate labradors.

Jack patted Rex's head. 'Da was telling me this was his first siring. Ah well, honeymoons take it out of a chap,' he added with a sympathetic grin as he took me in his arms, saying how great it was to be together again. How he had missed me and so forth.

And most important, with his parents' footsteps on the threshold, he whispered was there any chance – tonight? And where was I sleeping?

I guessed what was in his mind, for the same thought had occurred to me too. I needed his warm loving arms. But I shook my head.

'Not a chance,' I whispered. 'Your mother has taken good care of our morals, that's for sure. You are at one end of the corridor in your own room and I am in the guest bedroom at the other end of the house.'

'With the master bedroom right between us, who needs a chaperone?' said Jack with a groan. 'Those damned old floorboards creak like the wrath of God.'

As his parents entered, he managed a stage-whisper. 'Keep

your thoughts to yourself about Father McQuinn. Not another word – understand – about thinking this was murder.'

I wasn't thinking. I was sure it was murder.

Somehow we got through the social part of what was left of the evening while Jack and his parents pulled the world apart and put it together again, in Eildon and elsewhere. Inevitably there was a lot of talk about Jack as a bairn, the sort of family history no bride to be can do without. How proud they were! From Police Constable to Detective Sergeant and now promoted to Detective Inspector.

I smiled when they looked in my direction, those more urgent forbidden questions unanswered burning inside of me. Or was it heartburn from the strong drams that were being offered as a celebration of Jack's return and our approaching nuptials? After all, this was something of an occasion, the first time we had been united under the family roof.

We had a moment together as his mother went upstairs 'to see to things' and his father sternly led the reluctant Whisky and Soda outside 'to do what dogs had to do,' and took Rex with him to check the farm gates were locked.

Jack seized my hand across the table. 'They're so proud of you,' he sighed happily. 'Everyone in Eildon knows you are Inspector Faro's daughter.'

'But not apparently that I am a widow.'

Jack frowned. 'How's that?'

'As I am being introduced as Miss Faro, it seems that my marriage has been carefully removed from the record.'

Jack shuffled uncomfortably. 'Yes, well, you know what Ma's like.'

I didn't but I was learning fast.

Observing my grim expression, Jack said hastily, 'Mothers can be tricky. I expect she didn't want the world to know that her son was marrying a – well, a widow.' He managed to make it sound quite improper! 'It's just a mother's pride, only son and all that. No harm in it at all.' And shaking his head sadly, 'She's very sensitive –'

She wasn't the only one, I thought indignantly, giving him a sharp glance.

Clearing his throat as he did when he was embarrassed, Jack continued: 'You know how people talk in small communities, especially knowing you were related to the Catholic priest – with Da an elder of the kirk and that sort of thing.'

'How will it be explained in our banns being read each Sunday?'

'Not at all. It's quite normal for just the Christian and maiden name to be read out.'

As footsteps announced the returning parents, I guessed sadly that Jack wasn't too disappointed at his mother's authorised version of my life. What sort of a family was I marrying into, for heaven's sake? Were they direct descendants of the ostrich genus?

Jack smiled. 'Time for bed.'

And so it was. His mother followed us upstairs close on our heels and held open the door of my room, averting her eyes from Jack's necessarily chaste goodnight kiss.

As I closed the door, my last sight was of her leading him along the corridor to his own bedroom, so proudly, like a return to the childhood he had left a very long time ago.

The cosy scene even had the suggestion that a bedtime story might be on the cards.

As I sat down on the bed, I was so lonely. At that moment I had had enough of the Macmerrys. I longed for my bedroom in Solomon's Tower. I longed for Arthur's Seat and thought of Thane sharing his sleeping quarters in the stable with a horse called Charity.

Exhausted and lulled by drams, I thought sleep would be

immediate. That was not the case as my mind kept returning to the housekeeper's story.

Whatever her devotion to Father McQuinn, he had been murdered. As it was beyond belief that she should have hit him over the head with the altar candlestick in a fit of anger, the stranger who carried him into the house was most likely his killer.

Was this the same man who had concealed himself in the confessional when I was about to discover the body?

And however Jack Macmerry felt about it, this as far as I was concerned was one of my cases now.

Not a Discretion Guaranteed investigation for a middle class Edinburgh client, whose fragile reputation lay dangerously at stake, but a full blown murder enquiry.

9

Over breakfast next morning Jack broke the news that this was just a fleeting visit, to see that Thane got proper attention for his wounded paw and to discreetly check the security arrangements at Verney Castle for the Royal visit.

'This is strictly confidential, Rose. Not a word to my parents. The Chief Constable thought as I lived in the area it could be accomplished without raising too many alarms or suspicions.'

'Suspicions of what? Are they expecting trouble?' I said anxiously.

Jack shook his head. 'We have wind of Fenian activities in the area. May be just a rumour, of course.'

'Your father told me that the Verneys were an old Catholic family, loyal to the Stuarts. And that they had Irish connections.'

'That applies to a lot of us,' was the wry reply. 'But there are Irish men and women loyal to the Crown. I don't expect that his lordship has a Fenian terrorist hidden away in the priest hole. Nothing as dramatic. He has a blameless record but where Royalty is concerned, the police always take rumours seriously.'

Pausing, he wagged a finger at me. 'And you should know that from your early life with an illustrious Chief Inspector.'

I shrugged. 'On the contrary, he never confided in his family.'

'A wise move,' said Jack. 'Discreet surveillance is the word. And the reasons for my visit home have provided the Borders police with the perfect answer. I shall have to report back to Central Office – briefly, of course,' he added casually, 'as there is another pressing matter which fitted in very neatly to my secret mission.'

'And what would that be?' I asked, knowing perfectly well.

His eyebrows raised mockingly at that. 'I can't believe you have forgotten our wedding arrangements. Counting the days we are now,' he added with a happy sigh. 'How many is it?'

I ignored that. The reminder had not been strictly necessary. 'So I'm to be left here on my own while you go back to Edinburgh,' I replied rather sharply.

'Hardly on you own,' he said reproachfully. 'After all, you have Ma and Da to take care of you.'

'Take care.' How I winced at the words. He made me sound like a little girl which I bitterly resented as he went on sternly: 'You can make yourself useful. Ma will need someone to give her a hand.' And that final note of self-righteousness, 'After all, weddings are a woman's business.'

Never a good actor, he was relieved at having a man's excuse to avoid all the wearisome details and preparations. I felt angry, not for the first time, that I was marrying a man who didn't know me at all, aware again of those vast unchart-ed areas in our relationship. Heaven only knew what this ver-sion of the Rose McQuinn he loved and wanted to marry was like. I was certain I had never met her, or at best had only a fleeting acquaintance and, had I recognised her, suspected I would most likely have despised her.

Married friends of course would have all the answers. Soothing tales that such pre-wedding anxiety was common to all brides. But did all of them at frequent intervals put words to the question burning in their innermost hearts: Were they doing the right thing? Was it too late to step back?

I had the answer to that one. In my case, it was.

Besides I was different, I had no married friends on hand and I was no quaking virgin bride being led to the altar with the terrifying prospect of the 'wedding-night-and-what-to-expect' spoiling the glamour of pretty gowns and extravagant presents. I had been happily married before. This second formal wedding was merely to put the stamp of officialdom and the church's blessing on our relationship. Scottish Law already regarded us as man and wife under that quaint term, 'by habit and repute.'

Furious that Jack had lured me to Eildon on false pretences, to get his family's approval – or not – (the jury was still out on that one!) – he had used me and Thane's injury as legitimate reasons for his police business in the area.

Now he was leaving me not only to prepare for our wedding but with the investigation of a murder case. Last night I had had visions of us solving it together, now I was being told he had to rush back to Edinburgh with his security report on Verney Castle.

I groaned. Police business was an all too familiar part of my life, from childhood days onward. I had never been first, let's face it, in any man's life. Certainly not with my well beloved father Inspector Faro.

I had moved on to discover that my rival in Danny McQuinn's life was Pinkerton's Detective Agency and now, back on my home territory, hopeful with Jack Macmerry, I had to contend once more with Edinburgh City Police.

Aware of my displeasure, Jack said, 'I'm sorry, Rose. But you know what its like when Her Majesty intends a visit to Edinburgh.'

A sudden gleam of brightness in the gloom. Perhaps my stepbrother Dr Vince Laurie, junior physician to the Royal Household, would be with her.

'Maybe she will give Vince leave to come to the wedding. If the dates are right – I wrote to him, of course.'

'That would be great.' Jack grinned. 'Then he can give you away, as a member of the family. One problem solved.'

'Or he could be your best man.'

He thought for a moment. 'Yes. My parents would be thrilled to have someone with Royal connections sign the register.'

'When are you leaving?' I asked.

'This evening. On the train back to Edinburgh.'

'This evening!' I echoed. 'What about Thane?'

Jack avoided my eyes. 'Da says he needs a day or two to get used to the splint. I was counting on you being here. You can bring him back.'

'How do I do that, pray?' A dog the size of a pony would hardly be welcome in a compartment for six persons.

'In the guard's van, as I did,' said Jack, a mite impatiently.

I sighed. 'Well, I expect I'll find enough to keep me busy for a few days, things I'm intending to look into, like murder,' I added sweetly.

Jack grabbed my arm. 'Rose – are you mad? There was no murder. For heaven's sake, the housekeeper told you what happened.'

'What about the damp floor? Someone cleaned up the blood.'

'Of course someone did. Mrs Aiden. Just to look at the woman will tell anyone that she's that kind of person. Blood on a church floor. Cleanliness next to godliness. For heaven's sake –'

I had a lot more to add to that subject. I would have stamped my foot if I hadn't glimpsed out of the corner of my eye Mrs Macmerry hovering about just outside the kitchen door.

The terrible urge to scream, to throw something, was there but I wasn't going to give her the gleeful satisfaction of reporting my appalling behaviour to his father as: 'I told you so. She's not the right one for our Jack.'

So I fumed and held my peace and went through the ritual

of going to the manse, meeting the minister Reverend Linton and fixing the wedding in the austere Scots kirk lurking in the shadow of the Abbey.

June 21, on the morning of the Queen's Diamond Jubilee. A quiet ceremony indeed. No best man, no bridesmaid, Jack's parents as witnesses, before a congregation consisting of their friends.

The minister was clearly disappointed. As Andrew Macmerry was an elder of the kirk and Mrs Macmerry big in the Guild he had expected a stylish wedding of notable proportions.

Did we require a rehearsal? That wasn't necessary, Jack put in quickly. No, he didn't have a best man in mind.

As my father was living abroad there would be no one to give the bride away – he didn't want to raise false hopes by mentioning the nebulous possibility of Vince – however, his own father would willingly hold the ring.

What about a bridesmaid? This was asked with a smile.

I couldn't provide that either. A married sister in Orkney with an infant son, various well-off Edinburgh friends – mostly grateful ex-clients who I couldn't imagine making the journey for a small undistinguished country wedding.

I had a sudden vision of Nancy Brook, niece of our old housekeeper at Sheridan Place. But as I knew Nancy greatly fancied Jack, I felt bridesmaiding at his wedding might be both cynical and cruel.

Reverend Linton was clearly put out that the ceremony was to be short and sweet. No hymns, no wedding march, the vows exchanged, the ring, the blessing and away back to the farm for a dram and a piece of wedding cake.

No big deal. However, when I said so, this produced a weak smile. As a matter of fact he had rather a lot of commitments. Involvement in Jubilee activities, children's events, village fetes, competitions to be judged, and so forth.

As we left Jack took my arm fondly, sighed and said: 'Well, that's all fixed. And I think we should feel fortunate that he could fit us in on such a day.'

I didn't bother to point out that this particular day was his, or rather, his parents' choosing.

As we walked back to the farm, Jack's father was hitching Charity to the pony cart.

'All ready for you, lad.'

'How's Thane?'

'Just grand, lass,' he said following me into the stable where Thane, on a very long rope tactful enough to calm any fears he might have of captivity, jumped up to greet me. Mr Macmerry patted his head. 'You'll be great in two-three days. Just as well the lad brought him to me,' and with a shake of the head. 'Many's the beast I've saved aye, and good horses from the knackers' yard. All it takes is time and a bit of know how – and nature's assistance, of course.'

I put my arm around Thane's neck and said: 'He isn't used to being tied up, you know.'

'I guessed that, lass. But it's better for him meantime. We don't want him roaming about and getting lost.'

I could see the reason behind that. What if instinct drove him to try to get back to Arthur's Seat again? I guessed the rope hadn't yet been invented that would keep him back.

'I'll just have another wee look at his dressing afore I go out by,' said Mr Macmerry. 'Jack's waiting for ye.'

Jack was in the pony-cart consulting his watch, 'Fancy a visit to Verney Castle, meet the local aristocracy? Unless you have anything better to do,' he added with a grin.

I did. My prompt reply would have been that I had intended to visit Mrs Aiden to find out more about that mysterious stranger who had carried Father McQuinn into the house so fortuitously. 'I have to see his lordship,' said Jack as I took the seat alongside him, 'Police business. Shouldn't take long, if you don't mind waiting. You can have a stroll in the gardens. They are quite something. I used to be thrown out by the gamekeeper regularly for trespassing, when I was a lad.'

He paused and then added. 'It will look better if you are with me, make it more informal. Less like an official visit.'

So that was the reason I had been invited along. Not for my charming company, I thought cynically.

It took a lot longer to reach the castle by the road, than by the track where I had been apprehended by the gamekeeper and his savage dog and accused of trespassing.

We circled the estate by a bank of trees and a couple of fields leading through ornate gates, where a long drive twisted through tight shrubbery to emerge at the magnificent frontage of the castle, which I had seen from far above. The lawns sported a raised platform and canopied seating area.

Preparations for a Jubilee pageant, I decided, as the pony cart rattled across the gravelled forecourt and a footman appeared at the door.

Jack stepped down. A murmured conversation, heads turned in my direction.

'Would madam care to wait for you in the library, sir?' asked the footman.

I stepped down from the cart and shook my head. 'Thank you. I'll wait outside and enjoy the sunshine' Keen to be accommodating, the footman indicated a path through the shrubbery. 'Feel free to explore the gardens, madam. We'll ring the bell when sir is ready to leave.'

Jack grinned and they disappeared inside. As the door closed I had an instant's regret at missing a chance to view the library.

However the sun was warm and I love grand gardens, my life severely deficient in that respect during my years in the Arizona desert.

There were several inviting paths spread out like the fingers of a hand, twisting through tall well-manicured hedges. Small, shady, not to say chilly arbours, with stone seats under the watchful melancholy stone gaze of a number of underclad gods and goddesses, who must have found the long winter months somewhat trying.

At last I emerged at a large artificial lake with a boathouse. There were swans and ducks and a boy with a toy boat. He was about eight years old, immaculately clad in sailor suit and a straw hat tilted back over a mass of blond curls. A picture book child unaware of being watched and I regretted not having my sketchbook.

A cry of distress, he had lost his hold on the boat's rope. He was leaning forward, staggering, ready to topple into the lake.

I raced forward, grabbed his legs just as the rest of him was about to slide into the water and pulled him ashore.

The sleeves of that immaculate white suit were somewhat the worse for the experience but he wasn't grateful for my life-saving activity.

Pointing he yelled, 'My boat. Please get it back. Look, I've lost it!'

'You almost lost more than that, young man,' I said sternly. 'Just wait until your mamma sees you –'

He was unconcerned and continued to wail. 'My boat, it's drifting away.'

'Wait here, don't move,' I commanded and tore down a loose branch from one of the overhanging willows. 'I'll get it for you.'

Following the boat's progress around the lake and then, by lying flat on my stomach, with some careful manoeuvring of the branch, I managed to steer it safely shorewards.

'There you are now, no damage done,' I said ignoring the condition of my sleeves drenched in the process.

Hugging his boat to his breast, his smile was angelic. 'Thank you, thank you. You saved her! I don't know what would have happened if you hadn't been around.'

'You would have taken a tumble into the water and and got very wet indeed, I fear.'

He looked up at me and shuddered. 'I might have drowned. You saved my life. In that case I won't tell Ben that you were trespassing,' he added sternly, and holding out his hand. 'Very pleased to know you, madam.'

We shook hands. 'I take it that you live here.'

'Oh yes indeed. I'm Alexander. My father owns this place. What is your name?'

As I said: 'It's Rose –', the peaceful scene by the lake erupted as the fierce sheepdog I had met once before hurtled out of the shrubbery.

10

'Down, Billy – down.' commanded my small companion in a voice amazingly full of authority for one so young.

The sheepdog was closely followed by my old enemy the gamekeeper. His angry grimace showed yellow teeth identical in colour to those of his dog.

Ignoring Alexander he shouted, 'What are you doing here, miss. Don't you know you are trespassing. This is the second time I've caught you,' he added suspiciously. 'Molesting the young master, too. You had better come with me up to the house.'

'Stop, Ben. This instant!' Armed by his inborn right to instant obedience, the youngster at my side said sternly, 'This lady is a friend of mine. Her name is Miss Rose.'

The man's face underwent a rapid change of emotions, a quick succession too great for me to interpret and when he spoke again belligerence had been replaced by formality.

'Very well, young sir, but we'll see what his lordship has to say about that.'

Any further discussion was cut short at that moment by what sounded like the clang of a school bell from the direction of the front door.

I turned and said with great dignity. 'That is for me. My fiancé –'

I had almost said Detective Inspector Macmerry but something stopped me just in time.

Alexander took my hand, bowed over it gravely and, ignoring the scowling man and his equally scowling dog, said, 'Thank you – for the boat, I mean.'

'I'm glad I got here in time,' I said.

He said shortly to Ben. 'She saved my boat – from shipwreck, you know.' And to me, the bow, that angelic smile again. 'I do hope we shall meet again.'

'I hope so too,' I responded politely without any certainty that any such an occasion would ever arise.

At that Ben cut short any further conversation with a stern, 'You had better come with me, Master Alexander, you're all wet. Nanny won't want you catching cold again.'

Alexander nodded obediently and about to follow Ben, he turned. 'Will you be coming to our garden fete – on Jubilee Day?'

'I might.'

'Oh, please do. I would like that very much.'

Ben held out an impatient hand. I was conscious of his brooding expression. Not lust this time. Something else, sly yet triumphant. As if he had made a totally unexpected discovery.

Worse than his leers when we first met, it unnerved me. I was glad Jack was with me and I resolved to stay well out of the gamekeeper's way in future.

Jack was standing by the pony-cart in earnest conversation with the tall man holding the school bell.

As I approached, he turned, saw me and bowed. I decided I had never seen anyone in my whole life who looked so like a knight of old as Lord Quentin Verney. A thatch of white hair, white moustache, red face and regal bearing every inch of him suggested that he had just this minute stepped out of a suit of armour.

As Jack was about to make the introductions, the footman ran down the front steps, with an urgent whispered message to his lordship. Bowing again, with a smile and murmured apology, Verney disappeared indoors leaving Jack and I to step into the pony cart.

'Successful?' I asked.

'Indeed,' said Jack nodding solemnly. His noncommittal tone I knew of old. It meant there wasn't any further information forthcoming. 'What about you?'

'Oh, I had an adventure.'

'What kind would that be?' he asked cautiously.

'Well, I rescued a boat from shipwreck and fell in love.'

'You – what!' he laughed.

'I fell in love at first sight, just like the heroine of a romantic novel, with the handsome young master of the house.'

He guessed I was joking but felt obliged to ask, 'Does this mean I have a rival and will have to call him out and demand satisfaction.'

'You might. But not for a year or two. He's only eight years old.'

Jack laughed heartily, put an arm around my shoulder. I told him about the young Master of Verney as we set off back down the drive and, approving my life and boat saving actions, he consulted his watch.

'What shall we do now, Rose? I am yours for the rest of the day. My train leaves at eight o'clock. What say you to a picnic?'

'That would be lovely. But a picnic without food?'

He chuckled. 'I had all that in mind when we were offered the ponycart. Look under the seat.'

And there it was. A splendid basket, full of his mother's best baking and a bottle of her elderberry wine.

'Now I'll show you a piece of Eildon history,' said Jack, urging Charity along a steep and little used track. Below us the smooth line of undulating hills was scarred by the monstrous overgrown remains of what had once been a working quarry.

'And that,' said Jack, 'is where the men who built the Abbey in the thirteenth century got their stones from. Can you imagine this as a hive of industry, a thriving community, long before Eildon ever came into being. Thanks to the economic use of the ruined Abbey's stones by some enterprising farmers, they had no need for the quarry and it's been abandoned for years now. We were warned it was unsafe, a forbidden place and therefore extremely attractive as a place of adventure in my boyhood.'

Even in gentle sunshine it did not strike me as a place were I would care to linger or to explore alone.

Jack's next words confirmed that. 'There are all sorts of dangers, unseen hazards. Deep pits and caves and where most of the stone was taken out, a bottomless – so they say – pond. Two lads were drowned when Da was at school and that earned it a bad reputation with parents. There was also a gloomy suggestion that when anyone walked out of the house and disappeared, that was where you would find them – at the bottom of the quarry pond.'

'Not a great place for a picnic?'

He shook his head. 'It still gives me the creeps, but I thought you'd want to see it, intrigued as you are by unsolved mysteries. Besides there would have been no famous Abbey if it hadn't existed so conveniently close. Shall we drive on?'

We followed more twisting tracks which emerged at the course of a sparkling burn. This was Jack 's favourite childhood haunt.

When he wanted to get away from everyone, having been naughty, which he said, was often, or just disagreeable and out of sorts with the world in general, he would retreat to this dear spot.

'The number of times I fell in and went home sobbing, a drowned rat, my clothes ruined,' he laughed as sitting on a large stone we dabbled bare feet in the burn.

A very isolated place and as it turned out very convenient and secluded for the benefit of lovers as Jack's motive for the picnic became evident.

Feeling particularly bruised by recent events I was glad of some physical expression of my future husband's devotion and our lovemaking, always perhaps the most successful and united part of our relationship, left me feeling breathless, very fulfilled and at peace with all the world – and with Jack in particular.

By the time we went back to the farm I had almost forgotten my intention to investigate Father McQuinn's murder as soon as he boarded the train. I was very concerned, though, about Thane. He was never far from my thoughts, nervously wondering how he was coping with his new environment.

Did he feel trapped, as I did – did he long for home, for Arthur's Seat as I did? In the stable, Thane looked less forlorn and Jack's father indicated a neatly splinted paw. 'Intelligent animal, knows its for his own good. Never made a bit of fuss, most dogs would need a muzzle. A wee bone fractured, painful and could have lamed him for life. But we've sorted that out, haven't we, old lad. You'll be right as rain soon,' he added, ruffling Thane's ears and his dignity.

I put my arm around Thane's neck. 'How long will it take?' I asked.

'A week or so and we'll take the splint off. Jack can come back for him.'

So I was to be a prisoner too for another week.

'He shouldn't walk much, mind you,' Mr Macmerry added and I was relieved to banish from my imagination that ghostly herd of panic-stricken sheep with Thane in full pursuit and every farmer's gun at the ready trained on him.

'What is he eating? I mean, what are you feeding him?'

Mr Macmerry seemed surprised at the question. 'Usual wholesome food we give all our dogs. Grand appetite he has.'

I looked at Thane who confirmed this by licking his lips.

I was allowed to see Jack off alone that evening. As we walked to the station I gave him strict instructions that next time he came he was to bring my wedding gown, or more correctly my new Sunday best summer dress which I had purchased at Jenners spring sale. A bargain, I saw it in the window, fell in love with it and had to have it.

I'm not normally much of a hand with impractical ladie's gowns more appropriate to the better-off section of Edinburgh society. But this was a gem of its kind. Ivory muslin, with a satin under petticoat, sprigged with delicate cornflowers. A wide blue satin sash did wonders for my waistline and that was what finally decided me.

I felt it did not altogether meet with Jack's approval. 'You look like a little girl, all excited and off to her first grown-up party.'

And as I surveyed myself in the mirror in Solomon's Tower and smiled at the compliment, he stared over my shoulder, scowled and said very solemnly, 'It makes you look infernally young. As if I'm marrying a child bride.'

Then seeing the disappointment on my face he gathered me into his arms. 'You don't look like a woman past thirty. You look about sixteen.'

'I wish!' I suppose I was flattered – what woman wouldn't be? But whatever the outside shell, inside I was every year of my life.

In ten years of my marriage to Danny from twenty to thirty, I had lived through every sort of dire circumstance in Arizona. Poverty, deprivation, near starvation, terror from Indians – and bereavement. And the worst that can happen to a mother – the loss of the one beloved only baby after years of being childless.

And looking 'infernally young' as Jack described it could be a considerable drawback in my chosen career. I was well aware of my lack of inches and dressed accordingly, with the care of an actress in a stage play.

I worked hard at the image of a Lady Investigator, Discretion Guaranteed.

A dark outdoor costume, tailored and correct, its length adaptable for my bicycle, black boots with a heel to give an illusion of more than my four feet ten inches.

'Which of your bonnets shall I bring?' asked Jack.

I thought of the two in my wardrobe at home. Simple, unadorned but reassuringly respectable. Felt in winter, straw in summer, in which my wild mop of yellow hair could be suitably tamed and hidden.

I laughed. 'Neither would do. I want a simple wreath of blue flowers,' I said firmly, 'and don't forget my white patent shoes.'

They too were beautiful, from the sales and as I had very tiny feet, a bargain although not everyday wear and far less comfortable than my sturdy boots.

'You might well be coming back to Edinburgh before the wedding,' said Jack hopefully.

'On the other hand, I might not.'

'Very well. You can leave it to me.'

I knew I could do just that. Jack was very reliable.

As the bell rang signalling the train's approach, he said, 'I'm relying on you to do what you can to help Ma with the wedding arrangements and – and no bright ideas about that other business. You know what I'm talking about?'

I nodded in agreement. His stern reminder was unnecessary.

'Behave, Rose. I don't want you getting into all sorts of complications. Remember my parents have to live here after we leave. You have no idea what village life is like. They're very proud and have a fine reputation. We don't want them to be a laughing stock.'

A rather cruel assessment of my discretion guaranteed activities, I thought but I understood his sensitivity on the subject of his family.

The train steamed in, hissed impatiently at the platform for its intake of one solitary passenger. With Jack leaning out of the window and that last kiss exchanged, the loftily titled station master in his more lowly role as guard and porter, when required, blew his whistle.

I stood with my arm upraised until the trail of smoke disappeared around the bend in the track. Wished a polite good evening, the guard, anxious to return home, closed the gate behind me.

The railway station was on the same side of the village as the Catholic church, and I recognised this as a golden opportunity to call on Mrs Aiden to offer my condolences.

An informal visit to find out how she was getting on. But I wasn't fooling myself for an instant, I knew exactly what I had in mind.

The house door was open, no one heard my knock, so hearing voices I presumed it was all right to enter, to be greeted by the sight of a room packed with black-clad women. Prayer books and rosaries were in evidence.

Awareness of this new arrival in their midst put an end to all conversation. Heads swivelled in my direction, expressions anxious and embarrassed.

I knew the reason why. This was a wake for their dead priest and as a non-Catholic and a stranger, I didn't have any role to play.

However Mrs Aiden spotted me leaving, rushed over and said: 'Miss Faro, the funeral's on Friday. Our new assistant priest is already on his way, sent by the Bishop to help the Father – his rheumatism is – was – bad and the outlying districts a bit too much –' Her eyes filled with tears. 'Come to the funeral if you wish.'

Had she forgotten that I was related to Father McQuinn by marriage?

'I'd like to meet the man who helped you with him –' I said awkwardly.

She stared at me. 'So would I. But as I told you, I had never seen him before. That isn't unusual, a lot of strangers pass through Eildon on their way to the Abbey.'

'What did he look like? Could he have been visiting one of the farms?' I added loudly in deference to her deafness.

Mrs Aiden shook her head and seemed bewildered by the question. 'I didn't take much notice of what he looked like.' And with a stifled sob. 'He might have been Satan himself – for all I cared at that moment. All I wanted was a big strong man to help me carry the Father from the church into the house. I thought he might be still alive then. That we might save him. But we were too late.'

Wringing a handkerchief in her hands as she spoke, she was clearly at a loss as to why I was so interested and I felt bad for upsetting her like this

Tomorrow, perhaps in a calmer light, she might remember some important detail about the stranger who had arrived on the scene so fortuitously.

The man I regarded with utmost suspicion as his killer. The shadowy figure lurking in the confessional who, I wouldn't be surprised to discover, was also my stalker.

But why I should be stalked on my arrival in Eildon, I had not the least idea or what was the link with the murder of Danny McQuinn's elderly cousin.

11

Cheerful lamplight from the kitchen window illuminated my walk up the farm track. Somehow it failed to lure me into spending the rest of the evening by the fireside having a cosy chat with Jack's parents.

Their two topics of conversation would be a wedding – mine – and a funeral – Father McQuinn's. In no mood for answering awkward questions on either, I tiptoed past and went to the stable.

There Thane greeted my arrival with delight, springing up on his three good feet. I put my arms around his neck and sat on the straw beside him.

Charity looked down at us and snorted in thinly veiled contempt. She wasn't a particularly friendly old animal, kept herself to herself, I thought, as I whispered to Thane. Telling him all my troubles, my worries about Jack and whether I was doing the right thing. Or whether I had any alternative.

Thane seemed to understand and held out the splinted paw for my sympathy.

'I wish we were back home,' I said. 'How I long for Solomon's Tower.'

Thane understood that too.

I retired to my bedroom feeling depressed. The thought of being static with Jack's parents for another week was like being confined in a cage, a very comfortable well-fed cage, but still a trap. So I resolved that as soon as Thane was out of his splint and pronounced fit by Mr Macmerry, I would return for a respite, however brief, to Edinburgh.

Meantime, completely ignoring Jack's warning I would fill in my time with some discreet enquiries into the matter of Father McQuinn's untimely end.

I knew what I had seen in the church. I had seen a dead man – and he had been murdered. I wasn't convinced by Mrs Aiden's explanation. Or by the doctor or by Jack.

I stubbornly maintained, against all odds, the gut feeling that came with so many of my murder cases. To be clinched when tomorrow I tackled Mrs Aiden about that wet patch on the stone floor, the bloodstains so carefully removed.

This was the first clue.

Had she, despite the shattering and totally unexpected death and Jack's logical explanation, noticed that stain and felt that blood spilt in church was so sacrilegious that having seen the priest carried into the house, she had quickly returned to the scene armed with mop and bucket?

Common sense insisted that no one in a such a shocked state would have made the return trip to the church, or indeed that a busy cleaning-up operation with soap and water would have been in the forefront of their mind.

There was only one exception to this reasoning – the person who had washed the floor was Father McQuinn's killer.

Tomorrow, then, I would have all the evidence I needed.

But tomorrow, as it turned out, was not soon enough.

At breakfast next morning, asked the now usual question of what I intended to do today, realising there was little to be gained by being devious, I said that I would like to take the priest's housekeeper some flowers.

Jack's father nodded approvingly, 'Aye, lass. You do that. There's some fine roses in the garden.'

I looked across at Mrs Macmerry's rather sour expression as he asked, 'That all right by you, Jess?'

A brief nod in reply, she seized a basket and, following her into the garden, I watched how skilfully her secateurs released some of her choicest blooms.

'I expect she has vases in plenty, and I'd like my basket back.'

With the church house in view, I realised that once again I was to be thwarted. Apparently I was not the only one in the village with the same idea of bringing flowers to Mrs Aiden.

A small group of women were gathered outside the door.

As I approached their agitated voices indicated that something was seriously amiss.

White shocked faces were turned towards me.

'What has happened?'

'It's Mrs Aiden. She took a fall –'

'Fell down the stairs –'

'Is she hurt?' An unnecessary question – I already feared the worst considering what looked ominously like a Greek chorus of tragedy.

'She's dead –'

'Aye,' (with a sob) 'broke her poor neck in the fall –'

'The new priest discovered her –'

'Father Boyle –'

'Arrived off the Edinburgh train this morning –'

'Came expecting to conduct Father McQuinn's funeral –'

'Now he'll have two of them to put to rest!'

(This raised a fresh chorus of sobs.)

'Found the door open –'

'She never locked her door, Maggie –'

'And there she was, lying at the foot of the stairs–'

Although they didn't know me, they stood aside to let me into the house. Perhaps they thought that I had some business there, some authority.

Mrs Aiden was no longer lying at the foot of the stairs.

Voices from the kitchen indicated that she had been moved. Her body had been laid out on the sofa, the parlour occupied by the dead priest's coffin.

Dr Dalrymple, whom I had already met, was snapping

closed his bag and handing over a piece of paper, presumably the death certificate, to the constable, busily scribbling details in a small notebook, his demeanour solemn as befitted the occasion.

The new priest, Father Boyle, identified by a black cassock and a biretta knelt beside the dead woman, holding her hands, his lips moving in prayer.

The quartet was completed by a thin man in a tall hat with mourning ribbons, Mr Symons, local undertaker-cum-carpenter, standing by respectfully awaiting his turn, nervously flexing his measuring tape and trying to look unobtrusive and efficient.

The doctor saw me in the doorway clutching my basket of flowers. He shook his head. 'Sad business, my dear. Sad indeed.'

The new priest stood up. Tall, bearded, stern-visaged but otherwise undistinguished. He could have been any age between thirty and fifty. Somehow I had expected him to be a young curate.

Introduced to him as Miss Faro, which I had not the heart to correct, he asked, 'Were you a friend?'

'Not really. We had only just met. I was related to Father McQuinn by marriage.' Frowning, he regarded me solemnly. 'I see, I see.' About to explain, my words were cut short by Mr Symons, requesting the priest's urgent attention. Left standing there, I wasn't sure what to do next. The room was small for four large men, all towering over me. All with their own business in hand, they regarded me expectantly and with nothing else to contribute, I indicated the flowers.

'I came to – to bring her these –' And suddenly, near to angry tears, 'How on earth – I mean, falling downstairs – it doesn't usually kill someone –'

They looked surprised and uncomfortable at this outburst, and their embarrassed expressions said quite plainly that the last thing they needed was the presence of a hysterical woman. The doctor led me gently back into the hallway, followed by the constable who closed the door.

'Very unfortunate,' sighed Dr Dalrymple. 'Nearly all fatalities happen in the home, you know,' he added, meaning to be kind and reassuring while I bit back some searching questions about Father McQuinn's accident that was almost certainly murder.

'The poor lady was quite beyond my help when I was called,' the doctor continued as the constable approached us.

My introduction as Miss Rose Faro went uncorrected as Constable Bruce said, 'Father Boyle came rushing to my door, frantic to know where the doctor lived.'

I thought he was lucky to find the police house so quickly. It could hardly be called a police station, since at first glance Eildon appeared to be singularly lacking in such amenities.

'It was too late for me to do anything,' said Dr Dalrymple. 'Never a day's illness although she was getting very deaf. I can't recall the last time I saw her as a patient. She occasionally collected pills for Father McQuinn's rheumatism when it was bad in the winter, out in all weathers.'

The doctor paused, shook his head sadly. 'It was intended that Father Boyle should do the heavy work of visiting his scattered flock way up in the hills. Apart from rheumatism he seemed otherwise fit.' He sighed. 'But you never can tell. Hearts can give out any day and accidents are always looking for somewhere to happen,' he added gloomily.

'I realised the poor lady was dead the minute I saw her,' put in the constable. 'Cold she was, you know. Must have happened during the night.'

Looking up the short flight of stairs, the doctor nodded, 'Bedrooms are up there. I expect she was coming down in the dark for something. You will observe that there is a w.c. just

106

along the passage,' he added delicately. 'Caught her foot on a frayed part of the stair carpet –'

I looked up the stairs. There were ten of them, not very steep, up to the landing. Half way down, a torn rag of carpet.

We all had to move aside as a young woman arrived with several wreaths and went hurriedly into the parlour.

The doctor, muttering, 'Sad business indeed,' made his exit and I was left with the constable who was frowning at the flight of stairs as if they might provide an answer to the housekeeper's fatal fall.

Looking round, he gave a shout and sprang into action.

Where it had rolled, half hidden by a hall stand overburdened with cloaks, walking sticks and umbrellas, lay the guilty house-slipper.

The constable picked it up, turned it over in his hand. Old and worn, out of shape, accommodating bunions and corns. An old friend looked forward to as the comfort of Mrs Aiden's sore feet at the end of each day.

'Were you present when the doctor was examining her?' I asked. He nodded, still regarding the slipper with fierce concentration as if it might have some interesting information to impart.

'Did you happen to notice if there were any bruises on her arms?' He gave me a startled look. 'Not that I could see, she was wearing a long sleeved nightgown. Why do you ask?'

I turned my attention back to the stairs. 'It's just rather odd.'

'Odd, in what way?'

'Have you ever fallen downstairs?' I asked.

He laughed at that. 'Glory be – man and boy, more times than I've had hot dinners!' He looked at me, still puzzled by the question.

'I've taken many a tumble as well, constable. And the

house I live in has stone steps, spirals – much steeper than these.'

Suddenly alert and interested, he asked, 'So –?'

'Well, what's the first thing you – and most of us – do when you lose your balance and feel yourself falling?'

He frowned, thought a moment and said, 'Stretch out an arm or a hand – to grab something –'

'Me too. That's the natural way and we end up with nasty bruises.'

He nodded, looking puzzled as I continued, 'But to fall down a few carpeted stairs and break one's neck, constable? Doesn't that suggest to you that she fell stiffly, precipitated headlong down from a greater height than five feet. Enough to break her neck.'

'I see what you're getting at. As you say, it is unusual, you'd imagine she would have stumbled forward and rolled down –'

Deep in thought, the constable rubbed his chin.

'May I?' And taking the slipper from him, I turned it over in my hands, examining it carefully. The sole was worn thin and smooth with constant wear.

'Observe,' I said. 'There's nothing here to catch – no heel, no projection of any kind.'

'What are you getting at, miss?'

'It looks as if she fell with more force than would be justified by a slippered foot encountering a piece of frayed carpet.'

'Maybe you're right. But we'll never know now, will we?'

The kitchen door opened and Father Boyle looked out. He had heard our voices and seemed surprised to find us lingering by the stairs.

'Oh, you're still there. May we have a word, constable?'

As he disappeared I decided to have a closer look at that frayed carpet. Kneeling on the stairs, it was certainly threadbare at the steep edges. But that was not what had caused Mrs Aiden's fatal accident.

There was a cut, the kind made with a sharp knife, about six inches long, showing fresh and clean fibres against the worn threads.

I felt a sudden chill, a strange flash of insight which shook me considerably. If Father McQuinn had been murdered, as I believed, what about the man who had helped Mrs Aiden carry him into the house.

The mysterious passer-by, the stranger who was to have been the object of my enquiry.

Was it possible that he had also killed Mrs Aiden, so that any revelation of his identity would safely be buried with her?

But why? The burning question remained. For every murder there has to be a reason, a motive. Why should an unknown man come to Eildon with the express purpose of slaying the Catholic priest? And his housekeeper.

It just didn't make sense.

I went into the garden. Most of the women had moved beyond the gate.

Footsteps behind me as I walked along the road. The constable had followed me out. 'Nasty business, miss,' he said.

'More work for the Fiscal?'

He looked at me in astonishment and laughed. 'Not this time. Accidents in the home aren't for him. No suspicious circumstances.'

'You're sure of that, constable?'

'You mean about the stairs?' He shrugged. 'Interesting theory.' And pushing back his helmet to scratch his forehead, 'Quite an amazing deduction.'

Then echoing my own thoughts. 'But who would want to kill the priest's housekeeper?'

I considered telling him about the carpet, deliberately cut, but decided to keep that vital clue to myself for the time being as, shaking his head firmly, he said: 'Just coincidence, these accidents. Life's like that. But let's hope they aren't catching.'

Knowing the futility of argument, I said I hoped not and he went on, 'I understand you are getting married here in a short while, at the other church,' he added politely.

I said yes and he nodded. 'Known young Jack for years. Wish I'd had his luck.'

'How's that?"

'Big time detective, great Edinburgh crimes. Not like here. Never as much as a poacher most of the time, his lordship's gamekeeper sees to that with his mantraps. Then we have two fatalities in twenty four hours.' He chuckled grimly. 'Business is brisk.'

I remained silent and, regarding me curiously, he said, 'I knew your father, Inspector Faro, by the way.'

As Jack had warned me, news certainly got around. Doubtless Andrew Macmerry was keen to boast of his future daughter-in-law's famous connection.

'He was here on a case years ago. A great man –' and regarding me shrewdly, taking in my lack of inches, my deceptively gentle appearance, '– I dare say if you had been a lad you'd have followed in his footsteps.'

That infuriating assumption! 'I might well have done that,' I said coldly. Then another more productive reaction. 'Did you ever meet my father's sergeant, Danny McQuinn?'

He thought for a moment. 'Just a fleeting glimpse. I expect that was the young chap he had with him. Some connection with this area, I seem to remember.'

Good for the constable, I thought, and said. 'Danny McQuinn was my husband, so I am – was – related to the old priest by marriage.'

He gave me a startled look. 'You're married?'

'A widow – for several years now.'

'I'm sorry, miss – I mean, ma'am. You being Jack's fiancée,

Mrs Macmerry has always talked about you as Miss Rose Faro.'

Which confirmed that Jack's mother did not intend the world to know that her beloved only son was marrying another man's relict.

Watching my expression, the constable changed the subject quickly. 'Policemen run in the family, eh. So that accounts for your interest in our accidents?'

It was a question and when I didn't respond, he shrugged, 'Frankly I haven't had enough experience of real crimes in all my years in the force to immediately recognise the margin between accident and intent. There isn't much foul play in Eildon, you'll gather. We pride ourselves on our peaceful village. I reckon the sack of the Abbey must have been the last act of violence in this area.'

And without waiting for a reply, suddenly eager, 'I wonder what young Jack will have to say about Mrs Aiden's accident?'

'He doesn't know. He left last night shortly after Father McQuinn was found –'

He sighed. 'I don't suppose accidents in the home would have much interest for an Edinburgh detective.'

'Not if they were accidents,' I said.

He gave me a long glance and whistled. 'So you think Mrs Aiden might not have fallen – that she might have been pushed downstairs. It's a bit far-fetched – but –'

Stroking his chin, he looked suddenly very excited. His eyes gleamed. And at that moment I realised I had found an ally, someone who might be prepared to believe me.

On an impulse, I did something I had never intended to do in the whole of my stay in Eildon.

Opening my reticule, I handed him my card.

Reading it, his eyes widened and he whistled again. "Lady Investigator, Discretion Guaranteed.' I can hardly believe it – Mrs McQuinn. You look so – well –'

'Respectable, is that the word you're searching for?'

He laughed. 'You're just a young lass, no business dealing with nasty things like murders. What does young Jack think about – well, his future wife being in the same profession as himself?'

I smiled. 'He puts up with it.'

'Good for him. Most men wouldn't. Very unusual, a woman in what is strictly a man's world.'

And taking in my expression, he chuckled. 'He hasn't any alternative, eh? Is that it? Resigned to the fact that it was probably born in you, inherited it from your father. Well, well. I expect if you'd been a lad you would have joined the Edinburgh City Police,' he repeated.

I let that guaranteed assumption pass this time. I had no desire to argue with PC Bruce at this stage about the place of women in a man's world.

'It's been a great pleasure meeting you, Mrs McQuinn,' he said doffing his helmet to reveal that the cheerful still-round youthful face with the white moustache was late middle-aged, topped by a richly shining bald head. Smooth as a billiard ball, as Jack would say. A transformation that instead of adding ten years to his age made him suddenly more vulnerable.

PC Bruce was probably near retirement.

Smiling at me, apparently reluctant to relinquish my company, he said proudly: 'Perhaps you would care to see our police station?'

Which was exactly the invitation I was hoping for.

12

I followed Constable Bruce along the street. He marched rather than walked, brisk and smart as an old soldier on parade, occasionally saluting passers-by, mostly women out with children and shopping baskets.

At his side I felt uncomfortably aware of their eyes on our backs, anxious that his stern demeanour would not spread the rumour among local residents that they'd seen Jack Macmerry's intended taken into protective custody.

Finally we stopped outside an unassuming ivy-covered cottage. Set back from the main street with a path leading between two neat flower beds and a notice with the word 'Police' printed in large letters in the window.

There was clearly no pressing need for the law in Eildon. Had I been short-sighted or in a hurry I'd have passed it by and again I marvelled at Father Boyle's luck. Angels and a few well-directed prayers must have helped him find it that morning.

Mrs Bruce opened the door, with two small children peering behind her skirts. She was about my own age, once pretty but with a mouth set in hard unattractive lines.

The face of a young woman used to getting her own way.

'Do come in. You don't mind the kitchen, Miss Faro?' The village gossips had been busy and she knew who I was. The constable's apologetic glance told me that he would explain to her in due course.

Mrs Bruce was also something of a surprise, since she and the children were younger than I would have expected from her middle-aged husband.

Jack's father told me later that this was the constable's second marriage and Mary Bruce had for a short while kept company with Jack. His sly look hinted that she had had 'hopes' in that direction but had been disappointed.

Perhaps that was in Mary Bruce's mind as she set tea and scones before me and settled down at the kitchen table for a good old gossip. After all, Jack was a local celebrity and woman's chat about wedding dresses, receptions, guests and honeymoons would be passed on through the village like wildfire.

None of this, I have to confess, was of gripping interest to me, especially as the two children had decided I was a worthy target for their undivided attention. Drinking tea was a hazard, faced with keeping a good grip on the cup, eating a scone and bestowing smiling glances on the pair of little devils, while diverting the constant threat of those jammy hands clawing at my skirts.

No easy task as I endeavoured to respond to their mother's stream of polite conversation, interspersed with shrill instructions to her offspring to behave themselves, her hands constantly upraised, threatening imminent punishment.

Once again, in this scene of everyday life in Eildon, I was out of my depth. It was soon obvious that PC Bruce was by no means a stern disciplinarian at his own kitchen table. He smiled awkwardly, pretended not to notice and brought to mind Pappa's sage observation: that many a cock o' the walk in the Central Office was just a poor feather duster in his own kitchen.

After a particularly violent bout of infant screams, aware of my discomfort, he said, 'I brought the young lady here to show her our police cell, Mary.'

Mrs Bruce pushed the children aside and, loudly protesting, 'Police cell indeed! You call it that! It had better not be!' she followed us into the hall.

'It's just one room, with a few bars on the window,' said the constable apologetically. 'Not a proper cell.'

'And better not be ever, Tom Bruce, I'm warning you,' his wife repeated. Turning to me she added. 'I've told him that if ever he locks a criminal in there then I'm off, back to my ma, and taking the bairns with me.'

'Not much danger of that, I keep telling her,' said Tom with a somewhat subdued laugh. 'Besides, it would only be overnight, then he would be handed over to the official county police to deal with.'

'I've told you, one night is enough for us to all wake up in the morning with our throats cut,' was the angry response from a wife with so little faith in her husband as a stern guardian of law and order, that my immediate reaction was to wonder why on earth she had married him in the first place.

Eager to change the subject, he turned to me, 'Perhaps you'd like to see some of our records –'

'Records, indeed. Just a lot of old rubbish. Things I never want the bairns to see. It would give them nightmares, those awful pictures. Enough to turn a woman's stomach,' was Mrs Bruce's warning.

However, as both bairns were now screaming at the top of their voices and going for each other hammer and tongs, as one might say, she rushed off to prevent imminent fratricide.

The prison cell was fairly comfortable for a night's lodging. A bed with pillow and neatly folded blanket, chair, table and washing bowl, all patiently waiting for a criminal who never came.

As a place of correction and restraint I decided that with some minor additions, it could have done credit to many a wayside inn. In point of fact, it compared favourably with Sister Mary Michael's retirement cell in the convent in St Leonard's.

Although the barred window was a minor deterrent, the lock and bolt on the outside of the door would never have restrained a determined lawbreaker's bid for escape.

But PC Bruce was very proud of his cell, busily spreading documents on the little rickety table. Crimes from *The Illustrated London News,* various newspapers and broadsheets with very graphic and imaginative artists' impressions of gruesome stabbings, cut throats, hangings and sundry executions.

When I expressed the polite interest that was expected of me, he kept repeating that this was a great day, a great day indeed, having the good fortune to meet me.

I realised that he was practically bursting with pride. In a uniform never renewed and intended for his slimmer figure of some twenty years ago, each gesture threatened every tightly fastened button with explosion.

'All these years, Mrs McQuinn. And at last, not a poacher, not a kitten up a tree, not boys pinching apples but a real crime, the possibility of a real life murder,' he said, smiling blissfully at the prospect.

I reckoned that whatever his wife's emotions on the subject PC Bruce thought he had died and gone to heaven, for this was what he had dreamed of all his life and, had he not been a pious Christian, an elder of the Protestant kirk, I suspected that he might well have sent up a little prayer for just such an opportunity to solve a murder, to justify his long uneventful service. 'And now, let's have the facts – as you see them. Right from the beginning, if you please,' he said briskly, words he must have rehearsed constantly in the forlorn hope of such an occasion.

As I spoke, he produced a ledger from a locked cupboard. A log book, which was very seriously empty, it transpired, but nevertheless brought longings for my own casebook left behind in Edinburgh. Having any use for it in Eildon was the last thing I had ever imagined.

'To begin at the beginning, I am certain that Father McQuinn's death wasn't an accident –'

I was relieved that this dramatic outburst was received with none of Jack's disbelief. Apart from his eyebrows almost disappearing into his bald head, he made no comments, calmly taking out pen and ink he prepared to record each detail, listening carefully to my discovery of the priest and the blood stained candlestick, occasionally halting my story to ask me to repeat some detail and add a query of his own.

In so doing, he sucked in his lips, frowning and squeezing his eyelids shut in a manner that suggested deep thought and intense concentration and again I thought of how this was the moment he had longed for all his life, waiting patiently with that empty cell in the modest police house for his efforts to be appreciated, his skills to be put into operation.

What a loss to the Edinburgh City Police! What an asset his enthusiasm would have been to the Central Office.

'Let's have a timetable, if you please, Mrs. McQuinn. I like that, helps sort out things tolerably well.'

A man after my own heart, I decided, going over the events again in chronological order as he carefully wrote them down.

'So you went across to the church to visit your late husband's relative shortly after eight o'clock last night? That was the time when you discovered his body. You're sure of that?'

'I am. I gathered that was the time the Mass ended and I had been waiting at the farm, rather anxiously counting the minutes, as a matter of fact.'

I didn't want to go into details of why I hadn't told the Macmerrys of my reason for visiting Father McQuinn, as I added, 'I waited until their clock struck eight and left immediately.'

Repeating once more the gruesome details and my suspicions that there was someone else in the church, the constable asked:

'How long before you left and went in search of help?'

I shook my head. 'Not long. After making sure there was nothing I could do – that he was dead –'

His frown was an interruption and I added hastily, 'I have some experience in such matters – then I rushed back to the farm for Jack's father.'

'Did you not think the local constable or the doctor would have been more appropriate?' he asked a mite reproachfully.

'It would. Had I known where either of you lived – and there was no one around to ask,' I responded sharply.

He nodded. 'At that hour, you could be sure of finding Eildon deserted except for the customers at our local pub. What about Mrs Aiden at the church house next door? Did that not occur to you – to go to her for help?'

'It certainly did not. To go and tell her that the priest had been murdered! All I would have had were delays and a possibly hysterical woman to deal with.'

Again he nodded and I continued, 'As it so happened, Jack had just arrived off the train – and that delayed us – I'll spare you the domestic upheavals I encountered regarding the deerhound he had brought with him. So it would be about quarter to nine before we ran back to the church together. As I told you earlier, the body was gone, the candlestick had been replaced. The bloodstains had been washed off the floor.'

I waited a few moments while he recorded these details.

He sat back. 'And all in about half-an-hour. So what happened next?'

'Jack thought I had imagined it all. He's like that.'

Did I imagine that wry glance as I went on, 'However, when we went to the church house, Mrs Aiden explained what had happened. How she had found the priest lying at the altar when she went to tell him his supper was ready and a stranger passing by had helped her carry him back to the house.'

PC Bruce tapped his pen against his teeth. 'If Father

McQuinn was murdered as you believe, then it follows that this stranger who so conveniently appeared – and disappeared – might well be his killer.'

'My own thoughts exactly!'

'And this suggests that he was still lurking in the church when you arrived at roughly eight o'clock and heard those mysterious movements.'

He thought for a moment. 'So Mrs Aiden must have entered the church almost immediately after you rushed back to the farm. This stranger who was somewhere close by appeared and helped her carry the priest into the house.'

Pausing, he said thoughtfully, 'Did he then run back into the church and wash the floor and candlestick clean of bloodstains. Is that the way you see it?'

'Yes. There is only one problem. Where did he get the water?'

The constable smiled wryly. 'Well, leaving out the use of holy water, there is a horse trough in the street just a step away from the church entrance. And if their vestry is anything like ours, there are cleaning materials – mop and bucket, in a cupboard.'

Noting that down, he asked: 'When you came to the church house this morning, while Dr Dalrymple was writing Mrs Aiden's death certificate, it was about ten o'clock.'

He frowned. 'According to the doctor's rough estimate, the poor lady had been dead for probably five or six hours. I don't know much about time of death, but she was certainly stiff and cold when I touched her, regardless of the mild night temperature.'

We were both silent, then he continued, 'So if the killer returned to the house to silence Mrs Aiden, he would most likely choose the early hours as the best time to take her off-guard. And even if he didn't know Eildon, he could be almost sure of a village's street being deserted at that time.'

'So where did he go in the interval – from eight o'clock to say, three or four in the morning?' I asked.

'Our local pub is out. Closes at 10 promptly. There is a tea room provided in one room for the benefit of visitors to the Abbey and much frowned upon by landlord Donald, who has strong views about the propriety of women crossing the threshold of his public house.'

While I was wondering what use I could make of this information, he went on. 'Anyway, although it's open during the summer months it closes at five o'clock. So our killer couldn't have taken refuge there and he would have stood out like a sore thumb in the public bar since Donald and his wife are very curious about strangers, well-known as a source of village gossip. And our stranger certainly would not want to be questioned.'

'So we must presume that he returned to the church, which is never locked, and bided his time there,' I paused. 'You said he most probably took her by surprise.'

'That was doubtless his intention. And what better way to get someone off guard than to knock on the door at four in the morning.' He frowned and added. 'No, that won't do. She was almost completely deaf.'

I was picturing the scene. 'The door wasn't looked so he crept upstairs and – What then? Did she recognise him as the helpful stranger? He would need some excuse for coming at that hour. Perhaps begging a place to stay.' I paused. 'And then he threw her downstairs.'

PC Bruce mulled this over and then said triumphantly, 'Know what I think? She wasn't killed by the fall – I think she was already dead before he arranged that scene –'

'You mean he broke her neck – first.'

He nodded grimly. 'Yes. To make sure –'

'And then he took a knife and cut the fraying carpet to make it look like an accident. Thought of everything, didn't he?'

'Indeed he did. If we are dealing with two murders, Mrs McQuinn, we aren't dealing with an amateur,' he said grimly. 'We are dealing with a professional.'

Pausing, he regarded me intently. 'This man is clever, not just a bungling amateur, a burglar caught in the act, who loses his temper.'

He thought for a moment and said slowly, 'Our man is probably a trained killer, perhaps even a mercenary soldier, well-versed in the art of how to kill.' And rubbing his chin thoughtfully. 'So what brings such a man here. What is his mission in a place like Eildon?"

A chill went through me. A fragment of conversation from my days in Arizona when Danny told me how Pinkerton's trained men in unorthodox ways of survival, of dealing with dangerous outlaws and criminals, as well as those employed in that other side of their detective agency – a highly confidential and secret service for the Government. Such as permanently silencing those who were a danger or a personal embarrassment to the President or some influential member of the Senate.

'The Queen's Jubilee? Could it have something to do with that?'

The constable considered for a moment, shook his head. 'Here in Eildon? Surely not.'

I wished Jack had been more forthcoming about that police business as I thought about Mrs Aiden's attacker, hearing again Danny's words, 'They teach you how to break a man's neck as easily as snapping a twig.'

And I thought of how I had shuddered and asked quietly: 'Have you ever done that, Danny?'

Danny had looked away from me, smiled narrowly. 'That would be giving away State secrets, Rose. But let's say that in an emergency, if I'm called upon, I know exactly how.'

The constable was asking a question. He had to repeat it twice:

'What we need to know is where is our killer now?'

Still thinking about Danny, I shook my head as he continued, 'His job done – whatever it was, I expect he's gone from Eildon long since.'

I thought about that. 'But how did he get away? How did he get here in the first place. On foot, horseback, by carriage? What about trains?'

He shook his head. 'No, too public. Especially small halts like Eildon where there are so few getting on and off the three trains a day that any stranger would be remarked upon – and remembered in some detail. Far too dangerous for our man.'

These theories were all very well. But there was one missing ingredient.

'If these two deaths, as we suspect, were murders, for murder there has to be a motive – a reason. If you consider that the Jubilee is rather far-fetched – you know Eildon better than I do, you've lived here a long time-so what about a personal vendetta? Did Father McQuinn have any enemies? What about fanatical Protestants?' I asked.

He laughed. 'There aren't any that I know of in our community. You're talking about the bad old days. This is the 19th century – things are different now, folk are more civilised. Our very respectable Presbyterian church is anti-Popery but remember our local laird is a Catholic.'

Then he added soberly. 'The Father was a good kindly man, a real Christian gentleman and one I would have trusted with my life. I respected him and his beliefs although I'm not supposed to say that as an elder of the kirk. I think everybody in Eildon would agree with me. As for Mrs Aiden. She was popular with everyone, a kindly soul always ready to lend a hand to those in trouble.'

He shook his head. 'No, I think we can rule out personal

vendettas. This isn't Europe, you know. Passions in Eildon don't rise much higher than the fate of the harvest each year, cost of grain and what price the sheep and cows will bring at the Peebles market.'

Throwing down his pen, he regarded me gravely.

'And there you have it, Mrs McQuinn. I fancy we are dealing with something much more sinister than killing a Catholic priest and his kindly housekeeper. Do you know what I fear most?'

I didn't but he was ready to supply it.

'I fear that these two innocent victims are just the beginning.'

I thought about that. In his eagerness to see something more dramatic than the simple misdemeanours of a tiny village community, was he exaggerating, even hopeful that he was to see his lifetime's ambition fulfilled at last?

The chance to solve not one murder, but two!

13

The sound of a crash followed by children screaming and Mrs Bruce calling 'Tom! Come here – at once!' cut short any further discussion. With a murmured apology a rather red faced Constable Bruce sprang to his feet, pushed the ledger into the drawer and saying hurriedly that he would contact me later, I was ushered out of the house known as the local police station.

Feeling somewhat frustrated at this abrupt ending to what promised to be a revealing episode regarding the two deaths, nevertheless I felt quite buoyant and confident, no longer regretting Jack's absence at this crucial time. Once I was able to produce evidence that I had not imagined the whole thing I knew he would throw himself wholeheartedly into a murder investigation. But in his absence, I had found a local policeman who not only believed that the priest and his housekeeper had been murdered, but was prepared to take an active role in helping me solve the crime.

I wondered how Detective Inspector Jack Macmerry would react to this piece of news and, more urgently, when he was likely to return to Eildon.

Deep in my thoughts, walking back along the street towards the farm, I heard my name called and, turning, saw a small pony trap, the kind known among the gentry as a governess cart.

It had come to a standstill across the road and waving wildly, I saw the small figure of the Master of Verney.

'Miss Rose – Miss Rose! Over here!'

As I approached I saw that his balancing act in an effort to attract my attention was being somewhat ineffectually restrained by an attractive fair-haired young woman who had been driving the cart and was holding on to him.

Smiling, I hurried across.

He clapped his hands. 'I am so glad to see you again.'

The young woman at his side whispered, 'Please sit down, Alexander. Everyone is looking at you.'

A slight exaggeration as the street was almost deserted but she gave me an apologetic nod as if to excuse her charge's exuberance.

'Oh, do be quiet, Cousin Annette. This is Miss Rose, a dear friend of mine. You see –' and I was listening once again to the dramatic account of my rescue of his boat.

Breathlessly at the end, Alexander beamed on us both, remembered his manners and said, 'Miss Rose, this is my cousin Miss Annette Verney.'

As we shook hands she said, 'We are very grateful to you – we realised from the condition of Master Verney's clothes that it was more than a shipwreck you diverted.'

And suddenly I knew where I had seen her before. No longer wearing the garb of a novice this blue-eyed pretty girl was my aloof fellow passenger on the Edinburgh train. At that moment I felt rather gratified that my observations regarding her elegant shoes and neatly manicured finger-nails, the evidence of a well-to-do background, had been correct.

'Yes, Alexander,' she was saying. 'You may go into the shop and spend your pocket money. I will wait for you –'

'Miss Rose – she is to wait too!' It was a command.

His cousin glanced quickly in my direction. 'Perhaps – if Miss Rose has not some more pressing engagement?'

This was a question. I smiled at him and said of course, I would wait.

'Then you must promise not to be too long. Alexander,' said Miss Verney.

Alexander glanced at me sternly. 'You won't go away – you will wait. You promise!'

When I said yes he gave a whoop of pleasure, hopped out of the cart and raced into the general store.

Miss Verney smiled apologetically. 'The seat is rather hard but perhaps you would you care to join me.'

As I stepped into the cart, she added, 'I think I should warn you however, we may have to wait some time. Alexander spends much time and deliberation over his purchases, especially colouring books and crayons.'

I was somewhat embarrassed as I did not know whether she would wish to be reminded of our earlier encounter. The same thoughts were in her mind when she broke the silence.

'We have met before, Miss Rose. And I owe you an apology. I fear I was rather rude.' And cutting short my protests, she went on, 'You came upon me at a bad moment. I didn't feel like talking to anyone that particular day. As you can guess by my resumption of normal dress, I was at a crossroads.'

Pausing, she sighed and gazed towards the hills as if they might provide a solution. 'I was about to take my final vows – I had to decide whether this was my rightful vocation – against the wishes of my family, in fact, and I was on what was perhaps to be my last journey home.'

She paused again and I asked the obvious: 'Then you have decided?'

'Fate has decided it for me. When I was in New York with Alexander's mother, I made an unsuitable – alliance – against my family's wishes. Lord Verney is my guardian and there was a fearful scandal – I was under age and had eloped with a humble clerk in a shipping office. I was dragged unwillingly home and poor Amelia believed that by diverting my life and putting more suitable and eligible young men in my direction, the marriage annulled, I might forget and make a better choice.'

She sighed deeply. 'I chose instead to go into a convent.'

Pausing, she smiled for the first time. 'When I left the train that day there were surprises in store. Amelia is an invalid and it seemed that as I have some education she wished me to teach Alexander for a while. His former governess moved on recently and it is hardly worth while hiring a tutor – for the short while before he goes to prep school in September. I was happy to agree. And then I had an additional reason for secret rejoicing,' she whispered jubilantly. 'A letter forwarded by a friend in New York who is in my confidence.'

Again she paused, eyes shining. 'You cannot guess what happiness the contents of that letter held. I am now of age, and the man with whom I eloped and who I still regard as my husband in the eyes of God is on his way to Britain to claim me as his wife.'

Somewhat cynically I considered that had not Fate intervened, she might well have slipped into the thankless role of a young unmarried relative becoming an unpaid servant in a noble household as she turned to me excitedly.

'My one and only love. And I am to have my happy ending after all. Is that not a romantic story, worthy of any novel, Miss Rose?'

And I thought of my love for Danny. One love, highly unsuitable. How I had never imagined I could ever love again. Yet here I was about to marry Jack Macmerry.

I decided I had better tell her that my name was Mrs McQuinn when, at that moment, Alexander appeared clutching his purchases, his colouring book and crayons, proudly chosen alone and paid for.

Relieved to see me sitting beside his cousin, he was reluctant to let me go. Could I not come back with them for lunch? Oh please, please.

Miss Verney shook her head and said in grown up manner that this was very short notice and no doubt Miss Rose had other engagements.

I got the message. But it was also too late now to embark on explanations regarding my widowhood as Alexander refused to be placated. I had to promise that I would visit them, and see all his toys, his rocking horse which he had outgrown and his new train set.

I gave my word and Miss Verney added her smiling request for an early meeting.

Watching them drive off I thought of her confidences, perhaps she was lonely and I was left with the feeling that I had another friendship in the making.

Besides, with a touch of snobbery I would never have admitted to Jack, I was rather pleased at the possibility of seeing the inside of Verney Castle as a guest and how new friends in high places would impress my future in-laws.

Back at the farm I looked into the stable to see Thane. Jack's father was with him and he looked up when I came in and greeted me in astonishment.

'You will never believe this, lass,' and holding out Thane's injured paw, no longer in its splint. 'This animal is amazing. Such speedy healing! – I've never seen anything like it.'

'All thanks to you,' I murmured, as he went on: 'Nay, lass. I have no such powers.' And pausing to push back his bonnet and scratch his forehead, a familiar gesture I had observed indicating surprise and puzzlement, 'It is absolutely incredible. Injuries like that take weeks to heal but look –'

Thane obediently held out his paw for examination. It was true. All signs of injury had disappeared.

'It's like a miracle. Never seen anything like it in all my born days of working with beasts. Who on earth did you get him from? They should have kept him for breeding.'

Thane gave a faint shudder. In a human one might have said he raised his eyes heavenward in an expression of disgust. As for me I could only answer 'He was a stray – he more or less adopted me.'

Mr Macmerry shook his head in wonder and I had no logical explanation that I cared to discuss with him regarding the arrival in my life of the strange deerhound from somewhere on Arthur's Seat two years ago. And how he managed to live in that wild place, and feed himself – although that was not quite such a mystery as how he managed always to look so groomed and cared for.

I could have told him – maybe I would someday – how Thane's strange telepathy – or magic – had twice saved my life. But Magic is not a word I readily use, or care to ask others to consider, although I now suspected that instant healing might also be added to Thane's mysterious origins and his agelessness.

'Will he be able to walk?' I asked vaguely, the question somehow superfluous.

As if he understood, Thane raced to the door. That was as far as the restraining rope allowed him, so turning he ran back to us.

'There's your answer, lass. He's just told us himself,' said Mr Macmerry, frowning, regarding Thane in wonder and something more indefinable – almost awe, I thought, as he asked:

'I suppose you'll be taking him back to Edinburgh now.'

That was the last thing I wanted at the moment with two possible murders to solve. I said, 'Can he stay here – if it's all right with you? You see, there's no one to look after him back at Edinburgh while we're away?' I added lamely and I'd swear I blushed, aware of a sharp and reproachful glance from under Thane's magisterial eyebrows at this outright lie.

'Besides Jack wanted me to stay with you. He thought I might be needed,' I added taking refuge in a small bout of self righteousness. Mr Macmerry beamed 'We'll be right glad of that, lass. You're great company. You're a joy to have around.'

My feelings of resentment at this forced stay gave me a

twinge of guilt, although I suspected the dear soul was using the royal 'we' and that such sentiments were a little one-sided, especially as Mrs Macmerry appeared at the door with her basket of eggs at that moment.

Mr Macmerry sprang to his feet and began telling her all about Thane's miraculous recovery.

She didn't share his amazement and enthusiasm, unwavering in her regard of Thane with tight-lipped disapproval.

'Very well. He can stay, if you are willing to be responsible for him, Andrew Macmerry. But That Dog is not to be allowed in my house – you understand.'

Her eyes flickered in my direction, a reminder that those instructions included any ideas I might have on the subject.

And again to Mr Macmerry. 'Not in any circumstances. Whisky and Soda would never tolerate another dog.'

Her husband tried to placate her but I could see a nasty domestic storm brewing up, so I gently unhitched Thane from his post and led him out of the barn leaving behind complaints about 'That Dog' still thick in the air.

This was his first introduction to Eildon and what better than to take him across the field leading to the Abbey. Unlike my first visit, today there were cows grazing and as I am a little cautious in case one might turn out to be a bull, I felt very confident and brave with Thane at my side.

I wondered how he would react to them, but as soon as they saw him they all stood still like some group of bovine statues and then they huddled close together. If they didn't exactly stampede, they certainly moved very fast out of our path. Halting by the fence at the edge of the field, they turned their white faces towards us, their steady unmoving gaze following us as we walked away.

I was rather relieved and decided that this was doubtless their normal reaction to any strange animal, particularly a large deerhound.

Wondering how Thane would take to the Abbey ruins, I soon discovered that he found them very interesting indeed and sniffed around, tail wagging in very normal dog fashion.

On impulse I decided to take him up the spiral staircase where my stalker had lurked.

He didn't like it. He went halfway and then stopped looked at me imploringly. Do we have to go on?

I wondered if this was too much for him and if his paw hurt. When I patted his head and asked if that was so, he turned and went quickly up the stairs. As we reached the open roof we were met by the sunlight and a cool breeze.

Alongside the top steps, there had once been a door, perhaps leading into a tiny room for occupation by a lookout in troubled times. I went in and it was clear from Thane's behaviour that it had been occupied more recently.

He sniffed the floor eagerly especially one corner so I looked more closely and saw a rough blanket had been thrown down and abandoned. That and a stump of candle confirmed that it had seen human occupation.

Thane looked at me. Oh, if only you could speak, I thought as I had done so often when faced with the certainty that he had knowledge that would be invaluable if only he could communicate it to me.

I left him rooting about in the dark corners and went out on to the roof where I realised this was the very spot from where the stalker had watched me. And what a view he had. The entire village spread out before him.

When I came down, Thane was still investigating cracks in the stone floor. I could see nothing. Dark and gloomy, I hated the foetid odour, smells which indicated that it had been used for less pleasant purposes than a temporary sleeping place.

I called to Thane who seemed reluctant to abandon his inspection of that bare stone floor. Later I was to regret not sharing his enthusiasm for a more careful search.

As we left the sentry room and went back down the spiral stair, I had the satisfaction of having solved one mystery.

This was most likely where Father McQuinn's killer had spent those missing hours while he lay in wait to murder his next victim: Mrs Aiden.

Constable Bruce would no doubt be very interested in my findings, I decided, as we set off in the direction of the police station.

Thane had no need of a rope. I knew he was happy to be free of restraint as he walked close to my side but the absence of a lead clearly alarmed some of those we met who were of a nervous disposition.

After all, he was a very large dog and I was conscious that he was almost as tall as myself.

'You're walking very well, Thane,' I said, 'all things considered.'

He looked up at me. Indicating his now healed paw I said:

'How did you manage that?'

He looked away. In a human I would have said, he shook his head, if dogs were capable of such gestures.

The reactions of the cows in the abbey field I considered quite normal. But at our approach some of the village ladies who had dogs on leads looked mildly hysterical, seeing that he could have gulped down some of their small charges in one mouthful.

But what interested me most was the reaction of the dogs themselves. Large and small alike, they did not approach him, or bark warningly, depending on their dispositions. They merely melted obligingly and respectfully into the sidewalks as if royalty progressed through their midst.

By their behaviour I realised that dogs, perhaps cows and all animals, recognised the mysterious quality in Thane that was quite beyond human interpretation. Some additional sense, some fragment of consciousness lost long ago.

132

We reached the police station without incident. To find there was no one at home. At least that was the impression we were to be given, although I could have sworn that the lace curtain twitched and Mrs Bruce remained silent behind it.

Perhaps her children were having a midday nap. Perhaps she was afraid of large dogs. Or was it more likely that she was afraid I was to be a bad influence on her husband and might, by our mutual efforts, succeed in putting a dangerous criminal – a murderer – behind those frail bars in the prison cell!

14

Back at the farm, Mrs Macmerry was watching our approach along the lane. 'You haven't got That Dog on a rope,' she said accusingly, pointing out the obvious.

'He isn't used to walking with a lead,' I replied.

She sniffed. 'All dogs except for our two and Rex have to have leads whether they like it or not, and That Dog is no different from any others.'

I smiled and thought, how surprised she might be if she knew the truth.

Taking my smile as defiance she said, 'There's soup waiting for you and tea in the pot. Once you've tied That Dog up again.'

Smiling sweetly, I said that was my intention.

And Mrs Macmerry marched indoors, her lips tighter than ever, looking a little disappointed at my lack of argument if she had been hoping for a disagreement and spoiling for a fight.

After seeing Thane settled once more and promising him another walk soon, I went into the kitchen to be met by a delicious smell of baking.

Jack's father was seated at the table with the weekly local newspaper spread before him.

As I sniffed the air appreciatively he grinned. 'That's your wedding cake, lass. Jess has a friend in the village who is great at decorating. All three tiers.' And then with a guilty look, he added, 'I wasn't supposed to tell you. It was to be a secret.'

I smiled and said consolingly, 'I'll pretend that we never had this conversation and knew nothing about a wedding cake.'

We heard footsteps and I immediately sat down at the table and we both tried to look innocent.

'Perhaps you'd like to read all the local gossip,' said Mr Macmerry.

'Not much for a city lass, Andrew,' said his wife, 'there's only farm and church news, the parish pump at its best.'

'True enough, Jess. But there's something stronger for the headlines this week. Look at this.'

Mrs Macmerry leaned over his shoulder and read, "Body of an Unknown Man near Berwick." Well, I never. Wait till I find my glasses –'

'Don't bother, I'll read it for you, Jess. "The body of an unknown man was found on the railway embankment near Berwick Railway Station. The police are investigating a suicide or the possibility that he fell by accident from the evening train to London from Edinburgh on Monday.'

'Oh, that was the day before our Jack came home,' said Mrs Macmerry dramatically.

'Listen to this,' Mr Macmerry went on, '"A railway guard reported that the communication cord was pulled soon after the train left Berwick Station. When he went to investigate the compartment was empty and the carriage door down to the railway line was lying open. He saw nothing amiss but reported the incident to the rail authorities, as was customary. It now transpires that this was within a short distance of where the man had made his death leap."'

'Would you believe it, Andrew, that's the very same train our Jack gets when he comes to see us. You're not safe anywhere these days – as for those carriage doors –' said Mrs Macmerry with a shudder, as if Jack might be a future victim of just such an incident.

A knock on the kitchen door announced Dr Dalrymple. 'How's my patient today?' he asked Mr Macmerry and I learned what he had been at pains to conceal, that Jack's father had a suspected heart condition. He was becoming increasingly breathless on the hill to the up-by field and just the other day he had taken what he described as a queer turn.

Mrs Macmerry was in a state of shock over this. Why hadn't he told her, why had he kept it a secret? As if he had had a bad bout as she described it, just to personally inconvenience her.

Dr Dalrymple was put out at this revelation and the consternation it had caused. 'Andrew, I just looked in in passing. I presumed you had told Jess. I am sorry –' he added, looking anxiously at Jess who was on the brink of tearful hysteria.

On the other side of the table Andrew remained calm and smiling, shaking his head, stoutly maintaining that it was nothing for any of us to worry about.

'Let me be the judge of that,' said the doctor sternly. 'Now, now, Jess – there, there. Don't upset yourself,' he added with poorly concealed impatience.

As he opened his bag and withdrew a stethoscope, I tactfully withdrew to my bedroom feeling that the scene I had left suggested that he might now have two patients on his hands and would be handing out pills to both instead of the one he had come to visit.

I left my door open until I heard him leaving.

Smiling as I came downstairs, he waited in the hallway and, taking my reappearance as natural concern for his patient, he said:

'He'll be fine, lass. Nothing I can see for you – or Jess here – to get alarmed about. Don't worry, Andrew will be fighting fit for your wedding, aye and we'll see him dandle his grandchildren yet.'

I followed him down the lane. He didn't find it necessary to use a carriage, he said. Walking was good for him and for patients who lived further afield, well, he had a splendid horse who also needed the exercise.

I had a sudden idea and asked him if he could give me

something for indigestion. I explained that I was a martyr to heartburn and that I was also sleeping badly.

He raked me over with a doctor's shrewd gaze and shook his head. 'First diagnosis, you're too thin, lass, and not used to Jess's grand meals, I expect. Second diagnosis, for what it's worth, it's wedding nerves that's wrong with you. Stop worrying about all those wedding arrangements, lass. Rest assured, it'll all go like clockwork and you'll sleep fine after your great day.'

To my wan smile, he added, 'I can give you something from my dispensary if you'd like to come back with me. Just along the street.'

As I waited in the immaculate white-walled clinically-shelved room that would have done a hospital proud, he counted out pills, put them in neat little boxes and talked about the Macmerrys as if I needed reassurance about my future in-laws.

What a fine family they were, generations of splendid farm folk, while I racked my brains for a suitable opening to Mrs Aiden's recent demise. Guiltily I realised I didn't really need the pills either, well aware of the reason for my heartburn, but asking for a prescription had occurred to me as a fine subterfuge. I could hardly accost him in the surgery saying: 'There's nothing wrong with me, doctor, I simply wanted to ask you some questions.'

I certainly couldn't admit I might be pregnant. The village gossip would certainly find its way back to Jack's mother. So taking a deep breath, I interrupted the flow of reminiscences regarding boyhood days with Andrew Macmerry.

'You have had a busy week, so far.'

He agreed, and I continued: 'Was Mrs Aiden badly bruised by her fall?'

He stopped writing in his prescriptions book to stare at me over his spectacles. Obviously taken aback by such a question, he said: 'Her neck was broken, lass. Wasn't that enough?'

I wanted to say that there was not nearly enough evidence that her neck had been broken by falling down five stairs and that Constable Bruce and I had reason to suspect that her accident had been murder. But I held my tongue.

'Here are your pills,' he said handing me the boxes, just a trifle impatiently, refusing payment and when I insisted he said, 'I'll settle with Jack.'

He saw me out rather briskly, and I was very conscious that he was probably thinking Jack's future wife was a bit odd.

That mismanaged interview was not to be my last embarrassing encounter for the day.

The sky had darkened. A sudden shower of rain turned into a veritable cloudburst. Still some distance from the farm I was unprepared for such an eventuality, having left the farm in sunshine, without a cloud in the sky, with no thought of either hat or umbrella.

Looking round, desperately searching for shelter, I spotted the Eildon Arms and, remembering that they boasted a tearoom, I dashed inside.

And of course found myself in the Public Bar where a large selection of the male inhabitants enjoying their mid-day glass of ale, stopped mid-sip to stare belligerently at this female intruder in their midst.

None more so than the owner Donald, who I had been warned about.

Coming towards me, he said very loudly so that all could hear: 'Not in here, madam. No – ladies –' (that produced a snigger all round!) and beaming on his customers he repeated: 'No ladies permitted in the public bar, if you please.'

Outraged I stood my ground and faced up to him, all four feet ten inches of righteous indignation.

'And where then does one make an enquiry regarding accommodation?'

'Follow me.' Somewhat mollified he led the way along a corridor into a reception area, with a second door that led out into the street and which I had not noticed in my hasty arrival.

Positioning himself behind the desk he said: 'And when would you be wanting this room, madam?'

That was a tricky question. 'Not for myself, for – for a friend who was arriving from Edinburgh two nights ago.'

Taking out a register he consulted it, frowned and said: 'We had no guests that night.'

Squinting over the counter, it was obvious that there were no entries in the register for several days.

'No matter,' I said with a feeling of triumph for that part of my question was answered.

Donald was frowning, giving me very odd looks indeed. Aware that I was floundering in very deep waters, I decided to make my exit with as much dignity as possible and drawing myself up to my full height once again, I added, 'There must have been some misunderstanding, doubtless he will get in touch with us.'

'You are not requiring a room for yourself, madam?' he sounded disappointed at having lost a potential guest.

'No. I have accommodation, thank you.'

A sudden gleam in his eye, a flash of recognition. He knew who I was. I could read his thoughts. What was Jack Macmerry's bride-to-be doing testing out the Eildon Arms? Was she having problems with her future in-laws – already? There was no quick escape from an embarrassing situation. Beyond the window the rain was heavier now, running in streams down the street.

Beyond the desk I saw a glass door marked 'Tea room'.

'Are refreshments available?'

Closing the register in an impatient gesture he said coldly,

'If you wish. Take a seat and I will send someone to take your order.'

'A cup of tea will do excellently.'

Again the faintest gleam of interest. Why was Jack's intended wanting a cup of tea in the village? Had she quarrelled with Jack Macmerry or his rather formidable mother?

As he walked away I guessed that my advent at the Eildon Arms would make interesting discussion for his cronies in the public bar which would hardly endear me to Mrs Macmerry when, as it would, the gossip reached her ears.

I realised uneasily that I was not making a success of my approaching wedding either and once Jack's family got wind of my investigation of what I believed were two murders in their quiet village, I could hardly expect my popularity stakes to be high with my in-laws or their respectable friends and neighbours.

Not a very auspicious start to a happily married life for the future Mrs Jack Macmerry.

15

Looking round the tea-room of the Eildon Arms, I almost lost my nerve. It was as uninviting as the proprietor. Dingy and depressing with a preponderance of dark brown walls and dark brown tables and chairs, a room which had never seen the gesture of a woman's hands in a cheering vase of flowers.

A warning notice read, 'No Alcohol or Spirits Served Here.'

It could hardly have provided an enticing prospect for visitors to the Abbey and had it been unoccupied at that moment, I think I would have fled the dismal scene. However, taking courage from the presence of two women with a teapot and cups on the table before them, I sat down nearby.

The elder of the two women smiled. 'You have to press the bell near the fireplace there if you want service.'

Thanking her I did so and a moment later a young lad entered. Obviously hastily recruited and by his surly expressions sharing the same sentiments as Donald, it went severely against the grain having to serve despised womankind in a public house, this hallowed realm of men.

I ordered a pot of tea and no, nothing to eat. While I waited I considered what to do next and how to contact Constable Bruce with my new findings. It was obvious that as the stranger had not come to the inn here, he had spent those intervening hours in the sentry room at the Abbey with its sordid hints at recent occupation.

Outside the rain persisted relentlessly. Had it lessened even a modicum, I think I would have given up waiting and braved the deluge. Indeed I had almost made up my mind to do so, when the surly one arrived with a teapot, cup and saucer and a bowl of sugar and set them with an air of disapproval before me.

It was then I discovered that he had omitted the milk jug needed for what looked like a well-stewed pot of tea brewed some hours earlier and I suspected, reheated when necessary. However, I felt unable to run the gauntlet once more of those disapproving faces in a return to the public bar.

At the next table, the younger woman with a small child was taking her leave so I seized the opportunity of going over and asking if I might borrow the milk jug.

'Of course, please take it.'

Pouring some into my cup I returned it politely.

The woman smiled and pointed to the window. 'Easing off a bit now, thank goodness,' and as I was obviously a stranger to the Inn's tea room, she added, 'Taking refuge from the weather, are you?'

When I said yes, she nodded towards the closed door. 'They're not very hospitable. Hardly provide fare for visitors. All very rough and ready. But it's the best we can do until we can provide a proper tea-room or cafe. But you see our visitors are like yourself, mostly in summer – '

Then looking at me curiously, she said triumphantly, 'Wait a moment, I know who you are. You're Miss Faro, Jack Macmerry's fiancée.'

'That is so,' I said weakly. Once again, it seemed that Jack's mother had been very busy making sure no one knew my dread secret and it was on the tip of my tongue to correct her. Then I thought of the tedious explanation, of being a widow and so forth. I let it go.

'This is your first visit to Eildon.'

So that was common knowledge, too. I wondered if there were any secrets of our relationship unknown to them.

'Look, why don't you join me?' she said indicating the empty chair at her table. 'It's no fun sitting in this dismal room alone –'

Accepting her invitation, I had just moved over when the

sound of a horse-drawn carriage had her rushing over to the window.

A glimpse of black horses, a hearse and a coffin.

'That's poor dear Mrs Aiden. They're taking her back to Peebles. She'd have wanted that – to be laid to rest with her own family.'

Coming back to the table, she sat down, dabbing at her eyes. 'Poor dear lady. We were great friends. After my ma died, she was like a second mother to me. She will be sadly missed by everyone in Eildon, whether they were Catholic or not. It was all one to her.'

She was frowning, biting her lip, in the manner of one who has something on her mind and is undecided about sharing it.

'That awful accident, so close to poor Father McQuinn's heart attack. It doesn't seem right, somehow, both of them going so quickly.' She shrugged. 'I keep wondering – oh, I don't know.'

Now her wondering was interesting to me. 'Did you think there was something unusual –?' I began.

'Indeed yes. I keep remembering and I'm so worried, you see – well, the whole thing –' she shook her head '– it just wasn't like her.'

Pausing she looked across at me as if I might have some consolation to offer. 'After the wake for the Father I knew she would be terribly upset. I didn't go – I'm not a Catholic. But I knew I'd never sleep that night after all that had happened. Ned, my man, is a railway guard and he was on night duty, so I waited till our wee lad was settled. He's ten now and used to looking after himself.'

And shaking her head, she sighed deeply. 'I was – uneasy – somehow. So I went back to the church house to make sure she was all right – and I suppose to see if there was anything I could do to comfort her. I'd offer to stay the night if she needed me, although she'd said earlier that she wasn't afraid of

143

sleeping in the house with poor Father McQuinn lying in his coffin.'

Staring at the window she said, 'It was about midnight when I went across and – well, there was something odd. The house was in darkness but the door was open. I went into the hallway. Then I heard voices coming from the kitchen. The door was closed but she had a visitor already. She was talking to someone, a man's voice and I heard him cough.'

Again she paused. 'With my hand on the door I suddenly changed my mind. I didn't want to intrude on them.'

And looking at me as if for approval, she said, 'I thought it might have something to do with the Father's death, the arrangements for his funeral and so forth. Or perhaps the new priest who was coming to help him had arrived earlier than he was expected. Whoever it was, she had company, she didn't need me and she'd be all right. So I crept away thinking I'd be seeing her tomorrow morning.' And burying her head in her hands, she began to weep. 'But tomorrow was too late,' she whispered through her tears. 'She was dead when I got there – that dreadful unnecessary end.'

She shook her head. 'I could hardly believe it had happened like that. You see, she was always such a neat, tidy housewife and so careful about being on the lookout for anything that might cause an accident. I can't imagine her neglecting that stair carpet. Did you see it – torn like that?'

I said yes, I had noticed.

'Well, it wasn't like that the last time I was in the house a week ago and she would never have let it go unmended. She always used to say ninety per cent of prevention is better than ten per cent of cure. And that went for what she called accidents that were waiting to happen.'

Twisting her handkerchief, she stared miserably at the window. 'I don't know how Father Boyle will manage without a housekeeper, especially one as efficient as Maggie Aiden.

What a welcome for him, poor soul. But I dare say the ladies in his congregation will all get together and see him right until he finds someone –'

The village clock struck the hour.

'Oh, is that the time? I must go. Ned will be home and wanting his tea. He's on the train for London. Gets off that one and a couple of hours later, he's back on the next heading back to Edinburgh.' Smiling wryly she stood up, put away her handkerchief.

'It's been so nice to talk to you. Thank you for listening to me so patiently.' Then, with an embarrassed laugh, 'Going on, unburdening myself to a complete stranger. My name's Ina Fraser, by the way.'

I said I was pleased I could help and she looked at me quizzically. 'Do lots of people tell you all their troubles? I'm sure they do.' She laughed. 'There's something about you that invites confidences.'

It was my turn to look embarrassed and she smiled. 'Thank you anyway, it's been a great relief to talk to you. Remember me to Jack. God bless you both with a happy future together.'

A happy future seemed like a distant dream as she left and, with no desire to linger in that dark cheerless room, I went into reception, rang the bell, paid my bill to the surly lad and went out into the wet street.

The sudden storm had moved on and there was a gleam of blue in the sky. I took a deep breath, enjoying the delightful fresh smell of greenery, as if every bush and tree had bathed and enjoyed the heavy shower.

As I walked back to the farm I had much to occupy my thoughts. The conversation with Mrs Aiden's friend had been a revelation, another clue in the puzzle.

Who was her mystery visitor? Not Father Boyle, since he did not arrive until the following morning in time to discover her body.

That left only one obvious answer. If Mrs Aiden did not have a secret lover, which seemed unlikely, since her good friend who had just left would have known about that for sure, who was the man in her kitchen?

I decided that I knew he was undoubtedly the stranger who had arrived so fortuitously a few hours earlier and helped her carry the dead priest into the house.

And then promptly disappeared – to return again a few hours later to murder her.

It all fitted in. But the main obstacle remained.

The tantalising unanswered question – Why?

What was the motive for these two murders? Where were the missing pieces, the vital clues?

Another baffling question to share with PC Bruce.

I hurried back along the wet street but once again found the police station deserted.

What policing did he find in Eildon? I thought of his enthusiasm and the frustration of not being able to share my new theories with him.

Could he be relied upon to help me find an answer to this puzzle which seemed to have no logical solution?

16

Saturday was Father McQuinn's funeral. Men from the Protestant kirk also followed his coffin up to the little Catholic burial ground on the Verney estate, out of respect and liking for a good kind man highly esteemed by the community.

I walked at Andrew Macmerry's side, conscious of strange glances and whispers as it was unusual for women to go to the graveside. However I felt that Danny would have wanted me to represent him.

Father Boyle, in his new role as parish priest, conducted the short service. Difficult for him since they had never met, it amounted to little more than reading the appropriate passages from the prayer book. As it was, his words were almost drowned out by the heavy shower of rain which Eildon had been saving up as a suitable accompaniment for such a sombre occasion.

It added to its brevity as umbrellas were hastily raised while Father Boyle in his thin robes got thoroughly soaked, as if someone up there had been maliciously saving buckets of water to pour down upon the mourners.

As we scampered back down the hill, the ladies kept dry in the village hall while preparing a cold collation. I suspected that few of the non-Catholics would go along and Jack's father excused himself on the grounds of 'animals to see to.'

Looking round for Mrs Fraser, the dead housekeeper's friend, I told Andrew of our earlier meeting and said that I would stay in the hope of seeing her again. He seemed surprised at my decision and laughed a trifle cynically. 'Ina Fraser, the village gossip. Well, well. You can be sure that anything you tell her will be all round the village before you get home to the farm.'

Removed from his soaked robes, Father Boyle looked most unhappy. His hair still wet, cold and bedraggled, he was short with sympathisers, a little angry and impatient with the mourning ladies who fussed anxiously around him.

His emotions weren't hard to guess and I, for one, felt compassion for the irony that his first service should have been the funeral of the priest he had come to assist.

Doubtless the implications of what that assistance now involved weighed heavily upon him. He didn't stay long and Mrs Fraser, having rushed in at the last minute, watched his departure.

'The poor man, he'll be lucky not to have caught pneumonia.'

Her prediction wasn't far wrong. I was to learn the next day, meeting Mrs Fraser in the village, that there had been no service that Sunday.

'Poor Father Boyle caught a fever from his drenching and completely lost his voice. He'll be lucky if it doesn't turn into something worse,' she added as she continued the tale of woe.

Accepting only sympathetic offerings of soup from his female parishioners the priest then speedily sent them on their ways, saying he would retire to his bed and stay there until he recovered. Worse was to follow. They were absolutely forbidden to fuss over him. All offers of helping out until a new housekeeper arrived were firmly rebuffed.

Mrs Fraser went on about how he had emphasised that he had been managing his own life for many years now. As requested, I gathered that the ladies had retired crushed and disappointed, shaking their heads and sighing that this was so different from dear Father McQuinn's appreciation of their efforts.

I thought I would be expected to go to church with Jack's

parents that Sunday morning. I was wrong, unaware that it was known to invite bad luck for a bride-to-be to hear her banns being read. This was news to me and although Jack's mother looked askance, I came downstairs putting on my gloves and defying tradition on the grounds that I didn't hold with superstitions.

When I said we made our own luck, good or bad, she looked heavenward in alarm, as if I might be struck down on the spot.

There were hints from Jack's mother that the congregation who hadn't already seen me in Eildon would be very interested and curious, and so that his parents would have no need to feel ashamed or embarrassed, I dressed with more care than usual.

At last I was satisfied that I presented the picture of decorum in my best dress and jacket. With some difficulty and considerable use of hairpins, a major operation, I had managed to confine my unruly mop of curls under a staid navy blue straw bonnet.

As we walked the short distance to the kirk, Andrew Macmerry led the way with Bible tucked under his arm, his wife and future daughter-in-law on either side of him and on a perfect summer's morning that had never heard of yesterday's violent storm, we were greeted by birdsong on the outside of the church echoed by a good choir within.

I enjoyed the hymns and Reverend Linton gave a fairly innocuous sermon on the Good Samaritan, smiling kindly down upon us from the pulpit and putting at rest my fears that he might be a devotee of the present fashion of 'hell-raising' preachers.

My arrival had caused a flutter of excitement and a swift turning of anxious heads in my direction followed the reading of the banns for Rose Elizabeth Faro and Jack Andrew Macmerry.

At that moment, I experienced a sudden chill of fear, the note of reality – and finality. That I was trapped, with less than two weeks left, the door of my cage was closing. Suddenly conscious of being among strangers, I wished with all my heart that Jack could have been at my side for support.

Sunday dinner at the farm followed, with long time friends, the Johnstons and the Wards. Their conversation excluded me, full of 'remember when' and teasing personal innuendoes, the air thick with strange names, sons and daughters and grandchildren.

Then, as if suddenly aware of my presence and what it predicted to the Macmerrys with their one and only son, Mrs Johnston said slyly:

'Aye, you've waited a long time, right enough, Jess, but it'll be your turn to be a granny next,' at which sentiment Mrs Macmerry's blush outdid that of the bride-to-be.

'A wee lad would be grand,' said Jack's father and there were nods and smiles in agreement all around as the fate of the Macmerry farm, long in the balance, might thereby be decided.

As Whisky and Soda waddled closer to the table, salivating for scraps of roast meat, the conversation switched to the Annual Dog Show and Mrs Johnston, a lady of imposing proportions, who was in charge of catering, revealed that Mrs Ward could be relied upon once again to take first prize for her retriever bitch.

The talk turned to local farmers with sheepdogs who were to display their talents at the trials and gladden their owner's hearts while weighing down their mantelpieces with further trophies.

When I was upstairs removing my bonnet, Jack's father had taken them out to the stables to meet his remarkable patient

Thane and I was regaled with stories of animal lives saved by Andrew Macmerry's remarkable cures.

Thane had made an impression on the visitors.

'Perhaps Rose might enter him for some of the events,' Mrs Johnston suggested sweetly. 'He would be sure to win first prize,' she added with a sly look across at Mrs Ward.

I was glad Thane could not overhear such a remark since he would have regarded that suggestion with even less enthusiasm.

'He is such a splendid animal, you must enter him,' Mrs Johnston said to me, ignoring Mrs Ward's dagger-like glance in her direction.

'No,' I said firmly. 'I cannot do that. After all, he is just a visiting dog. It would not be proper.'

'That's true,' said a relieved Mrs Ward with a beaming smile. I was now her friend for life.

'He isn't a locally bred animal, ye ken,' said Mr Ward.

But Mrs Johnston staunchly refused to be defeated, and said to her husband, who was a Justice of the Peace, 'Of course we could adopt him, put him in a special category.'

Before Mr Johnston could pronounce judgement on this idea, I shook my head firmly and looking across at Jack's father, appealed for his intervention.

He smiled. 'Rose is quite right. I'm afraid it wouldn't be legal.'

Danger averted, I yearned to make my escape before the roast lamb and an abundance of vegetables followed by sherry trifle depleted all energy and thrust me in the direction of what I most longed for. An afternoon nap!

Instead, I opted for an afternoon walk and making my escape collected Thane and my sketchbook.

Walking through Eildon, the main street was busier than usual. The good weather had brought out carriages and a horse-drawn omnibus from Edinburgh full of visitors to the Abbey.

I tagged on to the group, following them across the field from which the cows had been removed but signs of their recent occupation remained a constant hazard to the walkers.

Thane was well-behaved, docile on his lead and I decided to linger on the outskirts of the group. Although after five minutes I knew I was learning nothing new, the official guide did credit to an account of the Abbey's history.

An actor born, he gave vivid life to the past, parading the ghosts of long dead bishops and monks, while the now smooth grass echoed with the bloody footsteps and battle cries of long-ago. Their shades marched through the quiet ruins, past empty stone coffins overlooked by gargoyles of devils and angels. Occasionally I glanced upwards at the shadowy heights of the Tower from where I was certain I had been closely observed upon my first visit to the Abbey. As if he read my mind, Thane was suddenly restless, eager to explore that nearby spiral staircase from which the group had just emerged.

Keeping him close on the lead rope, I let him lead the way quickly up the stone steps. He was quivering with excitement.

'What is it, Thane?' I asked. 'What's up there?'

The sentry-room was dingy and horrible. Empty and not smelling any sweeter than the last time, but once more Thane was intrigued by the stone floor, sniffing with dog like persistence at the cracks between the paving-stones.

Allowing him to explore, I could see nothing and said somewhat impatiently, 'Oh, do come away.'

He stopped, gazed at me imploringly and then at the paving. I went closer.

At first glance, nothing. Then I noticed a tiny bright glint of metal.

'What's this? Buried treasure?'

He wagged his tail furiously and kneeling down, I took out a hatpin from my reticule and scratched away at the accumulated dirt.

The tiny bright spot emerged as gold.

A gold wedding ring.

Wiping it clean on my handkerchief, my heart beat fast.

This was not just any wedding ring. What I held in my hand was the Irish betrothal ring: two hands clasping a heart. I knew it well, Danny had always worn the Claddagh that had belonged to his grandfather.

With Thane at my side, I knelt there shocked by my discovery. Of course, it was ridiculous, a coincidence. Such rings weren't all that common in Scotland but a visitor from Ireland might have dropped it.

I looked out of the window following the group's progress, decided that the ring must belong to one of the men. They were gathered round the guide making their way toward the exit gate.

Clutching the ring, I was halfway down the stairs when sense questioned that it was unlikely to have been dropped only minutes ago. Its condition, down a deep crevasse and embedded in soil, suggested that it must have lain there for some time.

Nevertheless, breathless, I raced toward the group.

'Have any of you lost a ring – up there in the Tower?'

They turned towards me anxiously, fingers were quickly examined. Sighs of relief as heads were shaken.

No, not ours.

The guide smiled. He didn't want to be involved. 'Just hand it in to the custodian, miss. Lost property is her concern.'

'I'll do that.' They drifted off through the gate.

Thane was sitting down, staring hard at me, whining gently. What was he trying to convey? There was something urgent, something he wanted me to understand. But for once, our telepathy failed.

All I could think of at that moment was that I must be holding in my hand Danny's ring that I had placed on to his finger when we exchanged our marriage vows in Arizona more than twelve years ago.

Danny was dead.

I felt ill, confused. If it were true, how had his ring come to be buried in the ruined Abbey in Eildon?

My mind raced back to the old nun at St Anthony's, Sister Mary Michael, who had been certain Danny had asked for her prayers less than three weeks ago.

True, she was over ninety years old and I remembered that Sister Angela had whispered soothingly: 'Mistakes regarding time are easy to make at that age. It happens all the time.'

She had given me other examples and I had gladly taken refuge in such consolation. But was it enough?

My legs suddenly weak, I sat down on the stone wall and there in the bright innocent sunshine of a summer's afternoon, I knew I was haunted.

Danny – was – dead.

Dead but not forgotten. His ghost still clung to me, never letting me go and in less than two weeks I was to marry Jack Macmerry.

17

In the following days I tried to get a grip on reality. I talked to Constable Bruce who, after our hopeful start, had made no progress at all on the suspicious circumstances surrounding the deaths of Father McQuinn and Mrs Aiden. Suspicious circumstances which I was sure were murders.

The constable was shamefaced, full of apologies, murmurs of domestic matters, sick children to look after while Mary was in Peebles where her mother had been taken into hospital. It appeared that the entire household was thrown into disarray.

As I was leaving, he said reassuringly, 'I haven't forgotten, you know. I'll get around to it as soon as I have a minute to spare.'

That wasn't quite consoling enough and left me feeling that as far as Constable Bruce was concerned, good intentions and police work came a poor second to his domestic life. Which was sadly, perhaps, the reason why, despite all those lofty ambitions, he had remained the village policeman and was unlikely to change now.

I had considered telling him about the Claddagh ring and changed my mind. He seemed to have enough matters to confuse him and how was I to explain sensibly and rationally my horrified reactions concerning its discovery? The ring had nothing to do with the two murders and I decided that it should remain in my possession until the Abbey was open again to visitors when I would hand it over to the custodian. I hoped to lay my fears at rest, to find that there was an innocent explanation, a coincidence that had nothing to do with Danny: some visitor had lost it on a previous visit.

Meanwhile l did my best to concentrate on the main reason

for my being at Eildon. Namely helping Mrs Macmerry with the wedding arrangements, the list of guests who would be coming, the presents which arrived almost daily and had to be acknowledged, the seating in the village hall – and all the preparations such matters involved.

I am happy to say that Jack's mother and I managed to get along quite nicely without any serious disagreements. As we sat at the kitchen table with our sewing and our lists spread out before us, I decided that although I could see no bond of great friendship being forged, at least we were both learning toleration in one of the universal bonds of womankind – a family wedding.

And of course there were daily letters from Jack, saying he would be home at the end of the week and most importantly, Thane had to be taken for walks so I spent any idle hours making my escape into the warm sunshine with him.

We explored the old quarry, which seemed to fascinate him, although I kept well away from the disused rusted machinery as well as the dark deep pond around which Jack had spent so many happy hours as a youngster.

One day Jack's mother ran out of matching pearl buttons for the petticoat she was making and gratefully received my offer to go down to the village shop. And there I had another encounter with Annette who was considering swathes of lace while Master Alexander Verney sat rather disdainfully on a nearby chair swinging his legs.

My arrival transformed his grumpy expression into instant delight.

'Miss Rose! How do you do?' He swung down from the chair, rushed over, bowed and kissed my hand in a most grown-up fashion.

Annette turned and smiled. I explained my mission for pearl buttons and she laughed. 'Then you are just the person I need at this moment. I cannot decide which pattern would go best with a ruby silk day gown.'

There were other customers waiting to be served and suspecting that this choice might take some time I said, 'I will be with you in a moment. I have my – my dog, tied to the post outside.'

'Allow me to escort you, Miss Rose,' said the gallant Alexander.

I opened the door and he yelled with delight. 'He is your dog, Miss Rose? I say, he is magnificent!'

I said his name was Thane and wondered how my arrogant Thane would react to being called a dog and the great fuss that was being made of him by a small boy who did not reach his shoulder. I was alarmed, I had never seen him bite anyone but with the boy's attentions, patting his head, ruffling his ears – there had to be a first time.

I was wrong. As always Thane was full of surprises and he looked quite pleased at all this admiration. In that curious cast of his countenance that made him appear to smile he looked delighted and full of forbearance, willingly giving his uninjured paw to be shaken.

Alexander looked up at me, his arm around Thane's neck. 'I will take care of Thane while you shop with Cousin Annette.'

When I mentioned this to Annette she looked out of the door anxiously and seemed taken aback by the picture of Alexander sitting on the pavement with Thane at his side.

She gave me a startled look. 'How extraordinary. Alexander is usually terrified of strange dogs, especially large ones.'

A little while later, the lace decided upon, the buttons purchased we emerged from the shop. The governess cart was parked around the corner.

'We must go now, Alexander. Say good-bye to the nice dog.'

Thane winced visibly. In a human his eyes would have

been described as raised heavenward in protest at such a description.

It was Alexander's turn to protest at this parting.

'Hush!' Annette said sternly, holding up her hand and turning to me. 'Perhaps we might walk the dog in the Abbey grounds – if Miss Rose has time to spare, that is.'

'Hurrah, hurrah!' said Alexander bouncing up and down with delight at this prospect which, however, presented some difficulties. We could not all ride in the governess cart, so it was agreed, reluctantly from Alexander's point of view, that Thane and I should meet them there.

'You are quite sure, Miss Rose,' said Annette. 'This is not imposing upon you?'

Independently we reached the Abbey where Alexander was waiting anxiously for our arrival, determined to be allowed to walk alone with Thane. This was agreed upon and, as Annette regarded the huge deerhound and the small boy anxiously, I assured her that Thane was well-behaved and could be relied upon not to pull Alexander off his feet.

Watching them scamper off across the grass, Alexander whooping happily, Annette sighed. 'The exercise will be so good for him. He is such a lonely child and spends far too much time on his own, reading and painting. A great pity that he has no brothers and sisters after all this time.'

As we walked together, always keeping them in sight, another reason for Annette's suggestion became apparent. It seemed that Alexander was not the only lonely one under the castle roof, as she took my arm and said, 'I am so glad we met, Miss Rose. You see, the choice of the right lace was very important,' and I realised I had been chosen as confidante.

Regarding me eagerly, she smiled. 'I have very few gowns, a much depleted wardrobe since I abandoned them all when I entered the convent as a novice. I had decided to forsake the world and to despise all such fripperies. I firmly believed

158

then that I would never in my life again yearn for even one elegant gown.

She laughed, suddenly radiant as she clasped her hands in excitement. 'I had forgotten somehow and now I find the world I abandoned is like a new discovery. The ruby silk was the only gown I could not bear to part with. I had an idea I might be buried in it some day,' she said sadly. 'You see, it was the gown I wore for my wedding in New York. The one I was wearing the day I met my future husband and it was his favourite.'

And looking round to see that Alexander was out of earshot she whispered. 'I have news of him. Letters are smuggled to me through a friend there who works for a publishing house. She sends me their catalogues which arouse no suspicion with my guardian and she manages to slip in my husband's letters unobserved. I should have gone mad without Sally's help. And today, I have had word that he is on his way. He will be here in a few days. I can hardly wait for that moment,' she added rapturously.

Of a more practical nature, I was aware of certain rather obvious pitfalls in this arrangement and asked, 'Where will you meet?'

'At Verney, of course. He insists on putting a bold face upon it and coming to the very door, to confront my guardian and claim me as his wife.' She chuckled. 'It will be a great surprise for him.'

That, I thought, was putting it very mildly indeed. Looking at her glowing face, suddenly so childlike and vulnerable, I felt extremely doubtful about her husband's reception. I could see nothing but trouble ahead, and that she might be wise to warn her guardian rather than have him angrily run off the premises, remembering the unpleasant gamekeeper and his savage dog.

She was waiting all smiles for my comments and all I could think of was a somewhat lame: 'Are you sure – I mean –'

'Of course I am sure – perfectly sure,' she interrupted, laughing, her eyes gleaming with delighted anticipation. 'I am of age now, there is nothing they can do. I came into my legal inheritance from my grandmother on my birthday last month and that means I can walk out of Verney with my husband and they cannot stop me. Naturally, of course, I hope they will be amenable.'

'Has your husband prospects of employment over here?' I asked.

That brought her up sharp. She frowned. 'He has not mentioned anything suitable but I imagine an organisation like the big shipping office he worked for in New York will have many suitable contacts over here to put his way. There are most certainly shipping offices in Edinburgh. Leith is a great port after all. And I do remember he indicated that much of the business he dealt with came through Scotland.'

How could I have the heart to disillusion her, to throw cold water over all her dreams and plans? To advise caution was rather too late in the day, but I felt that as her attitude towards this hasty marriage had been a trifle naive, so too was her taking for granted her guardian's reception and blessing.

As though aware of what my silence indicated, she said: 'I am not without means, Miss Rose. With a fortune of my own, we will soon find a good house in Edinburgh with a servant or two and perhaps a carriage.'

She sighed, smiled again at the dream. 'It will all be most agreeable. We shall live very comfortably but modestly to begin with until my husband can choose some occupation suitable to his talents.'

I must confess that the thought 'fortune-hunter' sprang unbidden to the forefront of my mind. She knew so little about this man, none of his background only that he was divinely handsome and a widower, somewhat older than herself. Romantic aspects are bound to appeal to a nineteen year old who had been carefully reared, waiting ready and eager to give up all the world for love. With not the faintest idea of what the real world was like, or the shady characters who inhabited the realms beyond a fine house, servants and a carriage.

I did not know her well enough, even though she was keen to make me her confidante, to tactfully bring up the subject of her promise to be governess to Alexander until he was ready for prep school. Or to remind her that she would be letting down both him and his parents, particularly her invalid cousin Amelia who had been very good to her.

It was time to leave. The reluctant Alexander, rosy faced and breathless, handed Thane's lead over to me.

'Have you given Miss Rose the invitation to my birthday party?'

Annette shook her head. 'I – I forgot, Alexander.'

'It is so important, Cousin Annette. And you forgot,' was the reproachful reply. 'What have you two ladies been discussing all this time?' Then to me. 'I shall expect you at three on Thursday, Miss Rose. You will come, of course,' he added anxiously.

'Please do,' Annette murmured apologetically, birthday parties having been the last thing on her mind as we walked together.

'I want Thane to come too,' he said. 'Will you bring him with you, Miss Rose?'

Annette looked somewhat taken aback by the suggestion. What would his mamma say; what about his mamma's little dogs, etc. etc. But Alexander firm in resolve would have none of it and at last an agreement was made. Thane would come to his party although I was also somewhat doubtful about the deerhound's reception by the yellow fanged Billy.

At the governess cart, Alexander suddenly dived a hand under the seat and took out a rather ancient toy dog, lacking fur and eyes. Obviously the much beloved companion of his infancy, he said somewhat shamefacedly:

'I would like Thane to have this. May I give it to him, cousin Annette?'

Annette looked bewildered. 'Are you sure, Alexander. Boxy is your favourite toy.' And turning to me, she whispered, 'He is never without Boxy, whenever he is unhappy, or has been naughty and punished, it is always Boxy he needs. The toy dog even sleeps under his pillow.'

Then a warning to Alexander. 'You will miss him dreadfully.'

But Alexander stood firm, shook his head. 'I want to give him to Thane – as a toy. I really have outgrown him.'

'Since yesterday morning,' murmured Annette shaking her head sadly.

'He is mine and I can give him to whoever I like. I want Thane to have him. That is my decision,' was the reply, the final voice of authority on the subject.

Annette looked distressed and whispered, 'Your big dog will just destroy Boxy – I have seen how long toys last with my cousin's pet dogs.'

She was echoing my fears exactly but there was nothing we could do watching her charge hand over his most cherished possession to Thane with both of us looking on, fearing the worst that he would tear the fragile toy to pieces on the spot.

But we were wrong. Thane sniffed at the little cloth dog, held it gently in his mouth, shook it several times and then looked up at Alexander who gave him a final hug and leaped into the cart shouting:

'Thursday, Miss Rose. Remember that's a promise.'

Walking back with Thane, I had an idea. I made a move to take the toy from him. In a day or two he would have forgotten all about Boxy and I could return it to Alexander unscathed.

But Thane would have none of that. With Boxy clenched between his teeth we walked back to the farm and in the stable he refused to relinquish it. Later in the day I looked in several times and there was Boxy lying close at his side, so the toy dog remained with him in the stable.

I shook my head. Here was a new version of Thane who not only made friends with a small boy but had taken to accompanying Jack's father to the up-by field where the sheepdog Rex apparently ignored him completely. That Thane was extending his activities and making new friends I could understand and was very pleased about it, but I also realised I had never even considered that Thane might enjoy playing with a toy of his own.

'What next?' I said relating the story to Jack's parents over supper that evening.

Mr Macmerry laughed. 'You don't surprise me, Rose. It's obvious you haven't had much experience with dogs or you'd know they love toys. Mind you, they have a very limited life. We tried it with ours when they were puppies, but anything we gave them was torn to shreds in a day.'

Not so Boxy, however, who Thane treated carefully and whose fate soon ceased to concern us.

As for Annette, I thought about her as I prepared for bed that night. I must confess I could see nothing but an unhappy future fraught with obstacles.

It was also perhaps for the first time in my life, that I realised I was now seeing from a completely different angle, the same headlong, headstrong future that my own family had envisaged when I sailed off to San Francisco to marry Danny McQuinn.

I had proved them wrong. And so my last thought before I fell asleep was that so too perhaps would the heiress Annette and her husband, the humble shipping office clerk. I wished them well.

18

When I came downstairs the next day the postman had arrived with Jack's almost daily letter. I opened it with excitement, watched by his mother, as I was, always eager for news.

'He should be home tomorrow,' she said complacently.

Scanning the first sentence, I threw it down in disgust. The crime trial in Glasgow was taking much longer than anyone had originally anticipated. There had been a change of jury.

'He says we are not to worry. Although he is a key witness he has been assured that he will be given time off to come to Eildon and get married – however, any plans for a honeymoon may have to be shelved for the present –'

I had been promised London, theatres, museums – I was furious. In fact, we were all unitedly speechless at such treatment and I went upstairs, leaving Jack's mother fulminating against the unfair treatment of the police. My main concern was wondering about the gown and shoes I was to be married in, not to mention my wardrobe for the honeymoon, all reposing in Solomon's Tower for Jack to collect and bring to Eildon.

The next moment I looked out of the window and all my miseries, my indecisions and fears vanished.

A carriage was bowling down the farm track.

What a carriage! With the Royal Coat of Arms and a coachman.

And what an occupant!

Who else but Dr Vincent Beaumarcher Laurie, Junior Physician to the Household of Her Majesty Queen Victoria.

Out he stepped, arms outstretched to greet me.

Hugged and kissed in that warm embrace by my beloved

stepbrother, more than a decade my elder. Reliable honest, sensible Vince.

Suddenly I was safe again. He had come to rescue me, take me back through the magic door leading to the safe haven of remembered childhood.

Or so I believed, in those blissful magical first moments.

The Macmerrys had come to the door. Jack's mother drying her hands on her apron, smoothing her hair to greet this unexpected visitor, worried at being taken at a disadvantage like this and looking round angrily, ready to blame someone – myself, in fact – for not giving her fair warning.

However, at second glance how her eyes lit up at the sight of the handsome carriage with its coat of arms.

A quick introduction to Vince and her first words were to ask which road he had taken. He shook his head and said he had taken the wrong turn, past the farm end road and had to go into the village to ask for directions,

Mrs Macmerry was delighted, mentally noting how many Eildon neighbours would be similarly impressed with this Royal connection.

Throwing a shawl about her shoulders she said, 'I must go and get Jack's father, he's in the up-by field. There's tea in the pot, Rose. Make your brother at home.'

Beaming on us both, she could hardly keep the pride out of her voice. I realised cynically that once again she had a way of amending and transforming relationships to suit her whims. As I was no longer a widow in the eyes of Eildon, so too Vince had been elevated from stepbrother to brother.

He didn't let her down either. Bowing, he gave her his most charming smile and put an arm around my shoulders, an affectionate squeeze.

And it was true, we were remarkably alike. The same eyes and nose, the same mass of yellow curls – but how those once boyish curls had benighted his early years! Despising them as far too frivolous for a doctor he had spent hours fiercely flattening them with hair oil. Where most men feared receding hairlines, to Vince this was a blessing.

He was of medium height, not tall like Pappa and I sometimes forgot that there was no blood kin between them. More than a decade before Edinburgh policeman Jeremy Faro met Lizzie, as a fifteen-year-old maid in a noble household ten years earlier, she had borne Vince out of wedlock. Marriage brought two daughters, myself and Emily, before she died in childbirth along with Pappa's longed-for only son.

How Vince had hated the stigma of illegitimacy, but had overcome it to emerge as a brilliant doctor, to eventually recognise and forgive his titled natural father as the latter lay on his deathbed, by which time Vince was to see his ambitions fulfilled and be appointed Queen's physician.

True, now in his mid-forties he was merely a Junior Physician to the Royal Household but the fact that his stepfather Chief Inspector Faro had been Her Majesty's personal detective and instrumental in saving her life on more than one occasion, had doubtless proved useful.

Her Majesty also extended her trust and reliance to Dr Beaumarcher Laurie as I was soon to learn.

'Tea?' I asked, seating him at the kitchen table.

'Haven't you anything a little stronger?'

'At ten in the morning! Shame on you, Vince. You do have some bad habits these days,' I said eyeing his waistline, his elegant waistcoat with its gold watch chain just a mite too snug.

'Tea it is, then.' A martyred sigh which quickly changed into laughter. He grinned, prosperous, happy and very well-fed.

Eating a thickly buttered slice of one of Mrs Macmerry's newly-baked loaves, he answered questions about Olivia and the children, and Pappa and Imogen's travels in Europe.

It seemed that Vince would be the only one of my family who might be present at our wedding.

'That's wonderful,' I said. 'Jack would like you to be his best man – if he gets here in time for his own wedding, that is,' I added telling him about the contents of Jack's letter.

'If he leaves Glasgow with only hours to spare, he won't have time to collect my clothes from Solomon's Tower. That's bad enough but he has a brand new suit, bought under duress I can tell you at Jenners sale, especially for the wedding. I've also bought him a handsome new shirt and cravat. Not that it would worry Jack. He has a certain lack of interest in sartorial matters.' I sighed. 'But I can just see us traipsing up to the altar letting down his parents in our shabby second best.'

Vince grinned. 'Stop worrying, Rose. It might never happen. Let's hope he is being unduly pessimistic,' he added soothingly. Then shaking his head, 'But like Jack, it seems I can't give you any guarantee of my presence either. I would be honoured to be his best man, Rose. If I can – but you have no idea what Her Majesty is like these days.' He shrugged. 'A veritable masterpiece of indecisions, constantly changing her mind not only from one day to the next – but practically from one hour to the next. And where she leads all must follow.'

He groaned. 'First it was to be Osborne immediately after the Jubilee celebrations and now it is Balmoral. Which is one of the reasons I'm in Scotland.'

The Queen's imperious indecisiveness was notorious and something I knew about from bitter experience. Many was the cancelled outing with Pappa that Emily and I could lay directly at Her Majesty's door.

'Then what are you doing here, if it has nothing to do with the wedding?'

He smiled. 'If you'd stop asking questions for a moment, I could tell you! It so happens that I'm on my way to Verney Castle.'

'Verney Castle! Whatever for?'

'To see Lady Amelia. She's a Saxe-Coburg, a third or fourth cousin of the Queen on the distaff side of the family. My visit is a medical matter,' he frowned, 'so treat this information as confidential. Lady Amelia has a rare blood disease, a subject that I have been studying. I have two conferences lined up, a paper to read in Paris and again in Vienna later this year. Her Majesty is interested in the subject and I am hoping to take some blood tests of the Royal family in general.'

He paused for a moment, as I refilled his teacup. 'You possibly aren't aware, although it's fairly general knowledge in the society they live in, that the Verneys are keen to have more children. Time is not on their side and young Alexander is the one and only so far. After eight years, they fear he is likely to remain so.'

Vince shook his head. 'I have no idea whether the blood problem is to blame, or whether I can help. But when I applied for leave of absence to attend your wedding here in Eildon, Her Majesty got this bee in her bonnet – or more appropriate, caterpillar in her crown – that I might be able to find the answer to Lady Amelia's problem. Infertility is the bane of queens, as you know, and of aristocrats who also need heirs. Happily it was never one that concerned Her Majesty personally,' he laughed. 'Rather the opposite, on her own admission she never cared greatly for having babies.'

And with a change of subject, 'I don't suppose you've had a chance to encounter the Verneys?'

I laughed. 'On the contrary, young Alexander is a personal friend of mine.'

When I told him how we had met, he grimaced. 'Spoilt brat, is he?'

'No more than one would expect from an only son and heir. He's a charming wee lad.' And leaning across the table I took his hand and whispered. 'I'm sorry for his parents but

I'm so glad that the Queen has given you a good excuse to come to Eildon.' I found myself blinking back tears. 'Oh, Vince, I do so miss you – and Olivia – and Pappa.'

'Me too, Rose. Me too.' Patting my hand he frowned. 'There's more to it than the Verneys' problem and I'm not sure whether –'

Pausing he looked guarded and then with a shrug he went on: 'There is a another matter. As I told you, the Court and everyone else believes that Her Majesty will go to Osborne immediately after the Jubilee celebrations. But Bertie has hinted that he would prefer to meet her at Balmoral.

'Heaven knows that they need time together to sort out their many differences and a suitable halfway house – or castle – would seem to be here at the Verneys. They are particular friends of Bertie's, or rather Lady Amelia is, he was sweet on her at one time, and he loves the Borders, comes to shoot deer in the autumn.'

Rubbing his chin, he regarded me thoughtfully. 'I don't know how much of this highly confidential matter I should be telling you, little sister, but I am sure I can rely on your discretion.'

I smiled and said he could always do so. 'Remember my motto – Discretion Guaranteed.'

He laughed and then his face darkened again. 'There is more, Rose. We gather from highly secret sources that there are rumours of possible Fenian activities in this area directed towards the Jubilee celebrations.'

This did not have the dramatic impact he had hoped for when I said, 'So I've heard.'

He sat up in his chair: 'You've – what?'

'Jack told me. The Edinburgh police are aware of it and he was over at the Castle seeing Lord Verney regarding security arrangements for the Jubilee.'

'For Jubilee read a Royal visit,' said Vince grimly.

'So where do you go from here?' I asked.

'The carriage from Holyrood Palace collected me off the London train at Edinburgh.'

'What have you done with the coachman?' I interrupted. 'Have you left him sitting outside all this time?'

Vince laughed. 'He's well used to that. I told him to go across to the inn and have some refreshment for half an hour. He'll take me to Verney Castle and then back into Edinburgh for the train to Ballater and hence to Balmoral, where I will await Her Majesty's instructions. The telegraph is a marvellous invention.'

'Not back to London this time?' Without awaiting a reply I said, 'Olivia doesn't see much of you these days.'

He smiled. 'Olivia is very accommodating, makes due allowance for a husband in Royal service. She doesn't feel deprived, I assure you there are plenty of advantages and benefits unknown to the average doctor's wife in Edinburgh. The children keep her busy and living in St James' means that they share tutors and governesses with the young Royals to their mutual benefit. Not a bad life-style, is it?'

Again he took my hand across the table. 'But rest assured I'll do my very best, everything in my power to be here for your wedding, and be Jack's best man. Promise! I'm sorry to have missed Jack though.'

I sighed. 'So am I. It's the usual story – one we both know well. Jack Macmerry is already married to the Edinburgh City Police,' I added bitterly.

'Just like Pappa,' he said softly.

'Exactly.'

'You do choose the wrong men, Rose. I'll give you that.'

It wasn't only Jack but Danny too in his mind as he sat back in his chair and took out a cigar from a handsome gold case.

Lighting it he gave me a searching look. 'It's taken you a long time to get this far – to the altar steps with Jack. How

170

long have you been together?' he added delicately. 'Nearly three years, isn't it?'

I merely nodded. Watching his cigar smoke carelessly make a pattern above our heads, he asked, 'Is there any reason for this sudden decision?'

I looked at him, sighed and said, 'The best in the world, Vince.'

19

It all came out then. I was telling someone, my dear Vince, for the very first time that I was pregnant. At once, it seemed the farm kitchen was transformed into a doctor's consulting room and across the table, placing his fingertips together, he asked the questions and I gave the answers.

At the end, he sighed, 'This isn't an unusual situation by any means, Rose. Rather the reverse, in fact.' He paused. 'Does Jack know?'

'Of course not. We've never discussed such possibilities.'

Vince's eyebrows shot heavenward at that and shaking his head, he said softly, 'He might even like the idea.' Watching my expression, he added gently, 'Don't you think it's about time –'

'I certainly do not. I would never want Jack to feel under an obligation of any kind.'

Vince smiled and leaned back in his chair. 'I hardly think obligation is the correct word, Rose dear. Jack simply adores you – he has been waiting for an opportunity to slip that wedding ring on your finger since I first met him.'

'So now is his big chance,' I snapped, sounding grimmer than I felt.

Vince looked at me sharply. 'I take it that you do want to marry him?'

'Oh yes – sometime. I'm fairly sure of that.'

'There isn't anyone else?'

'Of course not!' (Except Danny, conscience whispered.)

Vince smiled. 'I don't see the problem then. All seems pretty straightforward.'

'His mother is a bit of a trial,' I added weakly. 'Do you know, she hasn't even told people here in Eildon that I am a widow. Introduces me as Miss Faro,' I said indignantly.

Vince shook his head and, leaning across the table, he took my hand. 'Cheer up, Rose. You don't have to live under the same roof as Jack's mother. An occasional visit is all that will be required of you.'

I was silent.

'Come along, Rose,' he said just a trifle impatiently. 'This isn't the end of the world.'

'Oh, is it not? It might well be the end of my world though. I can't see myself pushing a perambulator while I search for clues.'

Vince laughed, obviously he found that image more amusing than I did. 'Then Jack might well be pleased about that too. After all, solving crimes is what the police are paid for.'

On an impulse I decided to tell him about my discovery of Father McQuinn's body and Mrs Aiden's mysterious death. He listened attentively but I was disappointed in his reaction.

'Accidents, both of them, surely.'

I was taken aback, having had expected him to be rather more concerned than a mere dismissive shrug.

'Surely it's obvious to you that the priest was murdered? – the candlestick, the bloodstains – so carefully removed afterwards.'

'The candlestick might not have been a murder weapon, perhaps he merely reached out to try and save himself as he fell. Besides who would want to kill them, Rose? Think about it. It doesn't make sense. Where's the motive? Remember Pappa's words. There must be a motive for murder. Find it and you're halfway to solving any crime.'

That was true. There was no apparent motive but I was certain that the priest had been murdered.

'Even Constable Bruce thought I might be right – especially about the housekeeper.'

Vince laughed, shook his head. 'Then leave it to your policeman to solve the mystery. That's his business, not yours,

Rose. You are here to get married in a few days' time, not to play detective. I should have thought that as bride-to-be, you would have more than enough to keep you occupied.'

I looked at him angrily. First Jack and now Vince. Men can be so infuriating and that goes for beloved stepbrothers too. I had expected better things of Vince so I told him about the stalker, the man watching me from the Abbey Tower shortly after I arrived.

He didn't find that in the least alarming. He grinned and gave me an appreciative glance. 'Let's just say that you're well worth watching.'

So here we were, back with a man's favourite taunt. Any pretty woman, a good excuse for a voyeur.

But there was more to it than that. Vince had another ready explanation. Scratching his cheek, he said seriously, 'Have you ever considered another possibility? That it wasn't you he was watching in particular, Rose. With this security scare about Royal safety and the Jubilee celebrations, perhaps the police already have the whole area under careful surveillance.'

I still had two more cards to play. The Claddagh ring lying upstairs in my jewel box, the ring I thought was Danny's. The message Sister Mary Michael had received, or believed she had received from Danny. Sadly I guessed that my very practical stepbrother would dismiss the former as coincidence and the latter as the confused memory typical of a nonagenarian.

At that moment, however, footsteps announced the return of Jack's mother with his father, commanded to change out of his muddy boots at the back door.

Vince was welcomed. Invited to take a dram – or two, which Vince did most willingly, it was some time before he felt free to leave for Verney Castle, the coachman already seated statue-like on the carriage as if impervious to time's passing.

As we walked outside with Vince, I said, 'There's someone else I want you to meet. An old friend,' I said triumphantly and led him to the stable to see Thane who greeted him with polite interest.

As Vince had never been quite certain that the deerhound was not another figment of my imagination, I was glad to watch his expression as Jack's father related the story of Thane's dramatic recovery and for the first time I observed that Thane was now devoted to Andrew Macmerry.

I was faintly jealous although I should have been grateful that he spent so much time in the farmer's company, since the walks I took him on each day were strictly limited in the kind of exercise a large deerhound needed.

At last it was time for Vince to leave. Suddenly he turned to me and said: 'I've been thinking about Jack's letter. If you're really anxious about your wedding gown arriving in time, you could come back to Edinburgh with me – I can't bring you back –'

'What a great idea,' I said excitedly. 'I can catch the evening train. It stops at Eildon.'

'Very well. I'll call for you on the way back from Verney – in about an hour.'

I promised to be ready. What bliss, I thought, a few more hours with Vince and the chance to be in my own home again for even just a short time would be extremely useful.

Should I take Thane with me, give him the chance to resume his old life on Arthur's Seat.

I wondered about that. Had living with a family changed him? Had we turned my mysterious deerhound into a mere domesticated pet dog?

I decided to rely on the strange telepathy we shared. I would give Thane the chance to accompany me back to Edinburgh in the hope that his reactions to seeing me get into the carriage with Vince would provide the answer.

It didn't happen. When Vince returned for me, Thane was not in the stable.

'He'll be off again with Andrew,' said Jack's mother. 'That Dog might be a very useful animal some day, if Andrew goes about it and trains him the right way.'

The thought struck horror into my heart. What had I done? Thane as a mere farm dog herding sheep was somehow a shaming thought.

Feeling somewhat sheepish myself, I got into the carriage beside Vince, consoling my conscience with the thought that Thane's disappearance was his way of telling me that he knew my mind and that he was quite happy to stay in Eildon and await my return.

Jack's mother rushed out as we were about to leave.

'Here, you'll need these,' she said handing us both a neatly packed parcel.

When we looked surprised, she said, 'Food for the journey. There'll be not a bite for you back in that place you live, Rose.'

I smiled. Like Mrs McQuinn she always found it difficult, not to say impossible, to get around to Solomon's Tower as my home.

'I've made some sandwiches and things so you'll not starve before you get back tonight,' she added sternly.

And then, with one of her more endearing smiles to Vince, her eyes actually twinkled, I thought as she said, 'And this for you, lad. There'll be nothing to eat on that train you're catching. This'll keep you going till you get to yon castle at Balmoral.'

We were both grateful, thanked her profusely. To be honest I certainly hadn't thought of food for the day and neither had Vince.

'Take care of yourselves,' and to me, she added sternly. 'Andrew'll see That Dog is properly fed.'

'Wasn't that nice of her,' said Vince and I cast aside anxious thoughts about Thane, eager to hear Vince's reactions to the Verneys.

As we bowled along so smoothly in the well-sprung carriage, I gathered he had been made most welcome, Lady Amelia a willing patient. That was all the information I could expect from Vince, respecting the law of confidentiality between doctor and patient.

'Lord Verney is an anxious husband, most amiable and concerned and they are a very devoted couple – but quite bewildered!'

'In what way?' I enquired.

Vince shook his head. 'There they are living in a castle, striving to keep abreast of modern inventions. His lordship is proud of being a model landlord, keen to impress on me that, like Her Majesty, he has electricity and even the cottages on his model estate, now have gas installed.

'As for the castle itself, I generally take little notice. I'm fairly immune to ostentatious wealth and only wish H M had not made it *de rigueur* to fill every tiny space with some *object d'art*.

'Verney Castle is an exception in that I have never seen so many original great works of art outside a gallery. Everywhere one looks there is evidence of wealth and there is the irony of it all. His lordship takes it as a personal affront that surrounded with so much of the world's goods, nature has denied them the simple blessing bestowed on the humblest mortals of an abundance of children. A blessing I have to say that many of his tenants would be pleased to avoid.'

Pausing he smiled and looked at me. 'I take it that you have not yet been invited to the castle –'

I shook my head. 'Indeed I have. I've been specially requested to attend Alexander's birthday party – and instructed to bring Thane too.'

Vince laughed. 'I wish I could be there. That will bring a

touch of mayhem to Lady Amelia's caste of small very noisy lap dogs.'

'Did you meet Alexander?' I asked.

'No, just a fleeting glimpse – Lady Amelia pointed him out – walking in the gardens with his governess –'

'Who is his lordship's young cousin, Annette Verney. And thereby hangs a tale –'

But the complicated story of Annette's love life was to remain untold as the carriage cornered sharply, narrowly avoiding collision with a farm cart and earning our inscrutable coachman a steady flow of ripe abuse.

'That was nearly a nasty accident,' said Vince as the coachman, having ascertained that we were unhurt, set off again. 'And talking of accidents, it was as well I had my bag of tools with me at Verney, as I had to administer first aid to Lord Verney's new secretary. Just arrived a few days ago – from Dublin. Fell running for the train.

'I had some patching up to do and I must say, the condition of his back and chest would suggest a lifetime in boxing or other aggressive sports, rather than the peaceful life one would attribute to a don from Trinity College.'

'Indeed?'

'Indeed. Dr Finbar Blayney had some very interesting scars for the scholar Lord Verney has engaged in the belief that he will add his expertise to cataloguing ancient family documents and his collection of art.'

'You sound doubtful, Vince. Was it just the scars?'

Vince shook his head. 'For a classics scholar, his knowledge of Latin was extremely shaky. There were some medical terms in frequent use which seemed well above his head. And you know how fond I am of my Latin tags.'

Pausing he grinned at me apologetically since they had been a sore trial to my sister Emily and I in childhood days.

When I groaned, he laughed. 'You still remember "*nunquam non paratus*"?'

It was my turn to smile. '"Always ready" is engraved on my heart!'

Vince grimaced. 'The simplest most common quotation that every schoolboy or schoolgirl with a decent education might recognise. But not so Dr Finbar Blayney, Classics scholar. He just frowned, stared at me blankly.'

And shaking his head, 'The incident left me with considerable doubts about his abilities to perform the cataloguing task that Lord Verney has in mind.'

'There might have been a simpler reason, Vince.'

'Indeed. Name one!'

I smiled. 'A very ordinary reason the clever doctor failed to diagnose. Perhaps the scholar is a little deaf.'

'Hmphh,' grunted Vince, who did not like to be put at fault.

And there the conversation ended. The carriage was now bowling along the Dalkeith Road. Arthur's Seat held the skyline to the east, dominating, majestic.

I felt a growing sense of excitement, once we reached Coffin Lane, Solomon's Tower would be in sight. I would be home once more.

20

The carriage stopped outside the Tower, its ancient stone suggesting that it had evolved independently as an extension of that extinct volcano, Arthur's Seat looming above us.

Waving the coachman's assistance aside, Vince handed me down and, taking the key, opened the front door. Staring into the dark interior, he asked anxiously: 'Are you sure you will be all right, Rose?'

I said of course and solemnly consulting his watch he sighed: 'I would love to come in for a while, but – the Ballater train. I have so little time –'

A kiss, a hug and an assurance that we would meet soon and he was back in the carriage, a hand out of the window. I waved back, watching it disappear down the road again towards the city, momentarily overcome by sadness at yet another brief interlude with Vince and that inevitable parting.

True, he always tried to leave me in good heart, holding on to the promise of an early meeting which, alas, mostly failed to materialise and, as I stepped into the Tower, I already had doubts whether he would manage to fit my wedding into Her Majesty's erratic and constantly changing plans for the Royal household.

However, my gloomy thoughts were soon overcome by the excitement of this temporary homecoming as I thought of the many times in Eildon when I had been longing for just this moment.

But like all such dreams the reality was somewhat different and homecoming not quite as I had imagined. I was alone for the first time in weeks and once inside the Tower with the door closed, I felt its vast emptiness, the high ceilings and stone walls closing in on me.

Suddenly I felt vulnerable, bereft without Jack, without Thane and even without the Macmerrys: Jack's father's warm geniality, his mother's warm food. How large, cold and dark the rooms seemed, the ancient tapestries on the high walls with their Biblical scenes somehow threatening.

It was as if in my short absence the ghosts of Solomon's Tower's long lost history had settled in again. The past had taken possession and I had become a resented intruder from a future world incomprehensible to them.

At that moment I realised how fortunate I had been in having found Jack Macmerry – at least I would never be lonely again – even if our short absences when duty called him away for days on end infuriated me. He was mine and he was my reality.

I wandered across the cold flagged stone floor into the kitchen, my footsteps loud and strangely echoing. This was not my usual kitchen. In my absence, a rare tidiness had set in. Bleak and sterile surfaces, a well-scrubbed table with cupboard shelves immaculate and starkly empty, apart from a few neatly stacked tins.

Opening the pantry door set off the scuttling sound of a mouse's hasty exit – although there had been little left for sustenance.

Up the stone spiral stair to my bedroom. The air was stale and I opened the window, moving aside spiders' delicate webs with a feeling that I was marooned in Sleeping Beauty's palace, especially as the garden below had become overgrown with weeds and in my short absence lush but alien vegetation had choked my pretty pot plants out of existence.

I turned round with a start as the cheval mirror reflected a ghostly image – a different 'me' from the Rose McQuinn who had stood before it just a short while ago.

Quickly moving out of range, I smoothed the coverlet of the vast ancient bed with its oak panels, its carvings of angels and Biblical characters which had escaped the ravages of invaders or changing fashion. Since the problem of moving it down the narrow spiral staircase was beyond man's ingenuity, the logical answer to its survival intact was that it had been built into the Tower sometime in the fifteenth or sixteenth century.

Beyond any guess of mine the vast procession of those who had been born and died under the once handsome tapestried canopy. But I was fond of my great bed and when I returned to slumber in its depths, I would be married. Jack would sleep at my side and we would take our place in its long cavalcade, its unwritten history.

With less than two hours before the train back to Eildon left Waverley Station, I quickly opened the wardrobe, gathered my wedding gown, bonnet and shoes, new lace camisoles, nightgowns and underwear. Closing the door, I had a fleeting thought for Jack and remembered just in time the handsome new shirt and cravat I had bought for him.

Packed in two valises, carrying one in each hand, they were evenly balanced, and no great weight. I had a quarter hour walk into Waverley station and thought longingly of my bicycle, out there in the garden shed, abandoned and forlorn. How I wished I could take it back with me to Eildon.

All this effort had made me hungry and I returned to the kitchen. Without lighting the stove or fire, never among my shining achievements, even boiling a kettle for the cup of tea I longed for would take hours. Grateful to Jack's mother. I eagerly unpacked the parcel of beef sandwiches, cake, apples and a container of milk that she had so thoughtfully provided and while I ate, on an impulse I wrote to Jack.

His almost daily letters were brusque and businesslike, irritable bulletins about the progress, or lack of it, in the Glasgow criminal court. Even the most imaginative reading between the lines could hardly have placed them in the category of love letters.

I never responded. Truth was, I always expected him to arrive next day. Now, in case he was not too busy or harassed with other matters to notice or feel anxious about my lack of communication, I assuaged my conscience by writing him an affectionate letter. I told him how much I was missing him and of my trip to pick up the wedding clothes, sealing it with the satisfaction that post from Edinburgh would reach him in Glasgow next day.

As my walk to the railway station would take me down the Pleasance passing close to the convent of the Little Sisters, I wished I had left enough time to visit Sister Angela, to once again be reassured that the old nun's certainty that Danny had written her belonged to the confusions of age.

I decided I would write to her. For a moment at the gates I hesitated, but then popped my note into the post-box and hurried on.

After Eildon's pure air, I was very conscious of the acrid smell as I reached the city centre. Edinburgh had well-earned Robert Burns' epithet of 'auld Reekie'. Even on an early summer evening, smoke from a thousand chimneys in houses cooking supper, as well as bakeries, laundries and small factories clouded the sunshine.

The peace and country air of the Borders that I had taken for granted was replaced in the busy city streets by carriages, cabs and horse-drawn omnibuses noisily clanging their way along the North Bridge.

Bicycles were now a common sight, especially among the young blades who regarded ringing their bells as a great lark. However this mode of transport was still considered somewhat unseemly for young ladies, as one newspaper described it; 'shamelessly revealing their nether limbs.'

As for the 'horseless carriage', the Benz motor-car I had

encountered last year as a phenomena in Orkney was no longer a nine-days wonder in Edinburgh. Adding its acrid belches of blue smoke to the air, it bounced along, drivers swathed in goggles leaning on the horn and putting pedestrians to instant flight.

Such behaviour occasionally aroused shouts of anger and indignation, including some fists shaken by gentlemen of an older generation who consoled themselves that such monstrosities were but a new fangled idea.

'The horseless carriage would never last, it could never stand the test of time.'

As I walked into the railway station, the air was heavy with yet another version of black smoke and grime. The train from London had just arrived and descending passengers were hurrying along the busy platform.

Edinburgh had long enjoyed the popularity of a holiday resort with Scottish families, particularly the nearby beach at Portobello. In more recent years, thanks to the Queen, towns and villages in the Highlands, particularly on Deeside now readily accessible by train were enjoying a boom in holiday accommodation.

This was evident by the dialects from south of the Border as harassed parents gathered together children and luggage, shouting for porters, as they hurried in the direction of connecting trains.

In the now emptied train which had arrived late and was leaving almost immediately, I managed to get a compartment to myself and, as we steamed out past the ruined Abbey of Holyrood Palace, I remembered that other journey on the way to Eildon, my fellow passenger the young nun who I now knew as Annette Verney.

So much had happened in the space of a very short time. Two fatalities: to Father McQuinn's 'heart attack', which I was certain was murder and as for his housekeeper Mrs Aiden, I was firmly convinced her fall was no accident either but was linked somehow to the death of the priest.

Staring out of the window I found myself recalling Mrs Fraser's remarks about having gone to visit her friend that fatal night, fearing that she would wish for company with the priest lying newly dead in his parlour. And how, on hearing voices, one of them belonging to a man, she had returned home without making her presence known.

This man I was now certain had probably killed them both, but I was well aware that there was little hope of finding a solution to the two deaths or of bringing their killer to justice before the weekend when, along with the Queen's Diamond Jubilee celebrations, Jack and I would be celebrating our marriage in the Scots kirk.

I sighed in exasperation, two unsolved mysteries to add to my log book. For a Lady Investigator, Discretion Guaranteed, two admissions of defeat I would certainly not advertise.

Outside the sun was setting, throwing a golden glow over the fields. Away to the west, the Firth of Forth glistened and the hills of Fife settled into sleep. A pleasant uneventful journey, through local stations including Musselburgh, Dunbar where we gathered a few more passengers.

At last we steamed out of Berwick, the shreds of a castle around the railway station as a reminder of the bad old days. Walls built by the Romans in the first century AD were still standing, remarkably preserved despite it all, for they had been of little interest or significance to raiders from the south when Berwick became a constant target for vengeful medieval English kings.

We would soon be at the whistle stop at Eildon. What news from Jack, I wondered –

Suddenly the train jolted forward and ground to a halt.

Doors opened, and the guard who I realised must be Mrs Fraser's husband ran along the track.

Passengers opened doors, leaned out of windows. shouts of, 'What on earth has happened? Has someone been hurt?'

I joined the curious, leaning out of the window.

In the next compartment, a lugubrious passenger saw me and nodded sadly: 'Aye, it'll be another o' yon suicides – d'ye no' ken, it was all in the papers last week.'

21

Craning my neck to see what was happening at the front of the train, I remembered Jack's father reading an article about a man who had plunged to his death down a railway embankment just out of Berwick.

Was this yet another suicide?

There was nothing to be seen through the smoke.

The minutes passed then, at last, the guard hurried back along the line to be greeted by anxious cries from the passengers demanding to know what had happened, what was the delay?

'Nothing serious,' he said. 'No one injured. A dead cow on the line – come through the broken fence on the field back yonder, slipped and fallen on to the line.'

Sighs of relief and murmurs of 'Poor beast' from animal lovers as he continued, 'We've removed it, so we'll be on our way now. No more delays, I hope,' he added cheerfully, and blowing his whistle the train, gathering steam, moved slowly off down the line.

Ten minutes later we arrived in Eildon. As I stepped down from the compartment, Fraser was talking to his replacement, the guard who had left the London train on its way north to Edinburgh and was rejoining it for the journey back south.

As I walked past, they were discussing the reason for the train's delay and as I reached the exit gate, Fraser caught up with me, saluted and said:

'Miss Faro? isn't it. My wife, Ina, has told me about you,' and stretching out his hands, 'Allow me to carry those bags for you, if you please, miss. They look mighty heavy.'

Thanking him, I gratefully put them in his keeping for the ten minute walk down to the farm.

Fraser was prepared to be genial. 'I hope the delay back there didn't upset you too much, miss,' he said apologetically. 'I dare say your fiancé's family would be worrying about you.'

Explaining that I had been in Edinburgh for the day, I said I was glad that the accident on the line was nothing serious this time. 'I must confess I was rather alarmed – I hoped it wasn't another suicide.'

'Aye, miss. The same thought went through my mind. So you heard about the poor chap who topped himself. I was on the train that night.' He shook his head. 'Strange business, it was, right enough.'

'Did they ever identify the man?'

'Not as far as we know, miss. But there was something very odd that didn't go into the newspapers. The police were very interested in why he took off his jacket and shirt, before he jumped.'

That did seem curious. But the disordered confused state of a man's mind in those moments before he decides to end his own life, are often inexplicable to all but himself.

'Presumably the garments were found in the compartment.'

'Not a sign of them, miss. They just vanished too. There was no one we could ask either as he was alone when he made that terrible decision.'

'You're certain of that?'

The guard seemed surprised. 'Of course, miss, or surely someone would have tried to restrain him and told us about it.'

'Then who was it who pulled the communication cord and stopped the train?'

He shook his head. 'Must have been someone passing the

188

compartment who saw the door standing open.' He thought for a moment. 'When we left Edinburgh that night it was a busy train and there were two other passengers in the compartment. One with a ticket to Alnmouth and the other passenger with a ticket to Newcastle – I met him later when the accident happened and we were making general enquiries.

'I gather there was a bit of an argument. The Newcastle gentleman asked me to find him another compartment. Said he had moved out because the Alnmouth fellow complained that he was feeling ill and pipe smoke offended him. I remembered him, sitting in a corner, all muffled up to the eyes, as if he had toothache.'

'Did your Newcastle passenger have anything to say about the man who fell? Was he behaving oddly? Did he seem depressed?'

Fraser shook his head. 'No, not in the least. That's what's so strange. The Newcastle traveller was very upset, apparently the man who jumped off the train had just sat there reading a book, minding his own business and ignoring him while the Alnmouth invalid grumbled about pipe smoke. Obviously that didn't bother him but Alnmouth apparently got off at Berwick when we stopped after the accident.'

'Surely that was odd?'

Fraser shrugged, he didn't seem surprised. 'If he was feeling ill as he said, perhaps he decided not to continue his journey and catch the next train back to Edinburgh.'

'I'm intrigued by this missing jacket and shirt – why the man discarded it we will never know, but if he left it behind, how did it vanish from the compartment? And there must have been other belongings, surely?'

Fraser shook his head. 'Nothing was found. The police searched but the compartment was empty.'

That was distinctly odd. Train passengers usually carry some possessions on even a short journey.

I could feel the Lady Investigator taking over, as I said: 'He had boarded the train at Edinburgh. What about his ticket?'

'It was a return half from Inverness to York –'

'So he was going back to York.'

Fraser shook his head. 'Aye, possibly. But you can never be sure – returns are valid for three months and business folk who find they aren't going back after all, often hand them on or even sell them cheap to someone else. The railways company trie to be helpful, but as he didn't buy his ticket at the Inverness station, just boarded the train there, they couldn't tell the police much.'

'What about his luggage?' The lack of it bothered me. 'Surely there would have been some clues to his identity.'

'Nothing was found, as I said. He might have had a trunk in the luggage van, of course, but they were all claimed and accounted for at London.'

'He could have put it on the train at Inverness.'

Fraser shook his head. 'The porter there was just a young lad and he couldn't remember anything about a trunk being loaded, it was a busy train and he couldn't identify the description the police gave of the poor fellow either. As for Edinburgh, it was the same story. I'm afraid porters only remember passengers who give generous tips.'

'Surely he was carrying some hand luggage, a valise, perhaps?' I insisted

'He had a small brown attaché case, the kind gentlemen carry when they attend meetings, but presumably that fell out with him. The only thing that I picked up – that had fallen under the seat – was the book he had been reading – poor gentleman.'

'Did it have a name inside?'

'No. It looked new and it was in some foreign language. I can't speak any other than the Queen's English. Never

190

learned it in the school I went to, foreign languages were just for rich folk not working men.'

'What did the police say?'

He shook his head. 'They were pleased I had found it, but it didn't help much in identifying the dead man.'

And my mind working rapidly over the evidence so far, I thought I had found another reason for the dead man's lack of interest in the two passengers who were arguing.

Was it possible that he had been a foreigner? If only the guard had been able to recognise the language of the book.

We had reached the farm track and I parted from Ned Fraser very reluctantly, regretting that with Jack's mother at the open door, there was no time for all the questions I still wanted to ask.

Fraser saluted, handed over my valises and said he would tell Ina he had seen me and that it had been a great pleasure having my company.

Thanking him, I thought it was more than a great pleasure, here was the kind of intriguing mystery that, with more time on my hands, I would have loved to solve.

22

Andrew Macmerry appeared from the direction of the stable yard and Thane bounded over to meet me, his effusive greeting a blessed relief. His absence from the barn when I left for Edinburgh had been faintly disturbing.

'We were in the up-by field – he must have known you were on that train, for the last half hour, not a minute's peace would he give me.' And pausing to gather breath, he added, 'I'm right out of puff. He had me racing back to the house here. What a dog, what a companion he is turning out to be.'

'How does Rex react to his presence?' I asked curiously, for the sheepdog had always been at Andrew's heels.

Andrew shrugged. 'I was a wee bit worried about that too, ye ken. But Rex ignores him, doesn't seem aware of his presence.'

Fondling Thane's ears. he frowned. 'Aye, Rex was always a possessive animal, growling and warning off any other dogs that came near me. But not Thane. I'll be right sorry when you take him back to Edinburgh with you. '

'Well, I expect Rex will be pleased.'

Shaking his head, he pushed back his cap and scratched his forehead in that characteristic gesture of puzzlement, he looked at me intently. 'It's as if – I dinna quite know how to describe it – as if Thane doesna even exist.'

And I thought, perhaps for Rex – he doesn't!

Jess Macmerry had come to the door and the two labradors aroused from their lethargy by the fuss and hoping that it meant food stared round her ankles somewhat defiantly in Thane's direction. Arms folded, Jess's expression said That Dog was still barred from the sacred precinct of the kitchen.

I said I'd take him back to the barn.

He was glad to have me back again, running round me in little circles, whining with delight, with an exuberance rare in him. And I must confess the delight was mutual.

I sat down beside him and told him all about Edinburgh and the guard's tale of the suicide. I realise that to normal people confiding in a dog is considered very odd and would be eyed askance. But Thane was more than my deerhound, he was my friend and I would have sworn that he understood every word I said to him, listening intently, his head on the side, occasionally raising those magisterial eyebrows in a puzzled expression.

I kissed the top of his head. 'If only you could speak, Thane – if only you could talk to me. I'm sure you know what I'm saying, and I'm sure you're clever enough to advise me.'

Andrew appeared at the door to say that supper was ready.

Walking toward the house with him, I asked if he still had the newspaper with the story about the man who had committed suicide from the London train at Berwick.

Andrew shook his head. 'We never keep old papers, lass. Jess uses them to wrap the eggs, or to light the stove, like as not.' And with a curious look. 'Why are you so interested?'

So I told him about Ned Fraser and his account of the suicide's strange behaviour, of removing his jacket and shirt.

That was as far as I got. We were at the kitchen door and I never reached the odd behaviour of the muffled up passenger with the Alnmouth ticket who presumably left the train at Berwick.

Jack's father roared with mirth and I looked at him indignantly.

'Lassie, lassie,' he chuckled. 'Never take a word Ned Fraser tells you seriously. He's a terrible gossip, every one in the village knows all about his tall tales. What he doesna ken for fact, he'll invent just to impress his audience.' As he was removing his boots on the doormat, I felt suddenly angry at having been so gullible. But whatever Andrew's reactions, it sounded beyond the bounds of possibility that the guard had made it up on the spur of the moment, just to impress me.

As we opened the kitchen door, ten o'clock was striking, and looking at the table groaning with good things, I realised that my delicate state of digestion would rebel horribly and would make me suffer cruelly for eating a large meal at this hour.

However, I had no option but to take my place at the table as I realised that this special effort by Jack's mother was all for my benefit.

The heaviest meal in the farm was at the middle of the day. For all farmer's wives, Jess included, this was the tradition. Their men and the farm hands had a hearty breakfast at six or earlier to set them up before venturing out to the fields in all conditions of weather, all year round.

After the lunchtime meal there was a break at five or six, another cooked meal, something substantial fried or baked, and quite different to the dainty sandwiches and tiny cream cakes, the afternoon tea, consumed in Edinburgh stores like Jenners by middle class ladies and their friends in all their finery.

Supper hardly existed, a sandwich or piece of bread and jam for any with hearty appetites, particularly Andrew or Jack, who were always hungry and whose constant nourishment was Jess's main concern. Missing a meal drove her into paroxysms of despair: they were sickening for something or they would starve to death, go into a decline, by morning.

And so in my honour, here was a table spread with a mammoth meal of soup, beef stew, apple tart and rich thick cream.

Struggling through the first courses, I was urged to second helpings. Refusing I was told, 'I don't suppose you've eaten anything all day but those few sandwiches I packed for you.' That was true. 'Then you must be hungry,' Andrew insisted.

Watching me eat, both of Jack's parents were full of admiration for Vince whose visit was destined to be a constant topic among their local friends.

How were the children – and Olivia, Jess wanted to know. And had I ever visited their apartments in St James' Palace?

Between mouthfuls I shook my head. Jess seemed taken aback at this lack of seizing a great opportunity to glimpse how the Royals lived.

Eyebrows raised. Surely your brother has invited you. My reply: Yes, of course and I hoped to go some day.

'You should have gone before you got married. You'll be busy then looking after a husband and a home,' she said sternly.

At last I sat back and insisted I couldn't eat another morsel, not even a piece of her delicious chocolate cake.

Disappointed at this lack of appetite, Andrew yawned. 'Well, you've had a busy day in Edinburgh, lass.'

With no more anecdotes of Vince forthcoming, Jess said, 'Time we were all off to our beds.'

At that moment there was nothing I wanted more.

'Before you go,' she added. 'You'd better unpack that dress for your wedding and let me see to it for you. It'll need hanging and pressing.' Cutting short my protests, which weren't very strong, she said: 'My irons need a bit of handling. You have to know when they're too hot.'

'Aye. Many's the shirt that's been sorely scorched.' This admission from Andrew earned him a dagger-like glance.

So I did as I was told, trying not to think uncharitably that I was being taken over. After all, I hated most domestic tasks and ironing in particular, so that warning was very timely. Poor Jack had been known to tackle his own shirts and collars in weary desperation, a fact I hoped would never reach his mother's ears.

Despite being weary I slept badly that night. Something more than Jess's supper was lying heavily upon my stomach.

I still could not believe Andrew's dismissal of Ned Fraser's story. As I went over the details, I knew there was a core of truth buried somewhere, some fact I was sure he had not invented.

The man with his face all muffled up 'like he had toothache'. Was there a link here? I had an uneasy feeling that the unknown suicide might have been the victim of a murderous attack – by the man who had a ticket to Alnmouth, but according to Fraser had disappeared from the train.

I remembered Ned's words about feeling ill, and deciding to leave the train at Berwick, to continue his journey when he felt better.

Or his mission accomplished, I thought grimly, had he merely slipped off the train and disappeared after making sure the train would stop by pulling the communication cord?

The scene persisted like the pieces of a jigsaw I sought in vain to set in order. I kept waking and remembering, sleeping and dreaming that I was on a train, a man was leaping from the door, pushed by a shadowy figure, his face concealed…

I sat up in horror. There was something, something important in that earlier conversation with Ned's wife Ina, that I should remember.

I groaned. Jess's apple pie was making its presence felt. Small wonder I was having nightmares for it lay like lead on my stomach. Gulping down some of Dr Dalrymple's remedy for heartburn with a glass of water and lying prone, I tried again to sleep.

Tomorrow morning I would tell Constable Bruce about

196

Ned Fraser's version of the suicide. I would be very interested in what reasons the constable might produce for a man who removed his jacket and shirt first before leaping to his death.

A man who carried no luggage on a return ticket from Inverness to York. A long journey, to have no possessions beyond a tiny attaché case which disappeared with him and a book. A book he had been observed reading when the train left Edinburgh which had fallen under the seat. Recovered later by Fraser who described it as being 'in a foreign language'.

But by morning I had changed my mind. In the light of Andrew's reactions my conclusions seemed too far-fetched to tell anyone, especially the disappointing Constable Bruce of whom I had had so many hopes, but who now seemed to be heavily involved in a domestic drama of his own.

With an uneasy feeling that he too might find Ned Fraser's story a subject for mirth and hint that I had been too gullible, I decided that first of all, I would look closely at all the facts.

I would write them down, all exactly as I remembered, as Ned Fraser had told me. This was my normal procedure when trying to solve a crime, a procedure Pappa had used when working on murder cases long ago.

Doing so, I had learned, triggered off memories and scenes that lay dormant and then rose to the surface. So often the result had been perfect. Perhaps this time it would work again and that frail elusive fragment, the clue to unravel the reason for the two murders, would emerge.

However, before I could write anything down there was a late breakfast ready waiting for me on the kitchen table. This was now standard procedure and as I struggled with porridge and bacon and eggs, Jess sat across the table and watched me kindly instead of busying herself about the kitchen.

She wanted to talk about Vince, all my earliest memories.

What had he been like as a student? Was he clever? And every time I said his name she managed a few smiles, lost in admiration for this clever doctor, the stepson of a police inspector who had risen in the world.

I also discovered that I had risen in the estimation of Jack's mother. My popularity had gone up several notches, a claim to fame worthier by far on account of an illustrious stepbrother with Royal connections than for my famous father. And to cap it all, when she asked what I was doing for the day, I said I was going to Verney Castle.

I had promised Alexander I would be at his birthday party.

'Then you must take him a cake I've just baked,' she said. 'An iced one with his name on it.'

I agreed that this was a kind thought indeed, but with a horrible feeling that the cooks at Verney would have thought of that already. I refrained from hurting her feelings by mentioning such a possibility.

When I said I would be taking Thane with me, that Alexander had met him and specially requested I bring the big deerhound, her eyes widened in horror.

'A beast that size in a great big castle. I've heard they have lovely rugs on their floors, not just linoleum and handmade rag mats like the rest of us,' she added darkly. 'I just hope he doesn't misbehave and make a mess on their expensive carpets. That would shame you, a body wouldn't know where to look.'

I assured her that Thane would behave perfectly, but she was still doubtful, shaking her head when I set off to find him. Once again he hadn't accompanied Andrew and was waiting for me in the barn.

We went for a walk to the Abbey and I considered returning the Claddagh ring in the hope that some visitor had lost it. How that would console me, for its presence in my jewel box was a haunting reminder of Danny.

The grounds were empty apart from a couple of gardeners. This time there was nothing of interest to Thane and on our way back to the barn, he saw Andrew walking across the yard and greeted him joyfully.

'A walk with you, eh? So that's what he was up to,' said Andrew stroking his head. 'Didn't want my company this morning. He just sat here and looked at me.' He laughed. 'His expression was almost human, I swear, as if he was telling me he had something more important to do. I expect it's just because he missed you when you were away and doesn't want to let you out of his sight.'

Maybe, I thought, just maybe that was the reason.

Jess was gathering eggs and poked her head round the door.

'Did Jess show you the nice brush she's bought for Thane?' asked Andrew. 'Just in case we were persuaded to change our minds and put him into the Dog Show?'

He grinned at her and she shrugged uncomfortably. 'Nothing of the kind, Andrew. I thought his coat might need a bit of brushing, going off with you to the fields every day in all kinds of weather.'

'His coat looks good. Have you used it on him?' I added, wondering how Thane would react to such attention.

Heads were shaken. 'No, we thought you would be the right one, Rose, he's your dog after all.'

'We'll leave you to it,' said Jess.

I was glad she wasn't expecting some sign of gratitude from Thane. Although he seemed devoted to Andrew, as if conscious of Jess's disapproval and calling him 'That Dog', he ignored her completely.

But to please her, I took the brush. Thane eyed it askance with a faint shudder. He always looked quite immaculate, so whispering 'Sorry' I laid it beside Alexander's toy dog.

In the kitchen Mrs Ward had just arrived and was sitting

down to a cup of tea, croaking, her voice heavy with cold. Between bouts of sneezing she told Jess that Dave had taken to his bed. He was much worse than she was.

I hastily declined their invitation to stay and chat about the wedding arrangements.

23

As I started off for Verney Castle, with Thane trotting at my side, without his rope as I couldn't manage that as well as clutching Jess's birthday cake. I wanted to give Alexander a present of my own from the village shop. Ten minutes later we were walking down the drive armed with cake, a handsome box of paints and a colouring book.

The sun had clouded over and a dark sky threatened rain. Perhaps it was the change in the weather and the drive that twisted and turned and seemed to close in on us, heavy with massive shrubbery, that gave me the odd feeling that we were being watched. The rhododendrons had bloomed early this year and now their petals were falling in the breeze, a sinister mass of scarlet petals scattering in our path like drops of blood.

Thane's behaviour too affected me in that walk. He seemed uneasy and as if aware that something was amiss, he would stop suddenly, a paw raised, alert and listening.

'What is it?' I whispered, my hand on his quivering shoulder.

Shaking himself, as if danger had passed, we set off again. A few yards further on, the procedure was repeated. It was all faintly unnerving, with the rumble of thunder far-off and heavy clouds leaning over the treetops.

We were within sight of the castle, however, when I had my first real cause for alarm. A black shape bounded up the drive towards us.

Billy, the savage dog. It was my turn to stop, to freeze in my tracts. I was near enough now to glimpse that open jaw, the yellow fangs.

Then something extraordinary happened. Within a few feet

of us the dog slithered to a halt so suddenly that he did a backward somersault and rolled over. I stared in amazement, for it was as if he had hurtled into an invisible glass barrier.

At that moment, his master appeared through the shrubbery, shaking a stick at us and shouting, 'Where do you think you're going, miss! No dogs allowed here.'

Grinning now, he pointed sternly at Billy as if to tell the dog to get on with it and see us off the premises. But Billy made no move. He cringed, belly down and whining, and ran to his master, his tail between his legs.

The gamekeeper was clearly taken aback and I seized the opportunity to step forward boldly and say, 'You are mistaken. We have been invited to Master Alexander's party.'

His eyes still on his dog, wondering what had come over the normally savage beast, so reliable about scaring trespassers, he shook his head 'You, miss. Not your dog.'

'You are mistaken,' I repeated. 'Ask Master Alexander, if you like. He especially invited my deerhound.'

'He did, did he. Well, we'll see about that, miss.' And calling Billy, who gave us a scared backward glance, he hurried ahead.

We followed at a leisurely pace past the marquee I had observed some days ago and the stands erected for the Jubilee celebrations. Anxiously I regarded the sky where the first drops of a fine drizzle were falling. So much for the birthday party which presumably would have been held out of doors.

At the steps leading to the front door, Billy was waiting for his master. A very docile dog, all fierce bravado vanished, he stared at us resentfully.

The door opened and his master emerged once more. Tight-lipped, calling Billy to heel, he walked past us towards the gardens his head in the air, without a word or a glance. He had been defeated.

Expecting a footman, the man who invited us to enter was rather stockily built, balding and in his early forties. He was well-dressed enough to be an upper servant.

'If you'll just wait here a moment, miss. You're early and the other guests aren't here yet. I'll tell him you've arrived.'

A thick Irish brogue gave a clue to his identity. This must be Dr Finbar Blayney, Lord Verney's new secretary.

I handed him the cake with a hasty explanation. Nodding, he leaned forward confidentially, a whiff of medicaments suggested the remains of some of Vince's administrations.

'There is a deal of trouble up there,' he whispered, indicating the great oak staircase which occupied the centre of the vast marble-floored hall. 'Her ladyship is having great difficulty in persuading the young master into a fine velvet suit which she considers, quite rightly, the most suitable garment for a birthday party. Master Alexander doesn't care for that idea at all, or for receiving his guests indoors – he had a fancy for the marquee out there.'

As he disappeared into a room on the right I had a chance to take in my surroundings. Verney Castle was a disappointment. I reckoned that castles worthy of the name should be ancient, majestic and romantic but this edifice was more in the nature of a vast square and rather ugly modern mansion house.

I felt a sense of pride that it was considerably less attractive in every way than my own Solomon's Tower, which could have been swallowed up entirely by the ballroom of Verney Castle.

A sound of excited children's voices, footsteps on the gravel outside. A ring at the doorbell and Dr Blayney appeared again, smiled at me apologetically and opened the door to the newcomers who scrambled across the threshold.

A bevy of youngsters, these were Alexander's guests, girls and boys, some tall, some small, but all around eight to nine years old, obviously hand-picked by Father Boyle who shepherded them into the hall, his commands to silence completely ignored as Dr Blayney said, 'Master Alexander will see you now,' and led us across the floor, along a handsome corridor and into an immense room, its panelled walls heavy with portraits of long-gone Verneys, interspersed with rather gloomy landscapes.

This then was the ballroom as indicated by that concession to antiquity, a minstrel's gallery. Under its vast canopy on a padded chair, as if he was Royalty, sat the unhappy Alexander.

My heart bled for him, for I have seldom seen a sadder lonelier little figure, his face red with embarrassment and blotched with tears looking angry and frustrated by a blue velvet suit, a lace collar and cuffs from which his thin wrists protruded. Just a mite too small for him, it obviously belonged to last year's celebration and had been hastily produced when the weather was considered too inclement to wear outdoor clothes.

That decision, I feared, had been made with little imagination, for the velvet suit was a most unfair choice for Alexander's spirited nature and conjured up immediate visions of *'And When Did You Last See Your Father?'* with King Charles the First's unhappy small prince being interrogated by the Roundheads. Painted by W F Yeams in 1878 it had proved enormously popular. There were cheap reproductions of it in every art shop and in homes throughout the land. I suspected its immediate success also accounted for the discomfiture suffered by many small boys whose parents saw the velvet suit with its Royal connections as *de rigueur* for parties. However, looking round the portraits in the ballroom I felt that the Verneys should have known better and could have shown considerably more ingenuity by a careful scrutiny of their own family portraits.

At Alexander's side, standing bolt upright, her hands

neatly folded, was Annette, in a pretty muslin dress, with a blue sash. She looked completely happy, her eyes bright with excitement as she recognised me. Excitement, I was later to learn, which had little to do with her young charge's birthday party as she leaned over and told Alexander to shake hands with his guests.

At this signal they broke ranks from the regimental straight line commanded by the priest and swarmed forward, the shy ones given a little push by Father Boyle who introduced them one by one, although he had clearly some difficulty in remembering all their names

But Alexander remembered the inborn manners of his class, as he inclined his head to the boys and bowed slightly to the little girls.

As Thane and I waited in the rear, I looked at the little group of children, the boys in their Sunday best suits with white collars and well scrubbed faces, their father's or big brother's hair oil slicking down unruly locks. The girls in stiffly starched party frocks with unsteady large ribbon bows like unhappy butterflies tottering atop of their curls. Nervous and overawed by such unusual surroundings, the high ceilings and highly polished floors, they would have all been a great deal happier, I suspected, rushing about out of doors.

All had one bond in common. They were not Alexander's friends, indeed some of them had never shaken hands with him or met him in person before. Their only remote contact a distant glimpse as he rode past in his parents' carriage or in the governess cart, driving with Annette past their doors on the estate.

The sad truth of the matter, I realised at that moment, was that Alexander had no friends of his own age, or of any age. This group of children had been chosen from amongst the tenantry as having the right qualification of a similar age to match the Master of Verney's birthday party.

It was awful. Who was responsible for dreaming up such a dreadful scheme, I wondered indignantly, not surely by his parents or anyone who knew him at all.

At that moment he spotted us, his face transformed by an expression of pure joy and excitement, he swept forward and bowing over my hand, threw his arms around Thane's neck, welcomed by having his face licked.

He wasn't really interested in my present which I put on a side table and watching this scene betwixt boy and dog, I don't know exactly why, because I am not made that way, but I found that I was blinking back tears.

Introductions over, Father Boyle was regimenting the children once again, commanding them to stand in line and behave themselves as the doors opened once again to admit Alexander's parents.

Like some royal presence they walked arm in arm down the line. Boys bowed, girls curtseyed and as they were inspected, an occasional noble hand reached out to pat a golden curl, or touch a boyish shoulder. At the end of the inspection Alexander's parents stood back and his lordship thanked these unlikely guests for coming to the young Master's birthday party.

It was Lady Verney's turn. Putting forward her best maternal smile she told the little group that as well as getting nice things to eat very, very soon, they would each be given a little present of their own as they left. Now wasn't that lovely?

Faces brightened at the prospect and Father Boyle commanded three cheers for his lordship and her ladyship.

As they were moving on, Lady Verney spotted Thane.

She froze and asked in an alarmed voice, 'Who let that dog in, pray?'

Annette stepped forward, whispered something and the two noble heads swivelled sternly in my direction.

I had no intention of curtseying but before I could even

open my mouth, Alexander said, 'If you please, Mamma, he is my guest. Thane belongs to Miss Rose and he is very well-behaved.'

Polite introductions followed but Lady Verney continued to look doubtful. As far as she was concerned this was a large fierce dog and she perhaps trembled at the possible fate of her own small lapdogs should an unfortunate encounter take place.

I was introduced by Annette as Miss Rose Faro and realised that today Lord Verney looked less like my first impression of a medieval knight and more like an overfed red-faced country squire. A disappointment indeed as he smiled and said:

'Ah, yes, we have had the pleasure of a visit from – from –'

Frowning having difficulty with the name he turned to Lady Verney who obliged with: 'Dr Vincent Beaumarcher Laurie, my dear. He is Miss Faro's stepbrother.'

'Indeed?' His lordship brightened considerably at that.

'Miss Faro is to marry Jack Macmerry – at the end of this week, is it not?'

I nodded and Lord Verney said, 'Macmerry, eh. One of our tenants.' And grasping my hand, 'Felicitations, Miss Faro. I trust you will be happy in your new abode on the estate. Like Eildon, do you?'

'Very much,' I replied as was expected of me. I hardly felt it pertinent to bring in Edinburgh as our place of residence.

'Excellent, excellent.' A slight inclination of the head and they departed once more regally progressing arm-in-arm and leaving Alexander to his fate with his room full of strange children.

24

Verney Castle had been a disappointment and so too were its noble owners. I was very unimpressed by Alexander's parents. They were a typical product of the aristocracy my suffragette impulses had taught me to despise as a vanishing breed.

For one thing, they had not the slightest idea what to do with children. After bringing them into the world, they considered that their work was done. Begetting an heir was all that concerned them, a son to hand down the title and keep the ancient line afloat. Their dealings with children in those early years were like those of the Royal family who, I gathered from conversations with Vince, seemed unable to dissociate heirs with property and failed to regard this valuable commodity as flesh and blood.

My heart ached for Alexander, a little boy who wanted warmth and tenderness – and friends who were not just background characters invited to his party to make him feel that he was popular.

Now I saw how important it was for him to have found Thane, who was to sit by his side, respectful and quietly accepting the occasional darting movements of the bolder children in his direction.

These children of poor folk in Eildon who were his tenants had no cause to envy the Master of Verney. I guessed that he would have exchanged places with the meanest of them any day of the week to have a loving father and mother and caring siblings of his own. Thinking further afield even the poorest children in those teeming squalid Edinburgh closes had better lives.

'No wonder Lord Verney was so desperate to have more

children, especially looking at his noble wife, pale and thin, a figure like spun glass, she looked as if the wind might blow her away,' I told Jack's mother later when she eagerly waited to hear all about my visit to the castle.

Fortunately the party had time restrictions. The guests came at half past two and were expected to leave at 4 o'clock prompt, after a few children's games like Musical Chairs, Blind Man's Buff and the Noble Duke of York which were the limits of Father Boyle's imagination.

Having become self-appointed master of revels his ingenuity began to fail and the sight of the doors opening to admit housemaids carrying trays of lemonade and cake raised drooping spirits and fraying tempers among the small guests.

It was painfully obvious that Alexander soon wearied of party games. All he wanted was to be with Thane, and prevailed upon by Annette in whispered asides to 'join in,' he did so reluctantly, craftily missing the last vacant seat in Musical Chairs and being the first caught and 'out' in Blind Man's Buff.

Dr Blayney looked in more often than was necessary, perhaps on his lordship's instructions to keep an eye on things. As I observed him lingering by the piano where Annette was providing music for the games, I made a discovery. The don from Dublin who had failed to impress Vince, alas, was also failing to impress the pianist although he was doing his best, offering to turn sheets of music which she rather impatiently said were not needed. I would have found this amusing had it not been so pathetic to observe this plain unprepossessing man with his shiny bald head and large bright red ears so completely obsessed by Annette. As she played his eyes never left her and it is doubtful whether he saw anyone else in the room through that haze of devotion.

As for Annette she did not even know he existed, except as a rather persistent irritation. He had all the impact on her that would have been aroused by a troublesome insect and she dismissed him in much the same abrasive fashion.

She had her own reasons for being oblivious of Dr Blayney's attention. During the interval, while the children were engrossed in lemonade and cake, Blayney had been cornered by the priest, but his eyes remained constantly seeking Annette.

She drew me aside and we walked to the window. 'I have heard from my husband. He will be here from Edinburgh tomorrow. Isn't that the most wonderful thing in the whole world,' she added, eyes shining in happiness. 'We are to meet as man and wife – at last. I can hardly believe it. It is like a dream come true at last.'

Feeling that a word of caution would not come amiss I said: 'Does Lord Verney know he is coming?'

'Oh yes, yes and I have to tell you that despite all my misgivings, Cousin Quentin has been very understanding. Of course, he realises that as I am now of age he can do nothing about it. Perhaps he is resigned to the fact and both he and Amelia have decided to accept the situation, give in with good grace.'

'And Alexander, how will he take your departure?'

She looked at me, clasped her hands. 'I won't be departing, I have agreed to stay here for a few weeks as governess meantime.'

'And how will your husband take that?'

She laughed. 'Cousin Quentin has been magnificent. He has promised us a little cottage on the estate, one of his new model houses – it has gas and a bathroom. So up to date. We are to have that until we find a suitable house in Edinburgh. Meanwhile as this will be our very first home, we want to spend time planning how it shall be decorated and furnished – Amelia has promised us a few things, some of the antique tables and paintings she no longer has room for, but naturally we will want to choose our own.'

I was delighted for Annette that she was to have her happy ending after all.

'I do want you to see our little cottage,' she added 'As soon as my husband arrives, we shall invite you over.'

Now I realised I was to meet the man in person and could make my own assessment. I hoped that he came up to expectations and that I had been mistaken, eager to be proved wrong regarding those grave doubts about fortune hunters.

'I shall be away on Saturday – after my wedding,' I reminded her.

'Oh, you must forgive me. I had forgotten. So many things happening. I did so hope you two could meet. I want you to like each other,' she added wistfully.

I could understand that sentiment in a home like Verney Castle, where I felt affection and warmth and friends were pretty thin on the ground and Annette's new husband, after their catastrophic elopement in New York would need all the allies he could gather.

'Then please come to our wedding. I'm sure Jack will be delighted.'

'You really think so? Oh, Miss Rose, we will be honoured to be your guests. A wedding, such a romantic beginning for this new chapter in our own lives, is it not?'

Dr Blayney was approaching, his curiosity aroused by this confidential looking conversation.

'The children are leaving now,' he told us, but Annette merely shrugged.

'Miss Faro and I have important matters to discuss,' she said crossly. And turning her back on him, she said, 'Would you like to see our cottage before you leave, Miss Rose?'

And so the unhappy man wandered off to where the children were gathering to leave the ballroom and shaking hands with Alexander. As they stood in a line of barely suppressed excitement, sternly watched over by Father Boyle, for them the most important part of the afternoon was still to come. The handing over at the front door, by a now unhappy and perspiring Dr Blayney, of a present for each of them.

Alexander watched them leave thankfully, his arm around Thane waiting politely at his side. In the race for presents, his guests had already forgotten him, but he did not care. For him the ordeal that began with the blue velvet suit was almost over.

He came over to us and said anxiously, 'Must you go, Miss Rose? Won't you please stay for a while.'

'I am walking Miss Rose over to see my new home, Alexander,' said Annette.

'Will you be bringing Thane?' he asked me and when I said yes, he turned eagerly to Annette, 'Please may I come too?'

She smiled: 'Of course. You may even show us the way – if you remember.'

'I will be back soon. Wait for me,' he shouted and raced upstairs, followed by Annette, as I realised this was the perfect excuse, the right opportunity for him to discard the obnoxious velvet suit and change into something more worthy of his age and the outdoors.

As I waited with Thane I wandered along the hall looking at the portraits when a door opened revealing a smallish, book-lined room that had the look of a study.

Dr Dalrymple emerged talking in a low voice to Blayney and handing him a small box of pills. 'These are for his lordship. He knows how to take them.'

Blayney held out his hand and said anxiously 'Have you something for me, like I asked, doctor?'

Putting his hand in his pocket the doctor produced a small phial. 'Yes, of course. These are for your earache. They should help. A few drops three times a day should help the pain, and once the abcess has burst you'll be hearing clearly again, the noises will all be gone, I assure you.'

'Do you think it will work?' asked Dr Blayney miserably.

'Of course it will, old chap,' was the hearty reply. 'You'll be good as new.'

Thanking him Blayney went back into the study and closed the door.

Dr Dalrymple was suddenly aware of Thane and I standing in the shadows

'Good party, was it? Sorry I missed all the fun, it was all over when I looked in with his lordship's prescription. Everyone enjoyed themselves?'

I said yes, resisting the temptation to add, Everyone but Alexander.

The doctor grinned and pointed to at Thane. 'I didn't realise pets were included on such occasions.'

'Alexander invited him especially.'

The doctor's eyebrows raised at that as he considered Thane in a manner that expressed disapproval for such an idea.

Then with a laugh, 'He is quite an unusual animal and I just hope he wasn't tempted to gobble up any of the small guests or her ladyship's wee dogs.'

I was used to such nonsense. I smiled politely but Thane gave me another of his despairing looks at the stupidity of humans as the doctor made his way towards the front door.

'Your own happy day won't be long now. You must be feeling very excited, just hope the weather stays fair. Give my regards to young Jack. I gather we're giving him a right eve of the wedding send off at the pub.'

That was news to me. Then I knew the reason why.

'Ladies not invited. A strictly male occasion,' he added, dashing down the front steps. 'A lad's last chance to misbehave before the doors of domesticity close on him.'

And a final warning as Blayney emerged from his study. 'Stay clear of this influenza – we have a few cases in the area. Unusual for this time of year.'

213

As the secretary went upstairs I thought about his earache. Those scarlet ears and the reason for his intent listening to every word of Annette's. If he was also somewhat deaf his confusion over Vince's latin quotation was easily explained and I felt sorry that my thoughts had been so uncharitable.

When Alexander rushed downstairs followed by Annette, I said 'Poor Dr Blayney, he seems to be having a bad time with an abscess in his ear. Must be terribly painful,' I added hoping that the knowledge would arouse some compassion and perhaps make her pay more attention to the secretary and treat him more kindly instead of that contemptuous manner of pretending that he didn't exist.

My strategy was not a complete success or indeed any success at all. She merely shrugged and said rather wearily, 'Is that so?'

Then as we walked out of the front door and down the steps she added almost apologetically: 'He's such a dull man. Supposed to be absolutely brilliant but he never has a word to say for himself. Heaven only knows why Cousin Quentin chose him as a secretary.'

I remained silent thinking perhaps he was only tongue-tied by his passion for Annette and that quite brilliant men are often shy socially and have little small talk. Alexander was racing ahead. 'Come along, Thane!' he shouted and they raced out and down the steps.

'Take care, Alexander,' said Annette. 'Poor child. He was very lonely and Thane has made such a difference. I keep saying to Amelia that he should have had a dog of his own by now, but she doesn't approve. She is very fond of her tiny lap dogs and argues that they should be enough for him too. She just doesn't realise that a boy needs a more robust friendlier animal as a playmate.'

And so we followed them as Alexander raced ahead,

whooping and shouting through the gardens and then across a tiny wood towards the little estate house.

Annette's new home had the look of a picture book cottage, but it was a page from *Grimm's Fairy Tales* waiting to play the role fate has destined in all of our lives.

25

The house wore all its attraction on the outside. Despite a gallant effort at furnishing by Lady Verney, the result was a curious atmosphere of trembling uncertainty as if the house itself might find some difficulty in coming to terms of living in a state of harmony with antiques and bric a brac that might vanish in a puff of smoke.

I have a curious awareness not, alas, shared by everyone, that houses absorb the personalities of their occupiers and I wondered if someone had died here recently. Perhaps the last tenant had expired before Lord Verney's modern refurbishments and the melancholy atmosphere of a funeral wake still lurked about the walls.

I was relieved to find that Annette was quite oblivious of anything in the least disturbing. She was beside herself with excitement, rushing from room to room, thrilled beyond measure for what was to be her 'honeymoon home' as she shyly referred to it and turning to me from time to time for agreement, so that I conjured up the polite and enthusiastic responses that were expected of me.

Alexander remained outside throwing sticks for Thane who was obliging him in taking part in this somewhat degrading pastime for a deerhound.

My eyes widened as I glimpsed them from out the window. Here was a Thane new to me, the existence of a Thane I had never dreamed of. I would never have considered throwing sticks for him to retrieve. However, he seemed to be enjoying the new experience and perhaps thereby proving how wrong I had been and that my mysterious deerhound who came from Dear-knows-where and was able to survive on the heights of Arthur's Seat was just an ordinary animal after all.

Watching the boy with the hound many sizes too large for him, I realised sadly that time was running out for Alexander and all the joy of these last few days would depart with Thane.

At that moment I wished with all my heart that Thane was mine, that I owned him and could give him as a gift to Alexander, or at least on extended loan till Jack and I came back from our honeymoon.

As we said goodbye to Annette, she told me again how excited she was that I should meet her new husband at my wedding. I smiled. Had she ever mentioned his name and I had missed it, I wondered, or did she, after so many tribulations, obtain intense satisfaction in defying her guardian – and everyone else – by referring to him in the proud title of 'my husband'.

My thoughts drifted compassionately towards the unfortunate Dr Blayney and his earache – and his heartache too, the latter of which could not be cured by a phial of Dr Dalrymple's drops but might lessen when Annette's daily presence was removed.

As I reached the drive by a short cut through the wood, there was something else nagging at the back of my mind, something vital I should be remembering in connection with the unhappy secretary but it was banished by the appearance of Father Boyle.

I emerged from the rhododendrons just a few steps away from him. We were obviously heading in the same direction towards Eildon. I guessed he had been returning Alexander's birthday party guests to their respective homes on the estate and he was walking head down, clearly either praying or pre-occupied with his own thoughts.

He did not look overjoyed at this interruption of his contemplation and looked askance at Thane who, taken by surprise, moved swiftly in his direction.

'Shouldn't your dog be on a rope of some kind?' He sounded alarmed.

'Thane came back to my side immediately and I said,' He is quite safe, I assure you. Remember how well-behaved he was at the party.'

Boyle made a grumpy sound of disapproval. I felt sure that he did not want to walk with us, but a measure of politeness demanded that unless he had some ready excuse for speeding ahead, he must accompany us to the village.

Feeling guilty that I was a relative stranger, not of his religious persuasion, when he would rather have been alone, embarrassment is always the surest thing to make me tongue tied.

My mind went blank about some topic to engage his attention.

I began with 'All your charges are safely back home again?'

He merely nodded but I persevered with remarks about how well behaved they were, such nice children, etc. etc. He merely smiled, a trifle grimly I thought, keeping his opinion to himself, his silence indicating that it had been no mean task.

I tried again and asked how he was enjoying Eildon and his new calling.

'Tolerable,' he said, 'tolerable.'

'Have you succeeded in finding a housekeeper yet?'

'Early days.' His mouth clamped shut on that topic and as further enquiries obviously were not encouraged, the alternative was to end all conversation and walk silently back. So I decided as a last resort to mention his predecessor.

'Father McQuinn was a fine man,' I said.

That interested him. 'He was indeed. A difficult man to follow. I did not have the pleasure, but I have heard a great deal about his sterling qualities.' A pause. 'You knew him then?'

'I met him briefly on my arrival at Eildon.' I did not care to throw cold water over this promising topic of conversation by adding that I had found him dead in the church and that I believed his death was no accident but murder.

'As a matter of fact, we were related.'

'Indeed?'

'He was a relative of mine – by marriage.'

That got his attention. 'Related to your family here?'

'No. He was cousin to my late husband.'

He frowned. 'Your – husband?' He managed an unsteady laugh. 'Forgive me, but I have heard about your wedding – at the end of the week, is it not?'

'Yes, but in actual fact I am a widow. My husband was Danny McQuinn. His cousin, Father Sean, brought him over from Ireland as a young lad. He used to visit him here from time to time.'

Father Boyle stopped in his tracks and looked at me, as if he was seeing me for the first time. 'This is very unusual. Why does everyone refer to you as Miss Faro and not by your married name as Mrs McQuinn?'

I decided that I had better explain. 'I assure you it is not my wish that I should be presented under my maiden name. It is a whim of my future mother-in-law who, for reasons of her own, preferred that I should be known as Miss Faro. Let us say she did not care for the idea of her only son marrying a widow woman.'

Father Boyle looked taken aback. 'There is nothing in the Bible against widows marrying again. Had you been divorced or something of that nature, or have some discreditable association in your past, there might have been an excuse for your mother-in-law's reactions. But this is quite extraordinary.'

'And very uncomfortable too for me, I assure you.' I did not add that I suspected my future husband was extremely jealous of my late husband and rather approved of his mother's behaviour in this delicate matter.

The priest managed a smile but had he been the clergyman in charge of our nuptials I realised that he could not have been more surprised by this disclosure.

'So you are Mrs McQuinn and your husband Danny was Father McQuinn's cousin,' he repeated. 'Well, well,' he added with a dry laugh.

'I presume you are used to confidences, Father.'

'Naturally.'

'Then I will be greatly obliged if you keep this information to yourself. It would greatly upset and severely embarrass my future in-laws. Besides, in a few days I will have yet another name – Mrs Macmerry – and everyone will have forgotten there ever was a Mrs McQuinn.'

The village was in sight, the main street with its decoration of flags strung across the road in preparation for the Jubilee celebrations.

'How pretty,' I said. 'Eildon is quite transformed.'

The priest merely nodded and we parted, with mutual relief I suspected, but leaving me with some qualms. It had been unwise to confide in anyone, but to confess to a priest or a doctor could not do any harm surely, I told myself, remembering his last words of consolation:

'Feel free to confide in me at any time, Miss – er Mrs McQuinn. Your secret is quite safe with me.'

As I walked up the farm road towards the house, I wondered how the ladies of Father Boyle's congregation felt about their new priest, so different from Father McQuinn, who had been loved by everyone.

I remembered Father Boyle's reactions to their gallant efforts to take care of him when he took a fever after conducting the funeral of his predecessor, his first official duty, in the heavy rain. No doubt he also had sterling qualities behind that unprepossessing exterior. Perhaps being brought up by Jesuits had something to do with his long silences and his disinclination for social conversation with the opposite sex, but I certainly did not envy his future housekeeper.

Leaving Thane in the barn where it was no longer considered a necessity to keep him tethered by a rope, I hurried across the yard, still troubled with guilty feelings about my revelations to the priest although I could not see him in the role of a gossip who would spread the news all round Eildon like wildfire.

But as soon as I opened the kitchen door, all thoughts of Father Boyle were swept from my mind.

Jack had arrived home.

26

Jack was laughing, seated at the table before an immense plate of food, benignly watched over by his doting mother.

He sprang up to greet me, a great hug and kiss. 'Where have you been, what have you been doing with yourself? How's Thane?' A dozen questions in quick fire without giving me a chance to reply. More kisses and cuddles.

His mother's reproachful, 'Your food's getting cold, Jack,' brought him – and me – down to earth again. I sat opposite him at the table while he demolished that plate of food, occasionally stopping to take my hand and devour me with a loving glance while I kept thinking how wonderful it was to have him here again.

How much I had missed him. As Jess went on to tell him all about the wedding preparations, the little gathering for me on the eve of the wedding as well as his stag night at the local, I was suddenly delighted that come Saturday I would be Mrs Jack Macmerry and we'd be away to London on our honeymoon. Andrew appeared at the door and, seizing her shawl, Jack's mother said, 'We're away to see the Johnstons. For a couple of hours,' she added tactfully.

I was grateful to the Johnstons for the prospect of time alone with Jack when Andrew said, 'The Wards are both down with this influenza, so it looks like they'll miss your wedding.' Remembering Mrs Ward's heavy cold and Dr Dalrymple's warning, I hoped they hadn't spread the infection.

As the door closed on his parents Jack hugged me and sighed. 'The trial finished last night, thank God. It's strung on and on and for a while I was sure that I was going to have to miss my own wedding.'

'The same thought occurred to me,' I said and kissed him.

'I just missed the last train, so I spent the night at Solomon's Tower,' and putting his hand in his pocket he took out three letters. 'These were waiting for you.'

I scanned the handwriting. From Emily in Orkney, from Paris – Pappa and Imogen. Brief letters, saying what I knew already, how sorry they were to have to miss the wedding – Emily was sending a present and Pappa enclosed a very generous bank draft to buy ourselves something we needed.

Jack was interested in the one without a postmark. 'This must have been pushed through the door.'

I didn't recognise the handwriting but suspected it might be from Sister Angela, a reply to my note and knowing how persistent Jack could be when his curiosity was aroused, thrusting it into my pocket I said casually, 'It will be from the nuns at St Leonard's, in connection with their summer fete.'

The frown that crossed Jack's face told me to be careful, that the words 'nuns at St Leonard's' conjured up Danny McQuinn for him.

So with a hasty change of subject: 'Only two days now, Jack. We had better go over the sequence of events,' I said firmly.

'A good idea. What have you been doing while I was away? How are you getting on with Ma?' he added anxiously.

'Improving considerably. We seem to be coming to an understanding. And she's making me a bridal wreath to wear instead of a bonnet.'

'She likes you a lot, you know. It's just that you are – well, a bit different from the lasses here at Eildon. Not quite what she expected. But you've won her over. As I always knew you would,' he added as we went upstairs to pack for a fortnight's honeymoon in London.

Jack watched as I spread my wedding gown along with my shoes and the rest of my trousseau on the bed. He sighed deeply. 'We could do with an old fashioned trunk.'

'Do you like these?' I asked proudly, laying down the new shirt and tie I had been hoarding secretly for him.

'Great! They look very expensive.'

'They were. Nothing but the best in the circumstances.'

And with his head in the wardrobe. 'Where did you put my suit, by the way.'

'Your – suit?'

'Yes, the one I bought for the wedding. You were to collect it from Solomon's Tower.'

'I – I haven't seen it, Jack.'

'You must have seen it, Rose. It was in the cupboard next to the wardrobe in our bedroom.'

I sat down heavily. I had never even opened the cupboard.

'Jack,' I whispered in horror. 'When it wasn't in the wardrobe, I presumed you must be wearing it for the Glasgow trial.'

'Then you presumed wrong!' he snapped and stared down at me angrily. 'Why should I wear my new suit for a crime trial in Glasgow, for heaven's sake? And the reason it wasn't in your – the wardrobe was that there wasn't room for it. You have every available inch of space.'

Letting that sink in for a moment, he added dolefully, 'And another thing, our tickets for London and the wedding rings are in the jacket pocket.'

'Oh, Jack, I'm sorry.' I couldn't bear to argue that I could hardly be blamed for that and near to tears I said: 'What will we do?'

'I take it you mean what will I do?' he demanded, angry again. 'There is only one solution. I will damned well have to go back on the train to Edinburgh tonight and collect it – and come back again – the day before our wedding. Dammit, dammit!' he added furiously throwing a pair of shoes on to the floor.

I burst into tears, said I was sorry, it was all my fault – even though I believed it wasn't. But he believed me, and contrite, hugged me and said it wasn't the worst thing that could happen after all. He'd pick up the train from London to Edinburgh when it stopped at Eildon. Spend the night at the Tower and be back tomorrow on the night train. 'Maybe I should take Thane with me,' he concluded.

I hadn't considered Thane being freed again on Arthur's Seat, back to his old haunts. I suddenly thought of him spoilt by all his new friends in Eildon and missing them. How would he readjust without us? Had we ruined him for ever by introducing him to this new world?

We heard Jack's parents arrive downstairs and dear Jack saved my face by explaining that he had to return to Edinburgh and collect his wedding suit which he had forgotten. So gallant of him, I thought as he added:

'I thought I might take Thane with me –'

There was a positive storm of protest from Andrew. 'Why do that – we were hoping that you'd let him stay here with us until you got back from London. He's happy here, you know.'

I left them to it and went out to the barn. To ask Thane what he thought about it. I realise that may seem very odd, but I was sure he always understood what I was saying to him. He listened, intelligence gleaming in his eyes and when I explained that we would be back in two weeks, would he be happy to stay here with Andrew, he licked my face. In a human I could only call it a smile of assent.

Hugging him, I went back into the house where Jess was making sandwiches for Jack to take on the train, a quantity sufficient to see him to London and back rather than the hour's journey to Edinburgh.

I decided to walk with him to the station and there we found that the train had been delayed at Newcastle by a derailed goods van and was running late. In exposed parts like Eildon a waiting room however bare and chilly is a necessity for winter travellers and even the summer ones are abundantly grateful.

As we waited I told him about Ned Fraser's extraordinary story about the suicide who had first removed his jacket and shirt and carried no luggage. I mentioned it with a certain diffidence expecting my account to be met with Jack's usual cynicism.

However Jack, who obviously did not heed Ned's reputation as a gossip merely nodded and said, 'We know all those details, Rose, and the police are looking into it. They are regarding it as death in suspicious circumstances.'

'A Fenian plot?'

He shrugged. 'Possibly.'

I considered this noncommittal response. Jack's discretion was even worse than Vince's, at times it could put a clam to shame.

'Do you agree with me now that Father McQuinn and his housekeeper were also murdered?'

'That has been added to the equation,' was the enigmatic response.

'At least you don't think I imagined it,' I said sharply. 'About the suicide – have they a suspect in mind?'

Jack shook his head. 'Let's just say there were some very odd passengers travelling on the train that night, sharing the dead man's compartment. Extensive enquiries are being made, I assure you.'

'Odd passengers indeed –'

I thought of the ones Ned had described. A man muffled up to the ears. A mere thought, that might have no relevance at all.

But at that moment the train steamed into the station. Jack was kissing me goodbye and it was too late to tell him –

'See you tomorrow evening.'

'Hope you'll be in time for your stag party.'

He grinned. 'Don't worry about that. Goes on all night –
See you at the church. Bye!'

The train moved off and from the steam Ned Fraser
emerged having changed places with the waiting guard.

He was exactly the man I wanted to see right now.

As we walked back towards the village, I asked him to
describe again the events relating to the suicide and he confirmed that the police were very interested in his story.

He had been asked for a full statement. He sounded
delighted at this sudden popularity.

'Tell me again about the passenger with his face all muffled
up,' I said.

'The one I thought had the toothache or something, you
mean, miss.'

'Yes. Was he tall or short?'

'Couldn't tell you that, miss. He was sitting down.'

I left him at the farm road, certain in my mind that I had the
solution to the suicide. Remembering Dr Blayney and his earache, I only wished I had Vince to go through his visit to the
Verneys again. Especially the bit about the don who had a
remarkable collection of scars for a scholar.

Was Blayney the man who was muffled up to the ears, who
had for some reason, as yet unknown officially but most probably concerned a Fenian plot, attacked the real Dr Blayney who
was sitting opposite 'reading a book in a foreign language'.

Having spotted his victim shortly after leaving Edinburgh
he had waited for the right moment just past Berwick and had
thrown him off the train, after first removing, for some reasons unknown, the man's jacket and shirt.

If only I had time to investigate. If only the wedding was a
still week away.

Jack's parents had retired so I sat at the kitchen table and
made careful notes of all that I had discovered. All that was

227

lacking was the real identity of Dr Blayney's impostor and – since every murder must have its motive – the reason why?

As I was writing I remembered that heavy Irish brogue and throwing down my pen, thought I had the reason at last.

The bogus don from Dublin was a Fenian terrorist who had sneaked into the Verney household. To make plans to assassinate a member of the Royal family who, according to Vince, was coming on a secret visit at, or around, the time of the Jubilee celebrations.

Tomorrow I must tell Constable Bruce, surely this would arouse him from his lethargy – here was a chance for promotion, a chance to shine in the annals of Eildon.

Almost too excited to sleep, I remembered the note that had been put through the door of Solomon's Tower. As I suspected, it was from Sister Angela and read:

'Dear Mrs McQuinn. I regret that we could not meet on your recent visit. I thought you would like to know that dear Sister Mary Michael had made a mistake. She confused Danny McQuinn with a message she had received from Daniel McLynn, an unfortunate youth once under our care and now serving a prison sentence.

I do hope this eases your mind. Yours in Christ, Sister Angela.'

What joy, I thought. Now at last, I can believe that there will be no just cause or impediment to my marriage to Jack. And that Danny McQuinn's ghost is laid at last.

At last? Not quite. But how wrong can one be?

27

Tomorrow would be my wedding day.

I awoke after a nightmare-ridden sleep about Dr Blayney, determined to get rid of the Claddagh ring. Its presence in my jewel box was a symbol of Danny haunting me with his memory as well as the fear that if Jack found it, I might have some explaining to do.

Now that was over. Free of Danny's ghost, I would take it over to the Abbey custodian today but first of all, I must call on Constable Bruce and tell him of my discovery of the bogus Dr Blayney.

I went across to the stable knowing that these days I could never depend on Thane going anywhere with me since he seemed to prefer Andrew's company in the fields. I have to admit I felt a sense of disappointment to see the stall he had been given next to the horse Charity was empty once again, although I fully realised that I should be grateful that Thane would be well cared for in our absence and when we returned from London he would go back with us to Arthur's Seat.

And casting aside my twinges of guilt about the effects of his sojourn of domesticity, I hurried down the gaily decorated village street to the police station.

The door was opened by Mrs Bruce wearing her most disapproving expression.

'Well, what do you want?'

I thought the answer was a trifle obvious, but I gave her my most pleasant smile and asked, 'Is Constable Bruce at home?'

She sniffed. 'He is.'

'May I see him then?'

'You may not, miss. And I will tell you why not. He is in his bed with the influenza.'

'Oh, I am sorry.'

'Not as sorry as I am, having to run this house single-handed.'

'Is he very poorly?'

'Very. Not eating a thing and a raging fever too. I can tell you I am at my wits end.'

There seemed hardly any point in such circumstances in asking her to give him a message, so weakly saying that I hoped he would be better soon, and to give him my best wishes, I had hardly got the words out before the door was firmly closed on me.

I met Jack's mother coming out of the grocer's shop with a laden basket over each arm. I insisted on carrying one of them back to the farm with her despite her protests. These provisions were for the bride's evening party and we had a long argument about the preparations, none of which she would allow me to help with.

'It's not the bride's place,' she said. 'It wouldn't be lucky,' she added darkly. I failed to see how making a few scones or setting a table could interfere with whatever fate had in store for me.

'All you have to do is talk to folk and look pretty, not that looking pretty will be any trouble to you,' she added with one of her almost-smiles.

No, she didn't need anything else from the shops. She had everything in hand and although she bitterly regretted the absence of Mrs Ward, now laid low with the influenza, Mrs Johnston and the ladies of the congregation would be delighted to help prepare our wedding reception in the village hall.

It was useless to argue, so with the Claddagh ring burning a hole in my pocket I set off for the Abbey.

The day was bright, the sun brilliant and I just hoped and

prayed a little that it would stay that way for tomorrow, that all would go well, in particular that Jack got back safely this evening and that the trains would not be delayed.

The custodian's office was open. He seemed surprised when I handed over the ring but very solemnly opened a ledger and made a note of when and where exactly it was found as well as my name and address.

'We keep them for three months and if no one claims them, they become the property of the finder.'

Thanking him, I never wanted to see the Claddagh ring again as I watched him open a drawer in his desk, tie on a label and place it in an open tin box. There were other pieces of jewellery, a weird assortment of rings, brooches, bangles and hatpins all similarly labelled as well as an untidy selection of larger articles: gloves, handkerchiefs, scarves.

He smiled at my exclamation. 'These are just the small things. We get visitors to the Abbey from all over the world. In that cupboard over yonder, I could show you umbrellas, parasols, cloaks, hats and walking sticks. Come back in the autumn. We have a sale for maintenance of the Abbey fabric fund,' he added encouragingly.

'Visitors from all over the world' might well include Ireland, and that was a consoling thought as I emerged once more into the brilliant sunshine of the ruined cloisters and walked back across the lawns.

Suddenly I had that odd feeling once again that I was being watched from the ruined tower. From the shadows high above me a figure moved.

My heart beat faster. Was my mysterious stalker still at large? If only Thane were with me.

A moment of panic. I fought back the desire to take to my heels and run for the exit when my name was called:

'Miss Rose! Over here.'

It was Annette standing at the foot of the tower's spiral staircase.

I walked across and she said: 'This is most fortuitous. There is someone I want you to meet –'

A figure loomed behind her.

'Miss Rose, this is my husband – Danny McQuinn.'

Blinded by sunshine I could only see the shadow of the man who moved forward. I felt faint with shock, a darkness swirled over me.

He grasped my hand. 'Miss Rose, delighted. Annette has told me so much about you. Please call me Danny.'

I stared at him. My eyes were in focus again. My heart had resumed its normal beat for this man was not my Danny. There was no facial resemblance. His swarthy good looks suggested Mexico in origin.

Annette was hovering, holding his arm. Amazingly, my violent reactions had gone unobserved.

'Meeting you like this was so fortunate,' she said. 'We were going to call on you, but Danny wanted to see the Abbey again. He knew this area well.'

'Yes, indeed. An amazing coincidence when we first met in New York,' said the false Danny, smiling at her.

She merely nodded, nervous and ill at ease. Where was all the excitement, the joy of fulfilment? No doubt unseen problems back at Verney Castle that her husband was unaware of as, still smiling benignly, he said:

'I had heard of Eildon before my family emigrated from Britain. My cousin was the parish priest here.'

And it was at that moment the terrible implications of this situation became evident. The existence of two Danny McQuinns was rare but not impossible but the possibility of two Danny McQuinns who both knew Eildon and whose cousin was the late Father McQuinn was asking too much of coincidence.

We were walking towards the entrance. I hardly heard a word that Annette was saying. I felt that my face was white and stiff with shock and hoped she did not notice.

What was I to do? I could hardly tell this doting bride that her new-found husband was an impostor. That would break her heart and send her scurrying back to the convent. From my personal point of view an impostor, a criminal perhaps, was even worse than the fortune-hunter I had originally suspected.

The Verney carriage had arrived and was waiting at the entrance.

'He has to go into Edinburgh to see lawyers and I have papers to sign.' Annette said to me. 'I know that you are very busy just now, but would you please come and take afternoon tea at our cottage?'

I looked at her. Even her voice sounded different, excitement and jubilation replaced by a businesslike precision. 'It is our last chance of a meeting before your wedding.'

The false Danny's own expression was inscrutable and I got the feeling then that whoever he was and whatever his motives for marrying the Verney heiress, love was not one of them.

'Alexander wants to see you again and I have promised him that you will come this afternoon,' said Annette.

'I presume you will be living in Edinburgh when you return from your honeymoon,' said the man at her side. 'The lawyers have promised me the keys of some suitable houses.'

There was a pause. Perhaps I was expected to contribute some helpful hints and information on the availability of Edinburgh houses, but I could think of nothing except my eagerness to escape from this nightmare situation.

'If we have to leave Eildon before Alexander goes to prep school, Father Boyle has very kindly promised to take over his tutoring,' said Annette. 'They already have daily Latin lessons but this afternoon Alexander will be excused.'

As Danny handed her into the carriage, she leaned out of the window and said again in that flat toneless voice, 'Please say you'll come, Miss Rose. For Alexander's sake.'

There was no way I could politely refuse that invitation. I was beginning to feel that confidences were implied. Perhaps the reality of marriage was more complicated than Annette had expected and I already suspected that I was the only friend she had.

And there was a stronger reason for going to visit them. I had to know more about this Danny McQuinn.

If only Jack were here, he would know what to do. And then I thought how this information plus all the tortuous explanations of Sister Mary Michael's mistake, the discovery of the Claddagh ring and now this impostor on our wedding eve would cast its grim shadow over our wedding.

There just wasn't time to wait for Jack and have his counsel. I would have to do it alone, come what may.

At that moment, all I could think of was saving poor Annette Verney – or McQuinn as she now believed herself to be – from the heartbreak knowledge would bring and that might destroy her for ever.

The fact that I might also be in terrible danger did not even occur to me.

28

I felt dreadful. I could hardly stagger up the farm road. My head throbbed, I was parched with a burning throat, and I ached in every limb.

Was this dreadful sickness all in my mind, brought about by shock?

As I walked through the kitchen, Jess, busy at the stove, merely glanced in my direction, nodded but didn't seem to notice anything amiss. I was glad of that. Conversation was the last thing I wanted as I crawled up the stairs and lay down on my bed.

If only my head didn't feel as if my brains were about to burst out, then perhaps I could think clearly what to do next.

Groaning, I looked over at the cases lying open, waiting. I hadn't the strength to lift a finger let alone deal with packing wedding garments.

Tomorrow at this time I would be at the altar in the kirk down the road exchanging my vows with Jack. If only his instructions had been clearer about the whereabouts of his suit for the wedding and I hadn't been so involved with my own affairs I might have thought about opening that cupboard.

Then Jack would have been here and he would have known what to do.

'Soup's on the table,' Jess called upstairs.

I tottered down, feeling very sick. But if I admitted to being ill then I knew that would cause such alarm and despondency in view of tomorrow's wedding, an all-enveloping fuss that I certainly was unable to cope with.

The table was set for one. Jess had returned to the stove and was taking a tray out of the oven.

'Go ahead, lass. I had mine earlier. Andrew took sandwiches with him. He's got a lot to do with the sheep up on the hill today and he doesn't have time to break off.'

She sighed. 'Two of the hands are down with this influenza. I hoped we'd escape – there's a lot of it about and that's not usual in the summer.'

Andrew's absence was bad news. In two hours, after I had a little rest which I hoped would make me better, I would be going across to Annette's cottage on the Verney estate. I had hoped to take Thane along to please Alexander.

Now I would have to go alone and before then I had to think of some means of confronting Danny's impostor.

At the moment, logical thought was like fighting my way through burning treacle and by the time I was ready to leave, I hadn't slept at all but had gone through and discarded any number of strategies of how I was to get Danny alone and get to the truth without involving poor Annette. Uppermost in my mind and most important of all was to find out the whereabouts of the real Danny McQuinn.

I now knew one thing for certain. The motive for Father McQuinn's murder had become crystal clear: He – and Mrs Aiden – had known the real Danny and whatever the reason for this deception, it suggested that the stakes were much higher than those involving a mere fortune hunter.

I kept returning again and again to the most realistic fear: a Fenian plot as both Vince and Jack had hinted. And an Irishman just arrived from Dublin suggested a very strong connecting link with the security concerns at Verney Castle.

How well Blayney fitted the equation, as Jack had called it, that the police were investigating as I thought again about the passenger muffled up to the ears who, I was now certain, had thrown the real Dr Blayney off the train and taken his place as Lord Verney's new secretary.

If the false Danny was involved in bigger issues than laying his hands on Annette's considerable fortune, then the indications were that he was working for the Fenians and in league with Blayney.

As for the Danny who had been my husband and might still be, was he still alive? Although I now feared I already knew the answer to that vital question.

Somehow, despite my weak legs and raging headache. I reached the cottage. Expecting to find Annette there alone, her conversation having indicated that her husband was going in to Edinburgh, I was surprised to find the door open and the false Danny rose to greet me.

He bowed but I ignored the proffered hand and demanded, 'Where is Annette?'

'She will be with us shortly. Won't you be seated. Annette is bringing Alexander down. A fine boy, don't you think, a worthy heir to the Verney title?'

I wasn't interested in his small talk.

I sat down at the table, glad of its support. 'Who are you?' I asked.

The question seemed to surprise him. He smiled spread his hands wide. 'I thought you knew that. I'm Danny McQuinn – Annette's husband.'

Aware that there was not much time and that Annette might appear at any minute with Alexander at her side and that I had not the slightest idea what would happen next, I said, 'You might be her husband but you are certainly not the Danny McQuinn who knew Eildon and whose cousin was the parish priest. That Danny McQuinn was – my – husband.'

Regarding me narrowly, all affability vanished, he said, 'So I gather – somewhat late in the day for my comfort, I can tell you.'

'Where is Danny? What have you done with him?' I cried.

He shrugged. 'The last time I saw him, he was lying on a bed in a shack in Arizona. He was a dying man –'

'How dying?' I demanded. 'Did you kill him?'

'Mercy, no. The Indians had saved me the trouble. He had been caught in an ambush while he was searching for the grave of his dead wife and baby that someone at the reservation had told him about.'

That sounded like my Danny. I gulped back the tears. 'When – when was that?'

'Three years ago. I had known Danny from my Pinkerton days. But alas, I had got into a tricky situation with the law and when we met again, my name was on every Wanted poster across two states. I couldn't afford to linger and seeing that Danny was not likely to last the night I decided on a change of roles. The dead man would be me and I would be him, safe from the law.'

'How did you expect to get away with that? I demanded.

'Setting fire to the shack was one obvious way –'

'You cruel devil!' I yelled, longing to strike him.

'I didn't manage – there wasn't time. The sheriff's posse was right behind me so I rode like hell across that red desert until I picked up a train heading towards New York. Using my new identity I got a job in a shipping office –'

He stopped and smiled. 'You know the rest. I met Annette Verney, an heiress who found me so irresistible that she persuaded me to elope with her.'

'What an opportunity for a fortune hunter!' I said.

'Yeah. That's what I was temporarily. But there were better pickings than Annette's fortune, which she has just turned over to me.'

He pointed across the table. 'The papers are there ready for me to take into Edinburgh. I've had a long wait – I didn't know she was under age back in New York and that I'd have two years to wait for my reward. Seemed a wise move to come to Britain and keep busy finding out all about the Verneys. An interesting family, so old, so wealthy –'

He paused and smiled. 'And with only one son – the heir to it all.'

There was something in his expression that made me say, 'Leave Alexander out of this.'

He shook his head. 'Now that would be a pity. I have to confess that kidnapping is something I'm rather good at. Wealthy parents will pay anything for the return of a child, especially an only son – or daughter. I was doing rather well – for a time.'

His face darkened, angry at the memory and I said, 'You didn't get the money and so you killed the child.'

He shrugged. 'Something like that. I'd been tricked – there was no money. Those rich parents had been warned. Things were hotting up in that New York shipping office so meeting Annette suggested a good chance to extend a lucrative career overseas.'

And suddenly it was all becoming clear, the diabolical plan he had in mind even before he went on.

'Annette was expendable, but what wouldn't a family like the Verneys give to keep their only son and heir alive and returned to them in one piece. Certainly it would be worth a few million dollars in anyone's language.

He wagged a finger at me.

'I haven't been idle and I've been in Edinburgh longer than Annette suspects, long enough to make certain useful contacts. You see, your Danny was a member of Caen na Gael, pro-Irish Americans devoted to the Fenian cause. Kidnap the Verney heir and blame it on the Fenians, especially with the Jubilee coming up, and everyone expecting trouble again from that quarter.

'I prefer to work alone but this time a partner was crucial.

And from him I learned that there was a snag. The village priest was a relative of the real Danny. And before my plan could succeed it was necessary that he and anyone else who knew the real Danny must be got rid of.'

'Which is where Dr Blayney came into your calculations.'

He looked at me wide eyed for a moment, no doubt taken aback by my clever deductions. The idea seemed to amuse him and he laughed.

'By a kind stroke of fate there was a new man, a stranger coming to Eildon, so my accomplice changed places with him –'

'He pushed him off the train and made it look like a suicide,' I said.

He nodded in agreement. 'It worked well, didn't it?'

I had to keep him talking. There was so much more I needed to know. But where was Annette, I thought frantically. Why hadn't she arrived? And I suspected from his frowning glances towards the door that he was getting concerned too, wondering about her long absence.

Playing for time, I asked, 'Why are you telling me all this? Do you expect me to keep it all a secret – for Annette's sake, perhaps?'

Across the table, a jeering smile from this man with a face like a Mexican bandit. 'No. I am telling you all this because you asked and because there is not the slightest possibility of you ever telling anyone else or leaving this room alive,' he added coldly.

My heart was thumping loud enough for him to hear it, but I gasped out; 'And how do you propose to accomplish that? Killing is one thing you may be good at, but disposing of the body is quite another matter –'

He shrugged. 'I am given to understand that that will be an easy matter. There's a quarry not far away with a very deep dark pool.'

'And how do you propose to get me there? Am I to walk or be carried?'

In answer he began to walk towards me, I jumped to my feet. But it was other footsteps I heard – outside!

Annette and Alexander. Too late to warn them!

The door opened – but it was Father Boyle who rushed in.

I was saved.

'Father Boyle!' I screamed. Thank God –

But the false Danny was shouting, 'Where the hell have you been all this time? And where's the kid?'

I looked at them in horror.

'I did my best, Hank,' Boyle whined. 'Thought it was going to be easy, just like we planned. No one suspected a thing. But the Verneys wouldn't even let me see him –'

'I thought Annette was in charge of him –'

'Not today,' was the grim response. 'The kid's mother was there and half the servants. I couldn't take them all on and grab him –'

'You weren't expected to grab him. You were to be taking him out for his usual Latin lesson.'

'Listen to me, will you. Seems the lad has a fever – covered in spots, that infernal birthday party, all those damned kids, like as not. There was no way he was getting out of bed, lesson or no.'

'Damnation – damnation!' Hank, the false Danny, looked ready for murder –

'So what do we do now?' asked Boyle and, as if aware of me for the first time, he pointed. 'What about her? I thought you were going to get rid of her like we said.' And looking towards the door, 'We haven't much time. We should get on with it –'

They turned to me standing with my back to the table. Knowing they were going to kill me it wasn't much comfort to know that I had learned the truth too late.

241

Father Boyle, not Dr Blayney, was the passenger on the train, muffled to the ears, who had killed the real priest. Even the reason for stealing his jacket and shirt was now perfectly obvious. He needed the priest's clerical garb. The book in a foreign language which had puzzled Ned Fraser was probably a Latin testament. And this was the man Mrs Fraser had overheard talking to Mrs Aiden when she had called on her on the evening of Father McQuinn's death. The vital clue in our conversation I had struggled to recall had come too late.

I groaned inwardly. Having got it all wrong, when I told Father Boyle that I was Danny McQuinn's widow I now realised I had signed my own death warrant. Like Father McQuinn and Mrs Aiden, they couldn't afford to let me live.

I heard Hank say: 'Now that you're here we might as well get on with it. I have to go into Edinburgh and collect the money before Annette finds out. It all fits in great. She'll be only too glad of my gallant gesture to hand it over to the kid-nappers for part of the kid's ransom.'

He chuckled at the thought as his partner snarled, 'And I'm coming with you. I want my share, don't forget –'

'All in good time,' said Hank as he sprang across, grabbed me. His hands were around my throat. Knowing I had run out of time and I wasn't breathing properly any more, in that fight for survival I saw their backs were to the door.

As one last hopeless gesture I would try the oldest trick in the world and distract their attention by gasping, 'Annette!'

It was as if my prayers had all been answered, for the door behind them opened and Annette stood there.

'Stop – stop or I'll kill you both. I mean it.'

And she held up a rifle. 'It's loaded –'

Hank laughed, released his grip on me and said: 'Annette – you wouldn't –'

'Oh yes, I would and I will.'

'Come on, honey. You don't really know how to use that thing,' he added in a wheedling tone.

'Try me! My guardian shoots over the estate every day and I learned how to handle a rifle long ago.'

But I saw doubt in both their faces. Could she really use that rifle – our last hope. He still didn't believe her, but confident in her love for him he said: 'You wouldn't kill your adoring husband?'

'No, I wouldn't – if you were my adoring husband. But you're just a criminal, a murderer. You wanted to talk to Cousin Verney. I was curious so I followed you to the stables. I saw you with – with – this man. I overheard everything.'

At that Hank waited no longer. He sprang forward. The rifle fired and he fell back, cursing, clutching his side.

Annette stared at him in horror. She thought she had killed him and for a moment she was thrown off balance by the realisation. It was a moment wasted for we still had his partner to deal with.

Without a second glance at the injured Hank, he leapt forward to seize the rifle from Annette. I ran to her side, but we were no match for him, he felled Annette with one blow.

Now it was my turn. I grappled with him knowing it was useless. Within the next few moments I would be dead.

But the door Annette had left open sprung wide –

A grey shadow sprang into the room.

'Thane!'

'Bloody dog,' the false priest yelled and raised the gun. Through the smoke Thane was caught in mid air. The bullet hit him in the chest. I saw blood on his fur. He staggered then shook himself and kept moving slowly forward.

I heard myself scream: 'No!'

I jumped across and tried to seize the man's rifle as he tried to shake me off, to raise it again.

For a moment that seemed like eternity I struggled with

him. He pulled free and hit me across the head. As I crashed to the floor, I heard the rifle crack again.

My last sight was of Thane moving through the air and falling, falling on top of Boyle's assassin.

He lay still.

The rifle fired again and my world exploded into darkness.

So this was death.

29

Once again, I was to be proved wrong. I was alive and when I opened my eyes again I was in my bedroom at the farm.

Had it all been one of my lurid nightmares? Faces, mostly out of focus, swarmed into view but before I could summon up enough strength to speak to them, they drifted away.

Jack, his father, Dr Dalrymple with a stethoscope cold on my chest, shaking his head sadly to shadowy figures in the room behind him.

Jess emerged most often, laying cold cloths on my burning forehead.

Once or twice I even thought I saw Thane but I was too weak to call out to him.

Besides Thane was dead. I had seen the bullet strike him. Perhaps I was in heaven, perhaps we both were, although I burned with a ferocity that suggested hell and made Dante's Inferno look like a Sunday school picnic on a bright summer day.

Once the cloud in my brain began to clear and I could grapple with logical thought, I felt bitter resentment too.

I am never ill. Determined to stagger out of bed I was glad of the proximity of that bathroom as I hung on to the furniture which behaved in a very odd way.

I was very sick indeed and on one of these forays I miscarried and lost the baby whose existence I had concealed from Jack for more than two months. My only reason, I told myself, was that I did not want him to feel he was obliged to marry me, despite Vince's reassurances.

But time had become distorted. Sometimes I heard church bells. The bells for my wedding? There's not a moment to lose. I must get out of bed –

It was all too much. I could get up in my mind but my body refused to obey, so after a few feeble attempts, I drifted back into the floating world of the unconscious.

One day the clouds cleared a little and Jack emerged.

Grinning down at me he took my hands and said, 'Hello, you're still with us!'

I said: 'I must get up. Is it today we're getting married?'

He smiled. 'Not today, dearest Rose. That today has been and gone – and you missed the Jubilee celebrations. But never mind, there'll be a wedding for us just as soon as you're well again.'

I tried again to sit up but the effort was too much.

'How long have I been here?'

'Nearly two weeks. You've been very ill. Dr Dalrymple didn't give us much hope for you. Said this was one of the worst influenza cases he had coped with – where the patient had survived.' Again he grinned. 'There's strong stuff in that little package, that's what he said.'

Overcome for a moment by the memory of it, he gripped my hand. 'It was terrible, Rose. We all thought you were going to die. You were so tiny fighting that terrible fever, lying there like a little doll. Ma never left you for more than an hour or two.'

'I remember her, those cold compresses were wonderful.'

He tucked the covers round me. 'Now rest. You'll be up and about again soon. We have a wedding to arrange.'

About to leave, he smiled sadly. 'Sorry about the baby – Dr Dalrymple told me, thought I knew –'

'I was going to tell you – I just wasn't sure – it was early days and I have lost babies before –'

He put a hand over my lips. 'Hush now! We still have each other.'

Next time he came I wanted to know what had happened at Annette's cottage. I was very confused and vague about it all.

Thinking back, much of what happened that day seemed like the delirium of a raging fever but I wanted an exact chronicle of events, especially the bit about Annette's husband, Hank Elder, the man who called himself Danny McQuinn.

Even now, the name could make Jack wince.

'He's in prison awaiting extradition to the United States to be tried for a list of kidnappings, mostly successful – until a child died when the rich parents didn't pay up. He must have thought he was in luck when he met Annette and read up about the Verneys. Not only an heiress but a prospective victim.'

'What about his accomplice?' I decided not to mention my suspicions about a Fenian plot concerning Dr Blayney that had all been so seriously incorrect.

'Crofts? He'll hang, for Father Boyle's murder,' Jack said grimly. 'Elder thought he'd made a good choice there since Crofts' family had worked for the Verney estate and as a lad he'd been a gardener at the Abbey. What Elder didn't know was that Croft already had a police record and was under close investigation for a number of crimes in Edinburgh and Glasgow.

'He might have got away with murder but he hadn't bargained for Father Boyle having any relatives who were expecting to hear from him. Like a mother taken ill suddenly in York – the reason for the return half of his ticket from Inverness and his last-minute change of plan. He was just looking in briefly to see Father McQuinn, to explain that he would be back as soon as he had seen her and made arrangements for someone to take care of her. When he didn't arrive, and there was no response to their telegraphs to Eildon – which Crofts collected and destroyed, relatives raised the alarm.

Having got most of it wrong before the influenza almost finished me, I said: 'How did you know about the cottage?'

'It was That Dog as Ma still calls him, you have to thank. Pa was working one of the fields close to the Verney estate when Thane started behaving oddly. As you know from the past, he can be very determined. He made it clear that he wanted Pa to follow him. And as Pa knows a thing or two about sheep-dogs rounding up their flock, he got the message that this was something important.

'We met them on the drive with Thane dashing back and forth and Pa puffing in the rear. The gamekeeper startled out of his wits by uniformed constables on the drive, said yes, we'd probably find Father Boyle with Alexander in the grounds at this time of day.

'We knew there wasn't a moment to lose – Thane was heading for a cottage at a great speed and we followed, arriving just after you'd collapsed.'

'But what were you doing at Verney Castle in the first place?'

'We'd come on the train to arrest Croft for the murder of Father Boyle.'

He smiled rather shame-facedly. 'Your disclosures about that night had put us on the right track and confirmed our suspicions about him –'

'Which you might have shared with me,' I said indignantly, realising that it would have saved me rushing in the wrong direction over Dr Blayney.

Jack shook his head firmly. 'I wanted to keep you out of this at all costs, Rose. For heaven's sake, think of the predicament. We were getting married within days. It was all arranged.'

'Hardly important, surely, when lives were at stake,' was my stinging response.

'Your life, Rose. Let's get that clear for once and for all. Your life is more important to me than seeing any criminal brought to justice. The last thing I wanted was you rushing off in your lady investigator role –'

He paused and shrugged. 'Which of course is exactly what you did and nearly got killed once again. You have more lives than the farm cat!'

I'd have liked to argue with him if I had felt stronger so I decided on a change of subject.

'What of Annette? She was marvellous.'

'A few bruises, shocked but otherwise unscathed. You can ask her the rest yourself. She's looked in every day and at this minute she is sitting downstairs having a cup of tea with Ma.'

Leaning over, he kissed me. 'I'll see you later.'

'With that cup of tea, please. I'm hungry.'

Annette came in and sat by my side. After the conventional remarks about how glad she was to see that I was recovering and what a terrible shock I had given everyone.

'Alexander sends his special love.' In reply to my question she said:

'He is very well, and of course he knows nothing of all this terrible business although I dare say when he is older someone will give him the story of the attempted kidnapping and why his Latin tutor was removed so quickly. A curious thing, when we told Alexander that Father Boyle wasn't coming back he was very pleased. Apparently he disliked him intensely. Children are odd that way, instinctive somehow.'

She smiled. 'The great news is that Alexander is now the proud possessor of a labrador pup. My insistence had not gone unnoticed and Cousin Quentin, having seen him so devoted to Thane, decided it was time the lad had a dog of his own.'

There was a short silence. I hardly dared to ask, 'What about you, Annette. What happened with – with – ?'

I couldn't call him Danny.

She shook her head and sighed. 'I think I knew the first minute I set eyes on him again that I had made a dreadful mistake. It was so terrible because there was nothing tangible, just this dreadful certainty. He looked the same, sounded the same but this was not the same man I had dreamed of and built up all my hopes on for the past two years. I think I had the answer when almost his first words were to ask had I come into my fortune yet and in our very first embrace in the cottage that was to be our honeymoon home, I knew he had never loved me at all.'

She looked suddenly stricken. 'I made excuses that night I was to spend with him. Fortunately he did not seem to care but it was a moment of revelation and I saw him for what he was. I knew then without being told that my cousins' warning had been correct. They knew more about the world and fortune hunters than I did. But I was headstrong and I mistook infatuation for love – for a man who was older, divinely handsome and whose life seemed so different from ours, so full of adventure.

'The awful thing was that I would have to live with my mistake – I could hardly run to my cousins – I would just have to believe that when I had lived with him for a while, got used to him again, I might find that I had misjudged him. Some hope!'

There was a pause and then I asked: 'But how did you find out – about the plan to kidnap Alexander?'

'He wanted to talk to my guardian urgently and he had seen him with the dogs heading towards the stables and would go after him. I was uneasy and knew somehow that I didn't want him to face Cousin Quentin alone. So I followed him.

'They didn't hear me. I heard voices but it wasn't my cousin he was speaking to. He was in a heated argument with Father Boyle. Where was the kid? Why hadn't he brought him along as they planned? And to my horror I knew I was overhearing that they intended to kidnap Alexander.'

She shrugged. 'Never mind what a fool I had been, all I

knew then was that I had to protect Alexander. Fortunately for me, I needed no excuses, since he was in bed covered in spots – a legacy of the children's party, perhaps.

'Then I remembered that I had arranged to meet you at the cottage and that you might be in danger. I had no idea what to do, who to turn to. There wasn't time to rush back to the house, explain what I had overheard and try to convince Cousin Quentin that I hadn't gone mad.

'But knowing that this man I had married was a criminal I decided to arm myself. I'm not much of a shot as you must have noticed,' she added apologetically. 'But I ran to the gun room and seized one of my cousin's rifles – loaded it – just to scare them. When I reached the cottage – '

She shuddered. 'You know the rest.'

'You were very brave. What will you do now?

'I will stay until Alexander goes to prep school as I intended originally. As for the future I have no idea, but something will pan out, I am sure I am in God's hands.'

'Will you go back to the convent?'

'Never! That phase is over for me. I know I haven't a vocation. My cousins are very kind, they have said there will always be a place for me as long as I wish and suggested that as I have a good education I might assist Dr Blayney in this huge task of cataloguing the library and the old family documents. Amelia said it would help to keep my mind off things.'

A sad smile. A pause. 'I have to say I was quite wrong about Dr Blayney. Under that rather plain exterior, he is a very kind and thoughtful man and I am perhaps learning, rather too late, that one should not be fooled and that there is more to a man than the elegant wrappings.'

And thinking of the lovelorn Dr Blayney, I said, 'Never too late,' thinking that perhaps Fate might have a happy ending for him.

As for Thane, he had survived. I had not imagined his

presence at my bedside. Jess had allowed him to come upstairs although it was strictly against her principles regarding That Dog.

'He was so desperate to see you, lass,' Andrew told me later. 'He sat at the foot of the stairs and refused to move. He refuses to go out with me either these days and even Jess saw that it would have taken a heart of stone to keep him out of the house and that seeing him might even speed up your recovery.'

After Annette had gone, Jess brought me that cup of tea and one of her freshly baked scones.

'You'll have to eat something,' she said chidingly, 'if you're ever going to fit that nice wedding gown again. You've got very thin, nothing but a rickle of bones,' she added encouragingly.

I suppressed a shudder having avoided any possibility of seeing my reflection in the bedroom's one mirror and I thanked her for the cold compresses and for taking such good care of me.

She nodded shyly. Roughly taking my hand and at a loss for words, I felt tears were not very far off.

'There's another craiter that's never been far from your side. I'll just get him for you.'

Jack came in with Thane and confirmed his mother's remarks. 'He's been standing vigil, begging to be allowed to stay with you.'

And so I was able to hug Thane again who greeted me joyfully. But I wanted to know what had happened to him that day. In particular the part he couldn't tell me about. How the bullet which had struck him had been removed, was it another of Andrew's miracles?

When I told Jack, he shook his head. 'You must have been dreaming. If a bullet had struck him in the chest, he would be dead.'

But I had seen it. I had seen him fall but there was not a mark on him.

'He couldn't have survived a rifle shot at close range like that. See for yourself, there's no scar, nothing.'

Jack shook his head sadly and kissed me. 'All part of your delirium, love. You had a terrible fever that day, remember.'

Over his shoulder I looked at Thane.

He winked back at me. We had our own secrets...